Southern

Crosses

Southern Crosses

A NOVEL

Lawrence Annen

www.southerncrosses.com

This book is a work of fiction. All names and characters are either invented or used fictitiously. I have used several actual locations throughout this book to give it a sense of reality for the reader. No inference to any person, living or dead, or any organization, public or private, should be made. The Pinellas County sheriff's office is used purely fictitiously. The folks I know from that organization are nothing less than consummate professionals who are a credit to the uniform.

Cover design by Brion Sausser

Acknowledgements

My life has been uncertain at best. I've had many great experiences along the way and made many close friends. Some are still here, some lost forever. I cherish each and every new experience I've encountered along my course, and smile with anticipation not knowing what is yet to come. Each step is new and unplanned. The events, as they unfold, are welcomed with a sometimes nervous expectation knowing potentially catastrophic results lay close ahead. Sometimes I take a step back and revel in the wonderment of it all. Thank you, for each one of you contributed in some way to determining how and where my path twisted and turned. It is to all of you whom I graciously thank for your unwitting contributions.

One

Pete Mitchell awoke to distant and muted electronic beeps for what seemed the thousandth time. There were always ten beeps, the series occurring every hour on the hour. The master stateroom, which occupied the aft portion of the sailboat, was generally quiet and comfortable, even more so since the purchase of his new mattress, which he had thought would let him sleep through anything when he first lay down upon it. Apparently he had been wrong. The vessel was presently berthed in his rented slip at the St. Pete Beach Marina, moored with 17 other sailboats along this section of the dock. Pete lived in a full-service marina complete with swimming pool, showers, laundry room, and a BBQ area — Central Florida at its finest.

The beeping began as a distant curiosity some time after he had fallen asleep, but it soon became an annoyance. He had quickly determined that the noise was not coming from inside his hull, for he possessed nothing that would make that type of sound. One time during the night, Pete went above deck just before the top of the hour. The now highly predictable beeps could not be heard from here; but one hour later, right on schedule, he heard the muffled familiarity of the beeps beneath his hull again. At least, he was pretty sure the noise was coming from under his boat, which in itself was highly unusual. He would only have to tolerate the disturbance for a few more hours because he was scheduled to set sail.

Pete's one man company, Shallow Water Salvage, had nothing scheduled for the next couple of weeks, and he had planned a vacation. Being the president, CEO, and sole employee of the LLC afforded him the opportunity to only contract the salvage and dive operations he chose to undertake. When a larger recovery operation came along, he had a list of experienced divers always available to make some quick cash. For the smaller jobs, Pete enjoyed the freedom of working alone. At the moment, business was slow, and he was going to take advantage of that fact and get away for awhile.

As grey shadows began to take on form with the approaching shards of sunlight creeping over the eastern horizon, the clattering of a bicycle dropped on the dock signaled that Frank, his neighbor, had returned from the doughnut shop with his breakfast and paper. Frank had been moored next to Pete for two years now, and they were casual friends.

"Morning Frank," Pete said as he poked his head over the top of the ladder and peered into the sailboat's center cockpit.

"Good morning, Pete. Are you heading out today?" Frank was balancing the paper, a sack with several doughnuts, and a large cup of coffee while carefully stepping from the dock onto his sailboat.

"Yeah, I'll be cutting the dock lines shortly. I should be back in a couple of weeks. By the way, I've been hearing a strange beeping sound most of the night. It's been happening about every hour. You know anything about that?"

"Oh, sorry about that. I picked up a watch at a garage sale yesterday. It only cost a couple of bucks. The damn thing was going off every hour and driving me nuts. It was so noisy I couldn't get any sleep. I was banging it on the dock piling trying to get it to shut up and it slipped out of my hand. I didn't see where it went, but I heard a splash."

"Try looking under my stateroom — it's evidently waterproof."

Frank laughed. "Apparently it's shockproof too, because I was banging the hell out of it when it slipped out of my hand. I'll fish it out after you leave."

"Great. See you when I get back."

Pete slipped below and prepared to get underway. He would have his morning coffee out at sea.

By the time the sun had ascended into full view just above the horizon, it was time to start the engine. Pete Mitchell was ready to quietly slip away from the dock and head into the Gulf of Mexico. With the last dock line cast off, he eased the 38-foot center cockpit Endeavour sailboat out of his home port slip as he had done so many times before. Thoughts of succumbing to sub-tropical breezes for the next three weeks erased any lingering stress induced by being tied to shore.

The freshwater tanks had been topped off, the batteries fully charged, and the fuel tank filled with 65 gallons of marine diesel. Most importantly, the reefer was properly stocked, including with his favorite adult beverages. Everything was ready for a nice relaxing time plying the breezes along the western shore of Central Florida. This morning's departure would take him under the Pinellas Bayway drawbridge, "Structure C (bascule bridge)" on the navigation charts. Once clear of the roadway, he would make the usual right cut out into the open Gulf. Were he to continue south and east, he would go under Structure E, which would lead him into Tampa Bay proper.

The bridge tender was unaccustomed to much Intercoastal Waterway traffic this time of the week, and three calls on the marine radio were required to gain her attention. The warning horn ultimately sounded as the large gates fell toward the pavement, stopping the weary early morning commuters. Pete smiled inwardly as he passed cars full of important people on tight schedules and wearing expensive business suits. He felt very comfortable and at home while shoeless and wearing his practical quick-dry shorts and tank-top.

When folks met Pete for the first time, they could tell he spent most of his time outdoors. He had a natural tan that fulltime Florida residents seemed to be able to keep all year round. His t-shirt revealed a well-toned upper body, the result of keeping active. He spent a lot of time swimming and scuba diving. Pete's blue eyes were those of an understanding and compassionate man, if you took the time to study them, but his eyes also revealed a hidden side — Pete was a man who could draw a line in the sand and would do whatever it took to make that line stick. His slightly weathered skin had grown accustomed to the salt air over the years, and his smile remained all natural and sincere. His trimmed moustache and squared jaw line gave definition to his military-style haircut, and he was well aware that the ladies liked his slight dimples.

Pete knew every system on board and was at ease with his boat. He had fixed everything at least once and most things twice, for sooner or later, everything on a boat needed to be replaced, greased, or repainted. When he purchased the 1984 sloop-rigged sailboat seven years earlier, he had named her the Southern Cross, and one day he would make it south of the equator and sail under the stars that were the namesake of this vessel. He had lived aboard since he bought her, and he was still learning new things every day. The sea was an unforgiving teacher, but Pete appreciated the challenges and approached them enthusiastically. He never was one for routines and business as usual. Pete never could quite fit into that mold others had found so comfortable in their daily lives.

The Southern Cross turned westward, slipping past the point of Pass-A-Grille beach and into the North Channel, easing seaward at a steady 6.2 knots. It was necessary for the engine to take the load from the sails every now and then. The 83 percent humidity made for a sticky sunrise, which many northern tourists found uncomfortable. Muggy was the word the weather guessers on TV liked to use. The lack of wind would not last much longer though. The sun would continue its daily climb, heating the concrete jungle and generating an on-shore breeze as the salty air rushed landward to fill the void left by the rising torrents of automobile exhaust choked air. Then the sails would come alive and the engine would be relieved of duty, probably a bit after 9:30 by Pete's estimate.

Pete savored the quiet open waters that were free from the slightest bit of anger-fueled emotions, and he hated the city streets that now lacked even plain old common courtesy. Drivers were talking on cell phones, working on last minute makeup applications, forcing down a rushed breakfast behind the wheel, even text messaging on BlackBerrys resting on steering wheels while they made their way through traffic. Just about every skill could be witnessed except those required for driving. It really felt good to not be a part of that lifestyle. A slight grin developed as the evidence of advanced civilization was steadily replaced by the sound of passive teal blue saltwater being cut by the bow.

Reaching the open water allowed Pete's thoughts to drift. The concentration required to navigate the confined channels evaporated as he began to think about his friend Sam Adams, who he was scheduled to pick up in two days.

Sam Adams and Pete had first met in Army Flight Training at Fort Rucker Alabama quite a few years ago. They were both in their early 40s now, and a lot had transpired for both of them as the years ticked by. Sam was still married and had a couple of great boys, one of them in college and the other planning to join the Air Force. Sam's wife agreed to let him take off on the occasional "Pete Adventure Vacation Package" every couple of years, but otherwise, Sam was a good husband and a great father and his little vacations with Pete were well deserved.

Pete and Sam had become close friends after both volunteered for U.S. Army Special Forces training. They were subsequently assigned to the same aviation unit, one that didn't officially exist. The challenge of flying the AH-6 Little Bird helicopter into the night in support of some secret faraway mission was always a source of personal pride for both men. It made them feel like they were accomplishing something great. The helicopter was basically a solid-and-sound machine, but it was just a little underpowered. Sam liked to say that the lack of excess power just upped the skill level some.

Years ago, they were flying the blackened machines in Africa just above the sand on a heading of 127 degrees magnetic, 0215 hours local time. The flight path was planned to keep them away from any of the North African desert villages just south of Mogadishu. The mission was simple and required one pilot and one co-pilot/gunner for each bird, with a total of 4 aircraft in tight formation while blacked out. They would fly a knap of the earth profile, a practiced maneuver that kept the aircraft following the rising and falling contour of the terrain to minimize potential enemy targeting opportunities. They adhered to the preplanned route until reaching a point where two wadis, dry riverbeds in the desert, came together below several rolling hills, the latitude and longitude preprogrammed into the internal navigation systems. They were scheduled to arrive at a particular spot in the desert at precisely 0235 and were to remain on the ground for less than 60 seconds.

Six Navy Seals were in the desert, which sounded strange to Pete and Sam from the beginning, and were scheduled for extraction. The specific mission details were never known to the helo crews. They were told only what they needed to know to complete the mission and nothing further.

Compartmentalization of information was a necessary security measure, ensuring that no one person in the field ever knew the entire battle plan. The main mission could not be compromised by an unexpected capture, and torture will push any man, no matter how tough or how trained, to talk.

Part of this planning included one extra helo taking up Slot #4 in the formation, just in case. Should one of the helicopters be forced to make an emergency landing due to mechanical problems, the crew

8

would destroy their abandoned helicopter and ride in the backup bird.

It wasn't a mechanical problem that nearly killed Pete in a controlled crash that early morning, but a shoulder launched weapon, an RPG. The point of origin was not immediately known, but the point of detonation was. The grenade exploded just behind the tail rotor. Enough shrapnel punctured the tail rotor blades to cause catastrophic failure of the anti-torque system. The only thing that kept his craft going straight was the slipstream racing along the tail boom like the wind along a weather vane. The entire aircraft was shaking itself to death as backup systems began to take over for the destroyed primary flight control systems.

Pete had kept them in the air sufficiently long to escape the immediate threat by putting as much distance between themselves and the unknown shooter as possible, but AH-6 could not stay airborne much longer. The controls were increasingly hard to hold on to, and stable flight soon became impossible. Jackson, the co-pilot/gunner, was already on the encrypted secure radio channel announcing their emergency as Pete scanned the desert ahead of the wounded helo for a spot to set the machine down. The green glow of the landscape through the night-vision goggles provided enough terrain features to make a rapid judgment call. He had no lateral directional control and so this had to be a run-on landing. He would have to use his forward airspeed to keep the machine straight while sliding the skids onto the sand. Pete had practiced this procedure time and again, but under controlled training conditions with a perfectly good helicopter — not in the desert at night with the back half shot to hell.

The trick was to start rolling off throttle from the collective stick on his left side while sliding to a halt. The throttle movements needed to be precisely timed as the forward airspeed slowed down, which caused the machine to lose directional control authority. The decreasing throttle reacted with the Allison turbine to produce proportionally less torque, keeping the machine from spinning clockwise. Should a sideways slide occur, the helicopter skids would bite into the terrain instead of sliding on top of it. Should the helo pass 12 degrees of tilt to one side, a condition known as dynamic rollover would occur. The weight of the engine and transmission up top would not only roll the machine but keep the machine rolling over. No amount of control surface movement, even in a perfectly good and fully functional helicopter, could stop the roll once it began.

The emergency landing was executed with a level of precision that would have made his instructor pilot back at Fort Rucker beam with pride. For a split second, Pete allowed himself to imagine the I.P. pointing at him and proudly proclaiming, "Yep. Did you see that? He's *my* student, and *I* taught him that maneuver." That fantasy quickly faded, however. The biggest glitch was lack of continued contact between the earth and the helicopter until he could bring his helo to complete stop.

The helicopter was on the ground sliding straight and had slowed to less than 25 knots when they suddenly reentered the night air. Pete never saw the shallow wadi. It was too dark and everything was happening pretty fast. Had he seen it coming, however, there was absolutely zilch he could have done to prevent what happened anyway. He felt the helicopter become airborne again when the front skids hit the lip of the wadi. The spinning rotor blades would no longer support the weight of the injured helo with lift, and gravity claimed them.

The 25 feet to the bottom of the wadi was slightly less than one full second, but it seemed an eternity. That strange sensation of everything happening in slow motion was in effect, but then the machine smacked the rock and sand hard enough to actually bounce. Enough torque remained in the engine and transmission to cause a 45 degree twist of the entire fuselage to the left while still moving forward. The skids dug sideways into the sand and caused the helo to roll six times, ultimately landing on its right side, which was just where Jackson was strapped in.

He would later learn that one of the Navy Seals was a pretty good medic and had quite literally saved his life, but the Seal didn't remove the torn piece of aluminum structure that punctured Pete's right lung just behind his shoulder blade. The aluminum framework had to be cut from the wreckage and left protruding out his back through the torn flight suit for the ride out. The onboard emergency extraction tool had to come from a different helicopter as this one was

11

inaccessible in the twisted wreckage. Pete had been placed across the laps of two of the Seals in the back of Sam's bird while the medic packed gauze around the chunk of metal to seal his lung from the outside world.

During the rescue, two of the helicopters maintained a tight cover overhead, repelling the original attackers with superior firepower. The well practiced maneuvers stained the tan desert sand with enemy blood. *Death From Above,* just like the unit patch proclaimed.

Pete's copilot/gunner was killed during the fourth roll, although nobody really cared about which roll it was that actually killed him. Rich Jackson was coming home with them for a decent burial. Nobody gets left behind. *Ever.*

Sam Adams had stayed with Pete for the first few days after surgery at an Army base in Germany. Even though Pete had been married for the past few years, he didn't expect his wife, Amy, to show up. Their union displayed all the traditional earmarks of a marriage destined for failure. Amy had been star-struck early in the relationship. The flying, being an officer's wife, the dinners and travel all held initial glamour that saved her from an extraordinarily small hometown in Iowa.

Amy had simply closed the door on the Army Chaplain sent to notify her of the accident, and she never went to Germany. She had cried for a while but moved away two days later. She couldn't take the nature of his job any longer, and her reaction was to just disappear and let the divorce happen in absentia.

The doctors subsequently removed the metal and repaired Pete's lung after cutting about 15 percent of it away. Two of his ribs were permanently shattered and had to be supported with surgical steel rods because they were beyond healing by themselves. When Pete was medically discharged, he was as emotionally scarred as he was physically marred. He had nearly lost his life which he knew came with the duty, but he had also lost his wife, and tragically, his Army flying career. Sam was the only one who stood by him through it all. Bonds that were created in combat and blood were lifelong and *never* broken.

Two

Pete's thoughts had drifted long enough as he made his way deeper into open ocean, the sun now more intense as it rose into the sky. There were always a handful of chores that needed to be tended to when underway. Pete methodically checked off each item from a well-used mental list as it was completed. The sail covers were removed, winch handles put into place, mainsheet line ready to pay out, jib blocks set, and lots of other little things. The auxiliary diesel engine would be relieved of duty as soon as the morning breeze freshened enough to allow the sails to take over the propulsion duties. For now, though, the Yanmar was purring along and happy in its task.

Pete had begun his southwestern turn and brought the bow on course, 240 magnetic. A gentle tap to the autopilot had given all steering commands over to the mechanical captain. Several deliberate scans of the horizon, from ninety degrees port to ninety degrees starboard, confirmed that he was alone. On a Tuesday morning, most of the boating community was landlocked in the 9 to 5 rat race. Boats sat on trailers in subdivisions, painfully ignored during the workweek.

The next item on the mental checklist indicated that it was time to go below and fix that great cup of coffee. There was something about making a pot of coffee while underway. You used all the same ingredients and duplicated each step precisely that you used in port, and even the time to percolate the brew on the propane stove was the same down to the nanosecond, but somehow it was just not the same. Everyone who had ever been to sea agreed that this phenomenon exists, but nobody could explain it. The damn coffee just got better the further away from shore you went. Today, the coffee was going to be fantastic; it was percolating and filling the cabin with that wonderful aroma as he passed the 5 mile mark from shore, even the tallest buildings now dwindled to nearly nothing on the horizon. He never opted to stay just 4 miles off shore when he took these trips, for then he could see the scars of urban development along the coastline, which really ruined a great view.

Pete got out his wide-bottomed stainless steel at-sea coffee mug and snuffed out the propane flame on the stove. Most of the chores were completed, and it was time to relax for a few minutes and take in the beautiful morning. Heaven should be something like this, he thought, as the boat quietly slipped along the surface of the sea and the full majesty of the open ocean bathed its lonely occupant in peace and contentment.

The first sip of coffee was just a bit too soon, as it always was, and his lips had that slightly burnt feeling. He blew the steam away and brought the coffee closer to test the temperature with his upper lip while enjoying the wonderful aroma. It was then that the Southern Cross let out a shudder, which was her way of calling for help. A low vibration echoed through the core of the boat all the way up the mast, making the shrouds and stays hum in the slowing breeze.

Forward thrust had been all but eliminated as she coasted toward a full stop. A grinding sound emanating from below reminded Pete of a dying blender crushing ice cubes.

Pete set the cup down so fast he missed the countertop, spilling the hot liquid down his right leg just below the knee. His bare toes took the brunt of the cascading liquid as he jumped sideways and three feet in the air to escape the scalding coffee. He then leapt up the companionway ladder, skipping steps, which rewarded him with a bruised left knee to go along with his burned toes, and into the cockpit to check the engine controls. His mind flashed through emergency sequences and procedures, researching his mental records trying to find a match for the alarming sound. Somewhere in the deep recesses of his mind a previous experience found a match for the noise and the remedy became immediately apparent. *STOP THE ENGINE!*

Pete reached the engine cutoff switch in the cockpit about the same time that a funny smell tainted his nostrils. He had jabbed the kill switch so hard he was sure his nail would be black and blue. The Yanmar diesel complied and quickly fell silent after giving one last tremor.

He then checked sternward and found the culprit, a crab trap float with its line securely wound around the prop shaft. This was not a normal fishing area for crabs, and the pots with buoys should not be here. Pete hoped that he had silenced the engine in time to prevent damage.

Pete pulled himself up onto the cockpit cushion to collect his thoughts and relax for just a minute. The Southern Cross was steadily coasting to a halt, the crab trap buoy line wrapped around the prop shaft and securely in tow. Taking a few deep breaths and rubbing his sore knee, he began to weigh his options.

His initial assessment was that his stalled boat was not an immediate hazard to other craft. Pete didn't believe that he was taking on water because the bilge high-water alarm wasn't going off. The shaft seal was presumably still in place and holding. If that seal failed, he could expect about 35 to 40 gallons a minute flowing along the shaft and into the engine room, only 20 gallons a minute less than the pump manufacturer's rating of 65 gallons. By comparison, a 2 inch hole 6 inches below the waterline could let in 55 gallons a minute. The pump was supposed to be able to move water out at a higher rate than what it could flow in — at least the specifications said it would.

This knowledge did not make him feel better about a possibly leaking shaft seal.

A close inspection would be the only thing that would satisfy him, and Pete went below to check the seal visually. Reaching the bottom of the ladder caused a quick shot of adrenalin to hit him directly in his chest as his feet hit water. "There was no alarm," he immediately thought to himself. One half a second later, he realized he was not standing in seawater but in spilled coffee, and damn, it *was STILL hot!*

Hopping out of the hot coffee and onto a rubber-backed throw rug gave him a reason to use some colorful language, but he refrained. His ex-wife always complained that he cussed like a sailor, but she said that being one didn't excuse such behavior. It was such a long time ago that she was in his life, but 10 years of marriage had instilled old habits that refused to evaporate and completely release him from the past.

Pete removed the deck hatch opening the compartment. A flashlight revealed that the shaft, just aft of the engine room, appeared to be fine. At least something was going right — everything was dry. There were no signs of water seeping in past the cutlass bearing. He replaced the deck cover, and then Pete refilled his coffee mug and returned topside. A quick look around established that he was still alone, and his coffee tasted as good as he knew it would.

The pain was easing some, but there was an odd shaped red welt along the top of his foot and three biggest toes. His left knee still throbbed a bit, but the pain was tolerable.

Pete set the mug on the cockpit table just ahead of the wheel and went forward to the bow. He disconnected securing pins and opened the deck compartment where he could reach the Danforth anchor that was resting in the bow mounting bracket. The 35-pound anchor slid effortlessly from its cradle, creating a small splash when it hit the sea. About 45 feet of line played out before it went slack as the anchor found the seafloor. The boat was still drifting forward at about 1 knot, which was just enough to let out some extra anchor rode and allow the hook to dig into the seafloor. The flukes of the anchor were designed to penetrate into the sandy bottom and bury deeper with every tug. The harder the tug, the deeper it went. Generally, the anchor winch had to be used to pull the shank of the anchor straight up and break the flukes free of the sand.

When the Southern Cross began a slow turn around the anchor line, he knew the anchor had set properly. The boat quietly came to a stop and was now pointed northward. This was not the first time in his sailing career he had had to cut line from the prop shaft, but it looked like a good morning to go swimming.

Pete grabbed his Spare Air scuba bottle from the forward storage locker, a mini-tank that was a bit smaller and skinnier than a 16 ounce plastic root beer bottle. The tank was spun aluminum, just like his normal size scuba tank, and held 3,000 PSI of air, or whatever he filled it with from his main tank. Full pressure delivered 55 to 60 regular breaths at the surface, and fewer the deeper you went. The small regulator was attached to the top of the mini-tank with a standard mouthpiece. Divers generally carried this mini-tank as an emergency backup should something go wrong with their primary scuba unit. It delivered enough air to safely surface from less than 100 feet.

He then donned fins, a mask, and a very sharp dive knife, and with the Spare Air gripped between his teeth, he stepped off the port side. Pete had unclipped the two sections of lifeline normally reserved for passage to the dock while tied up, allowing him easy access to the Gulf. The warm 82 degree water felt surprisingly good on his burnt foot, and the weightlessness helped stop the throbbing in his left knee. Pete swam under the stern and hung onto the rudder with one hand for support. The crab trap line had indeed wound itself around the shaft and into a tangled mess of nylon rope. About 45 breaths later, the crab trap was free to drift away and strike terror into the hearts of blue crabs everywhere. The line was cut from the shaft, separating the float from the metal trap dangling somewhere below. The float was on its own and already drifting aft of the stern. No worse for the wear, Pete climbed up the stern ladder and got back on the boat. It was time to finish that cup of coffee and get back underway.

Pete sat drying in the cockpit sipping the cup of coffee while letting an ice pack cool his left knee. He always kept one frozen in the reefer for use in the small cooler that he frequently took ashore when anchored out. He was sitting with his leg propped up against the binnacle, which held the compass and navigation instruments just ahead of the wheel.

By the time the ice pack warmed to the ambient temperature, he had finished the last of the coffee, which was now tepid as well. Pete stretched as he stood, and then he walked forward to retrieve the anchor and be on his way.

Three

Pete grabbed a portion of the anchor rode between the cleat and hawser on the deck, then pulled up the slack and gave it two and a half wraps around the winch drum. The power to the windlass had been energized prior to coming to the bow. The foot switch on deck was under a protective rubber cover to keep it dry, but there was just enough protrusion above the deck to allow the 12 volt electric motor to be operated by slight downward foot pressure. Each press of the foot switch started the drum turning, thereby winding the anchor rode up onto the deck. All that was required of the operator was to feed the loose end into the open deck locker.

The anchor rode began its slow grind back on board while dragging the boat closer to the area directly above the anchor. Once the boat arrived overhead, the shank of the Danforth would swivel and pull straight up, prying the two flukes free from the sand. The anchor always brought back a big wet clump of sand and required rinsing before replacing it in the mounting bracket on the bow toe rail.

The winch would always grind a little extra hard while prying loose the flukes. There had been times when the anchor was set so hard in the sand that Pete had to allow the natural rhythm induced by the waves to break it free. This time, however, the winch seemed to grind extra hard. Pete stopped to let the natural buoyancy of the boat maintain enough upward pressure on the anchor to help it break free, but there was not enough wave movement this morning for that technique to work.

He gave another couple of taps with the foot switch to help coax the Danforth anchor from the depths, but all that this accomplished was to pull the bow a little closer to the sea floor. Pete leaned over far enough to see the painted waterline on the hull. The winch had actually pulled the bow an extra 6 inches lower than the stern. He had never been set quite this hard in the sand before.

The only explanation that made any sense was that the flukes of the anchor had been fouled by rocks or a limestone ledge, which had happened to him twice before, but he had managed to get the line loose on both occasions. Pete went back to the cockpit after giving the anchor line about 20 feet of slack, started the engine, and swung the wheel hard to port to back him off the ledge in the opposite direction the anchor had set. He eased back at an idle. Rock ledges were not extremely common here, but there were some limestone outcroppings in the area. This one was probably marked on some fisherman's GPS chart plotter as his "secret" fishing spot.

As the stern swung around, he gave the anchor a little help by throttling the engine up to 1400 RPM. When the anchor broke free, he would need to put it in forward gear just long enough to stop any rearward movement. Any unnecessary dragging along the bottom would simply cause the anchor to dig in and start the process all over again. Pete had his hand ready to close the throttle while the engine created a small wake up both sides of the hull. This resulted in nothing more than a taught anchor line stretching forward of the bow. The Southern Cross was held firmly in place.

"Things have a tendency to come in threes, and this must be number three." Assuming of course you group all the little injuries into one sub-category. "Wonderful," Pete thought.

Pushing the throttle back to idle and hitting the engine kill switch eased the tension on the anchor rode. The diesel gave one final spit of cooling water out the stern and fell silent. There was nothing to do now but get wet again. He had to swim to the anchor since the anchor wasn't coming to him.

The last time his anchor had fouled like this he had been in the Florida Keys anchored off Islamorada, if memory served him correctly. The anchorage there was about 8 feet deep and the water a turquoise blue. It was so clear you could watch dinner scurry by on the bottom. That time he was sitting on the stern in his old deck chair while enjoying another beautiful summer evening with a cold Corona in his hand. It was about an hour before sunset with a nice warm tropical breeze blowing along the length of the boat as she weathervaned into the wind. The scene was from a postcard you might mail to your snowbound friends up north just to make them jealous.

Pete had seen a lobster rush out from under a limestone rock and scurry to the base of a brain coral about 15 feet off the stern. Without a lot of forethought, he set the bottle on the deck and did a really nice looking dive over the aft lifeline. Taking a big deep breath as he was midair allowed his momentum, along with a couple of kicks, to take him to the bottom directly over the lobster. Pete effortlessly plucked the lobster from its lack of cover and brought him back to the surface. He tossed the lobster onto the deck and made a mental note to lower the swim ladder first the next time he decided to do this. The lobster began to scurry forward along the deck while Pete got his foothold and climbed over the lifeline. The lobster was mere inches away from making good his escape when he was recaptured, sealing his fate.

This water was far deeper and the swim would not be so easy. He looked over the bow at the troubled anchor line. The visibility was a scant 8 to 10 feet. There had been a near miss with a hurricane about three weeks ago that had stirred up the Gulf of Mexico, clouding the water from Key West to Pensacola. It would be another week or so before the visibility returned to normal. There were not as many currents on the Gulf side of Florida as there were on the Atlantic, which slowed the clearing process considerably.

Pete brought all his scuba gear up on deck and started to get dressed for the dive. He knew he would not be able to accomplish this task by using the smaller Spare Air unit. He would be going too deep for too long.

He stood up the metallic blue aluminum scuba cylinder and rested it on the black plastic boot secured to the bottom of the tank. The tank was naturally rounded on the bottom so it didn't want to stand on its own. The added boot gave it a flat surface and also kept it from chipping the Gelcoat paint on the deck. This tank was the standard 80 cubic foot version with an operating pressure of 3000 PSI. Calm steady breathing at less than 50 feet would provide him with about 45 minutes of down time, allowing for a proper reserve.

The harder you worked, and thus the harder you breathed, or the deeper you went, the more air you required and less time you could spend on the bottom. But Pete figured this should be a quick 10 minute dive and he would need to go no deeper than about 45 feet. That depth also meant he did not have to worry about making a decompression stop during his ascent.

The buoyancy compensator device, commonly known as the BCD, a vest like setup with circular straps on the back to hold the tank, contained an integrated air bladder system with two separate air fill points and three air release valves. The BCD would allow the diver to constantly adjust his buoyancy through the dive. Too little and you kept bobbing up like a fishing cork, but too much and down you went to the bottom. The buoyancy changed with the decreasing air pressure in the tank, differing depths, salinity levels, and gear. An experienced diver could set his buoyancy at exactly neutral, allowing him to float a couple of feet over a coral reef without any swimming movement. You would then simply drift along with the current and watch the stunning live show pass before you, the only perceptible movement were slight ups and downs as you inhaled and exhaled.

Drifting along with a 1 knot current for 45 minutes could prove quite a challenge when you had to swim back to the boat. Drift diving like this usually required someone in a boat to follow your dive flag and pick you up when your air supply mandated your return to the surface.

The regulator consisted of the first stage connected directly to a valve on the top of the tank. There were four black hoses of varied lengths, a console with gauges attached to the end of one hose, another hose that attached to an air fill point on the BCD, and two second stage mouthpieces.

Everyone commonly called it an octopus rig as it somewhat resembled the creature but just short a few legs. The primary second stage delivered a low pressure air supply, while the other regulator stayed available as an emergency air source to another diver. The console had a pressure gauge on the top that displayed units in pounds per square inch with a depth gauge below it that had a recording needle to remember the deepest point of the dive. Additionally, this display had a smaller inset water temperature gauge. The back side of the console contained a magnetic compass, all the dials self-illuminating for dark or murky conditions.

The water was warm enough that Pete decided not to put his wet suit on, but the thin layer of neoprene not only provided warmth but offered some protection from jelly fish stings and other minor dangers of the sea and so he did not make the choice lightly. Without the buoyant wet suit, he needed to remove three pounds of lead weight, known as soft weights because they resembled pouches of shotgun pellets, from the designated pockets on the BCD. He just set them aside on the deck.

His shorts and tank-top would be enough for this quick dive. He wouldn't be down long enough for the cooler water temps on the bottom to become much of a factor. He did, however, need his reef gloves, which resembled golf gloves. They were light weight but designed to provide protection from touching sharp corals or barnacles.

Pete opened the valve on the top of the tank to charge the octopus rig with pressure. Everything sounded like it was holding just fine, no leaks. Next he tested the automatic inflator valve by depressing the fill button and seeing the BCD begin to expand.

The pressure gauge showed just over 3,000 PSI, a full tank. He quickly tested each regulator by biting onto the second stage mouthpiece and sealing the outer ring with his lips. A couple of breaths with each regulator assured him they were working just fine.

Pete next stood on the deck with the tank and BCD in front of his legs. He turned the equipment so the tank was resting against his shins and the BCD was open and facing away from him. He bent over at the waist, reached through the arm holes of the BCD, and firmly grabbed both sides of the scuba tank. This move had him face down looking at the tank upside down. He stood and heaved the gear upward over his head, releasing his grip on the tank at the precise moment gravity would slide the BCD down his arms to rest on his back. Pete was now standing bent forward at a 45 degree angle with his scuba tank properly in place. All he had to do now was fasten the chest and waist straps while he stood up straight. A little upper body shaking got the BCD settled comfortably into place.

He next adjusted the locations of all the hoses and clipped the gauge console in position. With everything properly secured, he put on his mask and snorkel. He checked the seal on the mask by sucking in with his nose. No leaks.

Reef gloves went on next, and then his fins. The scuba gear was quite ungainly on dry land, and even worse on the crowded deck of a sailboat. He worked his way to the side of the aft backstay, remembering to give the folded swim ladder a kick with his heel. The ladder dropped backward at its one hinge point, doubling its length, and the bottom half settled into the water. It's a lot easier getting back on the boat with the ladder fully extended, as previous experience had taught him.

He placed the second stage of his primary regulator in his mouth and took a couple of test breaths. Pete held his mask and regulator in place by putting the palm of his left hand over the front part of the mask and regulator, holding it firmly on his face. He reached around his back with his right hand and grabbed the girth of one of the securing straps for the tank and held it firmly. Just prior to stepping off the boat, he dipped his chin toward his chest to keep the back of his head away from the first stage connections on the back and top of the tank. When you hit the water, you don't want the tank valve banging into the base of your skull. A split and bleeding skull would be more than a headache, also drawing the interest of any nearby sharks.

One giant step and he was free of the boat. He entered the water with a splash. Even with the regulator in his mouth, he still held his breath, a primal instinct. It's very unnatural to inhale while poking your head underwater.

Pete bobbed to the surface initially due to the extra air in the BCD bladder. He was breathing on the regulator now and everything felt pretty good. He slowly released the air from the BCD by pulling a cord attached to the upper relief valve. He could feel himself becoming less buoyant and starting to sink. As he slipped below the surface, he turned to face the Southern Cross and then swam along the keel. He decided to take one more look at the prop shaft on his way by to confirm that everything looked good.

He reached the anchor line just below the surface at the bow of the boat, and he then pulled himself down the line toward the bottom. When Pete reached a point about halfway down, he could no longer make out the surface nor could he see the bottom. He was suspended in a featureless void where up and down became confusing, but he watched his bubbles to assure himself he was still headed toward the anchor. Then the increasing weight of the water caused pressure to build on his mask and ears, but a couple of puffs out of his nose cleared up both. The mask pressure equalized and his ears popped easier than they did on an airplane.

The depth gauge registered 38 feet when bottom objects began to come into view as shadows and silhouettes. It read 43 feet before he could see the outline of something. As he swam closer, he saw that, whatever the object was, it clearly was not a rock. The anchor line led him straight to a foreign structure, obviously manmade, a dark barnacle-covered flat structure going off to his right at an angle and toward the surface. The left side of this flat panel met a rounded base that had an outline that was the shape of a window.

When Pete reached the structure, he discovered that it appeared to be the nose of an airplane. The flat panel off to his right was the left wing, and it looked like the engine on that side had a severely twisted propeller. Everything had a thick layer of slime, barnacles, and sand on it, but this was clearly a high wing twin engine airplane that had quite obviously been here for some time. The original color of the aircraft paint had long been erased by time and obscured by sea life.

The anchor had securely set with the flukes pulling up through the thin aluminum skin on the bottom side of the wing between the engine and the fuselage. The wing root was one of the strongest parts of the aircraft, as it supported most of the load when airborne. The anchor tines had entered the skin upward and wedged in between the frame and a wing spar. It was not going to let go or bend for the anchor of a mere sailboat.

Most of the airplane's right and aft sides were buried in the sand, and the entire right wing and engine were either gone or completely buried. Years of settling and shifting sands were performing a slow natural burial of the wreckage. The occasional hurricane probably served to expose the airframe for a short period of time before it became buried again. Pete mused that the same cycle had continued for countless years across all the oceans of the world.

The Plexiglas windscreen was covered with silt and barnacles, but the outline was quite clear. More barnacles had attached themselves to the fuselage. The ones on the glass were reasonably easy to knock off. There was a large grouper stationed under the left engine intently watching events unfold in what he obviously considered to be his home territory. He would closely watch the invader while remaining just far enough away to make good his escape should it be required.

The windscreen was cracked and the upper half easily pushed inward. A swirl of silt further clouded his view, and instinctively Pete grabbed a bundle that floated slowly upward from the new opening. He could tell immediately that it was canvas or cloth, and it felt like clothing of some sort. Pulling it from the cloud of silt, he got a better look at what he was holding. It was an old style gym bag, the kind that had a zipper along the top and two big handles, an artifact from the pre-Velcro days. The zipper had long ago rusted into a solid strip of nonfunctioning useless metal.

To keep the bag from floating away, Pete gave a couple of fin kicks and was propelled over to the engine. The grouper backed off to a safe distance near the wing tip while maintaining a vigilant watch. Pete hooked the handles of the gym bag around the bent tip of the propeller and let the bottom try to float upward, securing the bag in place.

Pete always kept his small dive light in the forward pocket of his BCD, which he used to check for lobsters in crevices. Night dives required the use of the bigger light, but this little one provided enough illumination to allow him a limited view into the interior of the airplane. Getting his facemask up to the opening in the upper half of the windscreen afforded him a closer look. Pete was rewarded with the unexpected pleasure of someone looking back at him. Well, kind of looking back. The skeletal remains were locked into a never ending gaze toward the blackened instrument panel. The sight was a little startling at first, causing Pete to take a few unnecessary extra breaths, but death was something he had been close to before and he soon regulated his breathing once again.

From what he could see, the pilot's was the only skeleton in the airplane. A couple of the rear windows had apparently broken as sand had filtered its way into the aft portion of the cabin, partially covering what looked like several cargo boxes. As he peered harder, he could see that the boxes were flaking apart. They were covered in cloth, or maybe burlap. Then it struck him. He was looking at some unlucky smuggler's missing mother lode of marijuana bales.

Most of the silt had settled now, giving Pete a clearer look inside. He saw nothing else floating loose, but he did see the small metal placard below the dash compass that had the registration number of the aircraft on it. It came off easily, and he secured it in his BCD pocket. A couple of fin kicks toward the engine moved the grouper back a bit.

With the bag in hand, Pete began his ascent as he ran through a list of questions in his mind, which distracted him from the original task. Pete stopped 10 feet above the plane and reversed direction to free the anchor. Then he wondered if he needed to leave it set for now. A call to the Coast Guard had to be made, and they would start an investigation, including interviewing him, which would mean a further delay. He would have to stay on the hook and a CG boat would be here either late today or early tomorrow morning. He wouldn't be able to get underway until at least the next afternoon, he was sure of that. Sam was due to arrive as previously scheduled, and Pete didn't want to disappoint him by being late. The guy in here was just another forgotten drug smuggling pilot who didn't make it all the way to shore, and whatever family he had would not care if it took a couple of extra days to hear about his fate. He'd already been down here for quite some time, the airplane was obviously not going anywhere, and a good GPS fix would put the Coast Guard within 15 feet of this exact spot.

It wasn't easy, but after much tugging, the anchor finally came free. Pete had to brace his flippers against the underside of the wing while pulling downward on the anchor stock and working the tines back and forth. The stock was a crossbar connecting the flukes to the shank, which was ultimately tied to the rode. Lots of exhaust bubbles indicated how hard he was actually pulling on the anchor to get it loose. Once the anchor did break free, he half-walked and half-swam the anchor about 10 feet away and jabbed the flukes into the sand to keep it from fouling on the airplane again.

He then swam back to the left engine where he had left the bag hanging on the bent propeller for the second time while he freed the anchor. This was becoming too much excitement for the grouper, and the fish subsequently disappeared. Pete took a moment to watch it swim off into the distance.

Pete then began his ascent to the surface once again, this time with a long list of questions.

Four

Pete was glad to finally get underway again. He had given all his scuba gear and the exterior of the gym bag a freshwater rinse, and everything was drying in the sun on the aft deck. The gym bag's old style zipper was still secured by rust, and the bag was encrusted with a thin layer of marine growth. Pete knew that whatever was in it was probably in about the same shape as the skeleton. Paper air navigation charts would not have lasted long at all. A plastic-coated driver's license might have survived, but most likely not. If he did find some identifying information, he would pass it on to the Coast Guard — the investigators would probably like to know who the skeleton belonged to. Pete would worry about trying to get the bag open once he got underway. He didn't want to slip too far behind schedule.

He brought the swim ladder back up and secured it in place, then double checked the sails. As the lines were freed and ready to be hauled up into place, the morning breeze was beginning to blow onshore, which would give him a starboard tack for his southbound journey. Pete had pushed the MOB, or Man Overboard button, on the

GPS. The machine accurately recorded his exact position with today's estimated position error of 14 feet. You could lose sight of the person overboard within moments when the waves were as small as three feet. A bobbing head is very small when in a large body of water. By the time you can get a vessel turned around, you can miss the victim by several hundred yards and never see them again. The MOB position report would get you back to the exact spot for a rescue. With a couple more button pushes, he renamed this waypoint "Pothole" and saved it in the internal database.

Pete planned to hoist the sails while still at anchor. He untied the sail ties that held the Dacron mainsail to the boom, which prevented any wind from unexpectedly inflating the sail. The main sheet halyard is a line connected to the top of the sail that runs up the back side of the mast to a pulley, from which it then returns to the deck. Located on the starboard side of the mast, three feet above the deck, was a manual winch that took two and a half wraps of the main sheet around the winch drum. The boat naturally weathervaned as the mainsail grew to its full extension while Pete cranked the winch. The sail made a flapping sound as it luffed in the light breeze. The jib was the next to come out. With the onshore wind beginning to develop, the desired effect of holding the anchor rode away from the plane below was achieved. There was now no chance of the anchor fouling on the airplane again.

The headsail, or jib as it was also known, was rolled up on the forestay, which is attached between the top of the mast and the forward deck at the bow. The sail itself was rolled on a full length sleeve, making the forestay fat with fabric. The jib sheet runs from the bottom edge of the sail through a block mounted on the toe rail next to the cockpit. A second line runs from a drum attached to the bottom of the roller furling headsail and to the other side of the cockpit. By using the two lines attached to the headsail, you could let out or roll up a specific amount of sail onto the forestay. The strength of the wind determined how much sail was let out. With the morning's light breezes, the sails would be fully extended. Pete pulled the line back, causing the jib to extend fully back toward and just aft of the mast. This sail flapped gently in the breeze as the jib sheet was allowed to remain loose.

Once the sails were extended, he stepped on the anchor switch and began winding the rode back onto the deck. He fed the free end into the deck locker as it was released from the winch drum. The anchor arrived on deck easily and rattled into place on the deck mount. What sand didn't fall off as it dried could be rinsed off later. Pete replaced the pin that secured the anchor as the bow began to fall off the wind and fill the sails.

Free from the airplane below, the Southern Cross began a slow drift backward as a result of the breeze. Pete spun the wheel to the starboard side, bringing the Southern Cross perpendicular to the breeze, and the sails immediately filled with air, taking the shape of a pregnant woman's belly to the port side of the boat. The Southern Cross heeled slightly to port as she transferred wind energy into forward movement. She started slowly, then began to build up speed, and as she did, the apparent wind changed direction due to the boat's forward movement. Several adjustments to the tension on the sheets had the sails balanced and set correctly. The GPS read 5.1 knots. She would get up to 6 plus knots when the breeze freshened after lunch.

There were no apparent hazards along his intended course either visually or recorded on the area navigation charts, and as the bow swung to a course of 152 degrees magnetic, Pete punched on the autopilot, putting the mechanical captain back in charge once again. He double checked his course after scanning the horizon to confirm he was out here alone.

Sam was due to arrive tomorrow evening at the Southwest Florida International Airport in Fort Myers. Pete planned to sail the Southern Cross up the Caloosahatchee River, which ran through the middle of town. Sam would take a cab to the municipal marina and find Pete somewhere in the Philthy Pelican, a nice little marina bar facing the river. Knowing exactly where he anchored meant he could usually see the tip of his mast from the outside deck overlooking the river. He could also keep an eye on his RIB, the rigid inflatable boat, or dink, which was pulled ashore next to the bar. The dink had a hard bottom deck with a slight V shaped hull. The sides were large inflatable tubes you could sit on while running along. The 9.9 HP Yamaha outboard was old but worked well, and once you got the boat up on a plane, she really zipped along.

From his present position, the easterly turn into the river was about 80 nautical miles to the south. He was too close to shore to sail through the night via the autopilot. There were simply too many things to run into this close to land. A vigilant all-night watch would need to be maintained, which would mean 36 hours without a good night's sleep. Not a great way to start a vacation, he mused, but Venice, 33 miles to the south, was a great place to overnight, and the entrance to the city dock at Higel Park along the river was pretty straightforward. It was a nice city dock with room for a couple of boats, but if that was full, he could just drop the hook in the marked anchorage alongside the Intercoastal Waterway. Pete had been here a few times before and knew the channel was well marked. At his present speed of 5 knots, it would take 6.6 hours to get to the mouth of the channel. So he decided to spend the night in Venice and get an early start the next morning. That left him with about 50 nautical miles to go, which would take 10 hours if he maintained 5 knots. The Yanmar diesel would move him forward at 7.3 knots if he needed to make up some time. Planning for 5 knots on the sails was a pretty safe guesstimate, although he generally averaged a little over 6.

Pete brought his cell phone up on deck and checked the reception. He had one bar on the small LCD meter, which was about normal for this distance from shore. The coast was littered with cell phone towers, and the salt water helped act as a ground plane antenna, increasing the distance you could use a phone. He ran through the menu to Sam's cell number and hit the call function.

Three rings later, Sam picked up. "Pete, ya old swab. How's the trip so far?" He had obviously read the caller ID.

"Great. I've had a couple of glitches so far, but nothing that should change our schedule." Pete turned a little to the left to get the wind to stop making the loud swishing noise over the microphone. "I'll meet you at the Philthy Pelican. You still planning on making it in time for dinner?"

Sam heard the wind noises go away. "Yeah, wouldn't miss it for the world. My flight is due in a little after 5 p.m. I hope whatever problems you had with that old money pit of yours were not too expensive."

"No, the boat's fine. I did find an airplane though, sunk in about 40 feet of water, and some old smuggler who never made it to shore was still in it. I hooked the thing with my anchor, if you can believe that. By the way, are you at home or the office?"

"I'm finishing up a few things at the office, last minute paperwork and such. It keeps the government operating at peak efficiency. Are we going to salvage an airplane this trip?" Sam asked.

"No, I don't think so, Sam. It's been down much too long. I need to let the Coast Guard know it's there. Could you look up the 800 number for me?" Pete added, "I'm hoping they don't want me to go back to the plane, which would make me a day late picking you up."

"I'll do you one better than that," Sam responded. "I've been training with a CG pilot, a guy named Steve Holland. We have been designing an updated version of the Homeland Security refresher course for helo drivers in the unit. I can pass on the info to him and he can get it in the system, which should help avoid any unnecessary delays on your behalf. Give me what you have so far."

"Thanks. That will work great." Pete pushed the memory function on the GPS and brought up the Pothole waypoint. While waiting for the numbers to appear, he said, "It looks like an old twin engine airplane, maybe a Twin Commander. The pilot is now a skeleton so it looks like he's been there a while." The GPS came up and Pete relayed, "It's at 27 degrees 33 minutes 25 seconds north, 82 degrees 51 minutes 28 seconds west. It's in about 45 feet of water and half buried, so it's not going anywhere."

Sam wrote the information down and wondered briefly what the owner of the skeleton's story was. "Okay. I'll pass it on. Is there anything else I need to bring?"

Pete thought a moment and replied, "Nope. I should have everything. We can get any last minute things in Fort Myers. Just say hi to Sharon and the boys for me."

"Will do, and I'll touch base with you when I land. See you tomorrow night," Sam said.

"Roger that."

Both men pushed the end buttons severing the connection. Pete then quickly scanned the horizon and made sure the autopilot was maintaining a steady course. He looked back at the bag from the airplane and figured that now was as good a time as any to see what was inside.

***

Sam had flipped through a business card holder that was in his upper right desk drawer. He thumbed to the page that had Commander Holland's card with his contact information. Two rings later, a secretary answered the office phone with the standard official canned greeting. Sam was rewarded with a short round of industrial elevator music until he got through to Holland. Sam told him the details that he was aware of and relayed that this was not a rescue mission as the pilot was now only skeletal remains. He related that Pete was under sail and out of contact for the next few days. Holland asked the standard basic questions and wrote down Pete's name and phone number, the boat's name, his home port, and the location of the sunken aircraft. Holland told Sam he would get the report into the system and forward it to the Tampa Coast Guard station. They would then disseminate it to the correct local jurisdiction for a joint investigation.

The bag was stiff with drying salt and tiny crustaceans. Pete stayed on the aft deck with the bag so he could rinse the falling debris over the stern. Because the zipper would never function again, he tried to cut through the canvas side with his small pocket knife but soon gave up. Pete went into the main cabin and returned with his serrated folding rigging knife and began sawing on the upper edge next to the handle. After a little effort, he made it through the thick canvas and began cutting just below the upper seam.

The side of the bag finally gave way and opened up, revealing its contents to the first daylight in many years. The first thing to come out was a wad of long ago destroyed papers that could have been anything, from air navigation charts to a newspaper. Below that was a solid square plastic wrapped object about the size of a paperback book. The wrapping reminded him of the plastic tarps painters use to cover the floor when painting a ceiling. Remnants of nylon strapping tape were evident and still partially holding the plastic in place.

The next thing was rather odd, an old piece of 4 inch PVC pipe about 16 inches long and capped on both ends. It fit into the bag with no room to spare on either end. It was obviously waterproof and most likely the cause of the bag's buoyancy. Next was a thermos covered with green slime. The old red checkered pattern was barely visible. Pete hadn't seen one of these in a long time. He got the lid unscrewed with a bit of grunting. "YUCK! Was that a mistake!" he bellowed as he nearly gagged. The stench was terrible. Some oozing liquid started to spill on the deck, and Pete immediately held the thermos over the aft stern rail to let the contents drip into the ocean. There was no telling what it would do to the paint on the deck.

Pete treated the ocean with respect, but this was different. He wasn't going to store this rotten gel onboard until his next onshore garbage run. This strange elixir would have the entire boat stinking in no time. The problem was solved with a quick release of his grip. The thermos and its odd contents quickly sank into the water.

Pete picked up the PVC tube and gave it a shake. Nothing rattled inside, but it had some weight to it. He was immediately curious about the contents and decided to cut the pipe open. It was a neat little mystery, but he wondered about the legality of breaking into what could well be evidence by the fed's definition. He had salvaged it from the ocean, however, and so he had maritime claim to the contents. He didn't want to interfere with any possible investigation, but this was just too curious an artifact to leave it sealed. He wouldn't have that answer until he cut it open, so the decision was made.

The Southern Cross was running along just fine, the autopilot holding and the sails well trimmed. There were no other boats in view except for a large cargo ship heading north about 4 miles further offshore. He could comfortably leave the helm unattended for a while.

Pete took the PVC tube below along with the plastic bundle. He had a small workbench area on the starboard side companionway near the engine room hatch. He placed the items on the bench and removed a hacksaw from the tool locker underneath. Holding the pipe with his left hand, he began sawing on one end next to the glued on cap, using the rim of the cap as a saw guide. When the saw made it through, after 10 or so good strokes, he slightly rotated the pipe away from him and cut into the next section. He repeated this procedure until he was back where he started, completing the process, and the cap fell away. He held the open end up to the light and realized that he was looking at the ends of wrapped stacks of cash, lots of cash. The sealed vault had done its job, perfectly preserving the contents.

He turned the pipe upside down and pulled on the center stack of money. When the first stack came out, everything else simply let go and fell into a heap on the workbench. Pete was staring at a nice little pile of cash — twenties and fifties and hundreds. There was also a sealed plastic baggie with white powder among the pile, cocaine most likely. Picking up a pack of cash, he noticed that each pack had a standard bank wrapper with the bill denomination listed along with the total amount. A quick scan revealed nearly seventy thousand dollars. There was a small piece of notebook paper with an odd series of numbers on it as well. It didn't look like a phone number, just a string of seemingly random numbers, and it was circled, maybe a bank account number. There was one pack of cash that had the initials 'LA' written in ink on the wrapper. He confirmed that the PVC pipe was empty.

Thumbing through several stacks of money, Pete realized that all the cash had a date of 1984 or earlier on it. Well then, that was an easy bit of detective work, he mused to himself. The plane crash obviously happened pre-1985.

Next, he picked up the plastic book-sized package. When he started to open it, a small amount of water dripped out of the first two layers, but it didn't amount to very much. He peeled about 6 layers of plastic and noticed that there was a small bit of sand in between the last couple of layers. Pete found a final inner clear baggie that revealed its contents, a well preserved video cassette, but not the standard size tape everyone had become accustomed to. The white sticker on the front of the cassette was blank, sans the manufacturing information, but the cassette was about one third smaller than the commonly recognized VHS tape. Pete vaguely remembered the Betamax units built by Sony that had eventually lost out to the standard VHS tapes used throughout the 80s and 90s. The Beta lost the marketing war as it only recorded one hour worth of programming. When the VHS went to 3 hours, Sony relented and discontinued the Betamax tape, falling in line with consumer demand for the extended length tape.

The tape appeared to be in usable shape. Pete could see a small portion of recorded tape wound on the take up reel. He couldn't immediately recall knowing anyone who owned a Beta tape player. He wasn't sure if any of them even existed any longer. The cassette's exterior revealed nothing as to the contents on the magnetic tape. It could have been anything from the skeleton's private pornography collection to a wedding reception. There was only one way to find out. He would have to find a Betamax tape player.

Then he turned his attention to the coke. There are too many police agencies working along the coast, and it's not uncommon to get boarded by one of the many local law enforcement agencies on another training inspection. They were all generally very courteous about it, but it was something he didn't need to happen while he was in possession of a felony amount of cocaine. He could try the truth with a jury, but that was too much of a personal risk. The simplest answer is most often the correct one, and he decided immediately to toss the coke. What would the Feds do anyhow, arrest the skeleton for possession?

He took the coke above deck and slit the top of the sealed bag. With the wind at his back, he shook the powder into the winds off the aft port quarter. The baggie should go over the side as well, but he couldn't let it go. Some sea turtle would mistake the plastic baggie for a jellyfish and eat it. Turtles are unable to digest plastic and it eventually kills them. So, Pete took the baggie below and rinsed any traces of cocaine from the surface down the sink.

49

When the baggie was in the shore trash bag, he surveyed his odd new treasure, thinking about how to handle it. According to maritime salvage laws, the cash was his. Anything salvaged off the bottom of the ocean belonged to the finder, minus the State of Florida's cut, if reported, as long as what you found was not in a protected area or marine sanctuary. This aircraft did not meet the guidelines of an archeological site, so there were no worries there. Being cash, it was not something he could readily report on his taxes as extra income, but Pete wasn't hurting for cash. Nevertheless, a nice little windfall should not be so easily dismissed, he told himself. He was certain that he would do the right thing and turn it in for the investigation, with no mention of the coke, and the money would sit in an evidence room for a few years and eventually be returned to him and he would then report it on his taxes. Pete didn't need any complications with the IRS.

Pete removed the bank wrapper with the initials on it and the note paper that contained the numbers. Studying the numbers a little later could lend some clue as to their hidden meaning. He secured the loose bills with a couple of rubber bands he had hanging off the end of a pencil at the navigation station.

He did need to stash the money and tape for now. Boats, by their very nature, are not very secure and prone to burglary when in some unfamiliar ports. Thieves usually targeted the dinghy and the outboard motor if left unattended for too long. When they saw you go ashore and take a cab into town, a watchful crook knew he had a little extra time on your vessel while at an anchorage. So, every boat needed a good hiding place for valuables.

Pete's hiding place was in the galley. He pulled out the silverware drawer and lifted on the front once it reached the stop. He slid it out from the inside rails that held it in place. The wood panel above the drawer on the inside could be pushed up on the back end about a half of an inch. The top panel would then slide inward 8 inches or so, revealing a hidden compartment that normally contained his cruising cash, one expensive watch he never wore, and a .45 cal stainless steel Smith and Wesson semi-auto model 4505 along with 3 extra magazines. The magazines contained eight 150 grain semi-jacketed hollow points each.

He kept the weapon here so he would not have to declare it when he made his Caribbean trips. The Bahamian authorities were funny about Americans with guns. You were supposed to surrender firearms when clearing customs, and they would give them back when you cleared out several weeks later, assuming they could find it. Mostly they couldn't. So, it was easier to check the "No Weapons or Firearms" box on the customs forms. Any normal customs inspection would miss this hiding spot, and if one of the agents was getting a little too close, Pete would open a cold beer. It was only polite to offer one to your guests, and thereafter the inspection usually became much less formal.

One such inspection had become so informal that Pete had to escort the wobbly Customs Inspector ashore once the beer ran out. He did have a new lifelong friend though, and never got inspected at that port again.

The cash and tape filled up what was left of the void where the gun was stashed. He pulled the panel forward, letting it drop back into its slot, and replaced the drawer.

The Southern Cross maintained a steady southbound course through the tame waters as Pete prepared lunch below.

Five

The world is shades of grey this time of the morning. It's not until the sun actually rises above the horizon that the world takes on its color. When there is a high overcast, which usually occurs during an approaching frontal system, the bottoms of the clouds take on the direct color of the sun before it has a chance to strike terra firma. This is where the old saying "red sky in the morning, sailor take warning" comes from. But this was not the case this morning, no sir. Today there was a light breeze that held that crisp fresh salt air smell that has attracted men to the sea for generations. It was Pete's favorite time of the day, with coffee, naturally.

He had arrived in Venice a half hour before official sunset the previous evening. The approach to the marked entrance was about as easy as it gets, and he made the right turn following the river past the Crow's Nest Marina, which passed on his starboard side. He found the city dock full, so he picked up a mooring ball in the anchorage and settled in for the night, the Southern Cross secured against the currents and changing evening breezes. Venice is well known as a protected anchorage, and it fills quickly when a storm is approaching, but this evening found only half of the mooring balls in use. A short line attached from the ball was attached to the forward cleat on the bow. The mooring ball itself was usually attached to a large concrete weight buried in the sand via a heavy chain. None of the boats on the mooring balls had enough room to strike another vessel when they swung with the wind. It was a secure system.

Pete enjoyed two scrambled eggs along with link sausage, one pre-made biscuit, and an orange. He sat up on deck in the cockpit with the little table extended that was attached to the forward side of the binnacle. "Yes sir, a beautiful morning," he thought. Breakfast was over about the time the colors of the world began to appear, and he would thoroughly enjoy his second cup of coffee out to sea. Pete got busy with preparations to get underway again.

Within a half hour, it was officially daylight and Pete released the mooring ball. His engine dutifully motored him from the overnight respite and took him on the short journey back into the Gulf of Mexico. There was enough of a breeze this morning to start sailing early. The sails were hoisted and the engine quieted. Once the transmission was in neutral, the prop would spin freely in the boat's slipstream, making a faint whine. He had listened to the whine long enough that he could accurately judge the boat's speed by the pitch of the sound.

Pete got the bow settled in on a magnetic heading of 165 degrees, and the sails were trimmed. He was making 5.3 knots, and the speed would increase as the day grew older and the winds freshened. He should easily make the 46 nautical-mile journey and still arrive in time for dinner. With the autopilot firmly in control, he scanned the horizon for any potential hazards to navigation. Finding none, and with his second cup of coffee in hand, the day was off to a great start.

***

Petty Officer Thompson had arrived at his desk at 0740 hours. He was a little early, which was usual for him. The Coast Guard facility was located in the Salt Creek Marina district, whereas Sector St. Petersburg had been his duty station for the past 18 months. He thumbed through the morning's incoming message traffic that had been left by the overnight duty shift for anything that needed immediate action.

One item requiring attention was the report of a sunken aircraft located off the coast near the entrance to Tampa Bay, just west of Egmont Key. The aircraft was listed as low priority, non-emergency, and not a hazard to navigation. It had been forwarded from the US Coast Guard District 7 office in Miami for today's Duty Desk Officer to follow up. From there it had been relayed via the C.G. Station, Washington D.C. The report originated from a local boater on a sailboat documented out of St. Pete Beach Florida. Thompson noted the odd routing, but he had been in the Coast Guard long enough to know that sometimes the abnormal was the normal.

The United States Coast Guard is primarily an emergency response organization dedicated to saving lives, not salvage operations, and the Guard had no officially trained scuba divers. The rescue swimmers were the best in the world at what they did, but scuba diving was not on the Job Task Analysis. If a craft was below the surface, it was handled by local law enforcement or other jurisdictional institutions. Petty Officer Thompson would keep an active link while the local investigation took form, however, monitoring the operation to see if it was a prior Search and Rescue operation assigned to the CG. Sport divers had been known to stumble across sunken pleasure craft in the past, clearing up unsolved cases that remained on the books.

Thompson had worked closely with deputies from the Pinellas County Sheriff's Office in the past. Specifically, he had become friends with Deputy Sheriff Brian Dawson, who was a fulltime marine patrol deputy assigned to the Special Operations Division. Thompson had aspirations of becoming a deputy sheriff and joining the unit at the end of his Coast Guard obligation. He waited until 0830 to give Deputy Dawson a call.

Within a half hour, deputy Dawson was in his immediate supervisor's office explaining the information he had just received from the Coast Guard. They looked up the latitude and longitude of the aircraft on a chart and determined that it was within their jurisdiction. Sergeant Miller then checked the weather and decided to assemble the dive team for lunch at 11:30 at the local Denny's. They usually got a table in the back room normally reserved for larger groups, and of course an added perk was their 10 percent law enforcement discount. The team would receive a briefing during the noon repast and set out for an afternoon dive. The weather looked good and the seas were generally quiet, forecast to be two to three feet offshore with the bay and inland waters a light chop. It promised to be a good dive.

The dive team arrived at the coordinates by 2:00 p.m. and set the anchor in the sandy bottom. The sheriff's office dive boat was painted identically to the patrol car theme, and it had a closed cockpit area for bad weather while the aft deck was open and could easily handle six divers. There was also room for two Stokes stretchers made of wire mesh that allowed the water to drain while hoisting a body onto the boat.

An initial check of the area with the depth finder didn't show any outstanding features on the bottom, which surprised no one. The depth/fish finder wasn't anything fancy, but given the county's budget, it was the best they could afford. They would find the airplane the old fashion way, by getting wet.

Two divers got suited up and entered the water. One of the divers, Deputy Dawson, had a reel with about 100 feet of white nylon cord rolled up on it with a stainless steel D-ring clip attached on the end. The duo made their way down the anchor line to the bottom, and once there, Deputy Phillips checked the set on the anchor and determined that it would hold during the dive. Dawson clipped the D-ring to the rode above the anchor so it was free to swivel 360 degrees. The divers had used this search technique many times before and understood it well. The diver with the reel would grab the end of the line and pull enough line out so that it stretched across his chest from hand to hand, about six feet. He did this again, giving himself twelve feet of line, about the distance you could see. Deputy Phillips maintained his station at the anchor and would guide the line around as the swimmer made a complete 12 foot circle. The swimmer wouldn't know when he had made it completely around the circle and depended on his partner at the anchor to give him two sharp tugs on the line.

When he got his two tugs, he stopped and ran out another twelve feet of line and began swimming again while keeping the line taut. It was about halfway around the third circle that Dawson sent four long tugs down the line. Phillips left the anchor and swam along the white cord leading him to his partner. The bottom was flat, sandy and covered in scallops among the sprigs of sea grass. "Something to remember," he thought to himself.

They were at the buried back end of a sunken airplane. The right wing was mostly buried with only a portion of the twisted propeller sticking above the sand. The top of the tail was visible in shape only. It was completely encrusted with barnacles and assorted crustaceans. They swam over the left engine toward the cockpit. As they crossed the forward part of the wing, they noticed a grouper move from under the wing and off into the distance. Deputy Dawson had removed a pelican marker from the pocket of his BCD. The pelican marker is about the size of a soda can, the bright yellow hard foam type material attached to 75 feet of thin cord. The free end was securely tied to the propeller shaft with a clove hitch knot. When he released the marker, it began unwinding by itself as it floated to the surface.

The other deputies on the boat saw the brightly colored marker break the surface, indicating that something had been found and marked. Deputy Collins grabbed the large float marker, which resembled a neon orange basketball, from its holder on the aft portion of the deck and set it on the swim platform. The float marker had 75 feet of half-inch braided line attached to the bottom of the mooring ball and 5 feet of three eighths-inch chain on the other end of the line. Once Collins was in the water, he was handed the chain, which required him to add extra air to his BCD to remain afloat. He then snorkeled to the pelican marker with the chain and buoy in tow, switching to the second stage regulator to begin his descent. By simply letting air out of his BCD, the added weight of the chain would slowly take him to the bottom. With the chain dangling below and the air in the BCD trying to float him, it was easier to descend feet first. Collins followed the pelican marker line down, slightly lancing himself in the butt with the tip of a propeller. Fortunately, the tips of the blades were bent backward, so he was only lightly bruised. He would have to talk to someone during the next cookout or poker game about their choice of a marker tie-off point.

Collins attached the chain to the propeller shaft and removed the pelican marker line. He would haul it back to the surface to keep it from fouling on the marker buoy. He could see the other two at the nose of the airplane near the windscreen where there was a hole. Just past them was a grouper intently watching all the odd activity as three steady streams of bubbles hurried toward the surface. Collins gave a few fin kicks and was quickly above the other two divers, who were looking into the cockpit of the airplane.

He watched as the other divers pried the remainder of the right side windscreen free from its bracket, dropping it next to the cockpit. One of the divers used his high intensity dive light to illuminate the cockpit area. Just as reported, one skeleton was sitting in the pilot's seat patiently awaiting rescue.

Collins fin kicked until he was behind the other two, and he picked up the piece of Plexiglas, an old habit from years of collecting anything and everything as evidence. Collins ascended with his line and broken windscreen by tapping his auto inflate button on the

BCD. Two very short bursts of air gave him enough positive buoyancy to slowly rise without effort.

Upon reaching the surface, he swam to the stern of the dive boat, flipped the windscreen on the swim platform, and handed the pelican marker line to one of the guys standing there. Collins gave a brief description of the aircraft and pilot while the marker was reeled in. He advised them that the skeleton could probably be removed through the opening they made in the window. There was a center post that split the windscreen in half that needed to be removed first, however. This aluminum T-bar ran from the top of the frame to the instrument panel.

Sergeant Miller told Collins to go below and have the other two come up for a briefing prior to extracting the pilot. Collins refit his mask and slid below the surface in a flurry of bubbles.

Several minutes later, the three divers were floating behind the patrol craft with the BCDs inflated to give them plenty of buoyancy while holding onto the swim platform with one hand. The seas were fairly calm, so they could remain here for the briefing. Besides, Phillips had to pee.

Sergeant Dan Miller was fully briefed regarding what they knew of the scene thus far. He decided to have the skeletal remains removed today and begin the formal investigation as mandated by the standard operational procedures manual.

Four divers returned to the bottom, this time armed with one large red-handled bolt cutter, two submersible body bags, a couple of dive lights, and a roll of cordage. The body bags were made of a nylon material that had very small pores and was designed to receive a body underwater and to contain any extraneous material attached to the corpse. When the bag was pulled onto the swim platform, the salt water would escape through the tiny pores, trapping any solid material inside the bag.

Prior to getting the call for this assignment, Collins had been fishing off the police dock, which was frowned upon by his superiors. He generally stood between two of the hoisted boats and remained out of view of the public for the most part. This of course excluded the view enjoyed by 82 homeowners who resided in the condos just across the channel. But when left unsupervised it was fun to try to catch the tarpon or sheepshead that frequented the docks. Collins always kept a small baggie of frozen shrimp in the cooler for bait at the dock, along with the bottles of water and Gatorade. The cooler was stowed on the boat prior to leaving the dock for this dive.

At the end of the briefing, Collins insisted on taking the shrimp back down with him, citing his love of nature and the fact that a hungry fish was hanging out near the wreck. Collins even pointed out how the fish was a potential witness and may need to be interrogated as to what he might have seen. Sergeant Miller tossed the bag of shrimp at Collins, who caught it midair. "Talk less, dive more,"

Miller said while using his bare foot to shove Collins' head underwater.

The grouper was waiting for the divers when they returned and took his normal station some distance away. The bolt cutter made short work of the center frame holding the remaining windscreen in place. With one cut to each end, it freely departed its center position, but divers would have to be careful as it left a couple of sharp aluminum shards protruding at the site of the cut. The remaining windscreen on the copilot's side was forcibly removed with a bit of tugging and pulling. It was then dropped to the side of the airplane. The divers had to wait a few minutes for the stirred up silt to settle so they could see again.

Collins had pulled a few shrimp from the package in his BCD pocket, and he moved a few feet to the side to put the grouper in just the right spot for a shrimp. Collins held the shrimp up and released it in the gentle current. It floated to within two feet of the grouper's snout. This guy knew a free meal when he smelled one. The grouper shot forward, closing the distance between him and lunch in a blur. The shrimp quickly disappeared, as did two more that came floating his way.

With the silt clearing, the dive team continued their quest. The body bag was unfolded and opened. It was held in place at the nose of the aircraft by two divers as the other two approached the open cockpit from the top. With the increased visibility, they could see that the skeleton was fully clothed. The material was tattered and algae covered, with the seatbelt and shoulder harness holding the remains in place. The straps were cut with a dive knife and allowed to fall away. Now for the tricky part.

The two divers on top attempted to lift the skeleton in one piece by holding what remained of the shirt's short sleeves, which was a dismal failure. This poor guy was literally coming apart at the seams. The skull slowly sunk to the floor, giving it something different to look at after fifteen or twenty years, and the song "I Fall to Pieces" started to play in Collins' head. If he was on dry land, he figured this would be the appropriate time to start singing the lyrics.

There were a lot of bones that stayed with the pants, and some stayed inside the shoes, but most simply fell into the interior of the cabin. This was going to be a pain in the ass, thought Deputy Stephens, but someone had to go inside. He motioned his intent by pointing at himself and then pointing inside the airplane, then gave the OK signal to the other divers and subsequently received an OK in reply.

Stephens began removing his BCD, a procedure practiced many times. He first took off his fins and dropped them onto the empty copilot seat inside the airplane. The BCD with the scuba tank slipped off effortlessly as it was weightless under water. He removed four pounds of the soft weights from the BCD and slid one two pound bag into each front pocket of his swim shorts. Without wearing the weighted BCD, he would have to keep fighting his natural buoyancy and use up his air prematurely. Holding onto the first stage of the regulator and the top of the tank, he backed into the airplane feet-first, careful not to slice himself on the newly cut aluminum. When he was all the way through the cockpit window, he pulled the tank in with him and set it on top of his fins in the copilot's seat. He couldn't get very far behind the front seats because the cabin was filled with deteriorating cargo. His exhaust air quickly filled the roof area of the cabin, and the excess eventually spilled out the top of the windscreen opening and rushed toward the surface.

The regulator hose was long enough to allow Stephens to position himself behind the pilot's seat where he could easily hand the skeleton parts out the front window. He began picking up bones off the floor and seat of the aircraft a few at a time and handing them out the opening. The body bag was rapidly filling with bones and clothing fragments. Collins was carefully placing the bones into the open body bag while wondering which part of the body they came from. He was looking at what he thought to be a femur when he looked up to grab the next group of bones. The image in front of him appeared so unexpectedly and startled him so completely that he sucked in a deep breath and held it for several seconds. When he realized what he was looking at, he almost lost his regulator because he was laughing so hard. Stephens had removed his mask and placed his chin on the dash of the airplane. He kept his regulator in place but held his breath so no bubbles floated up. Next to him on the copilot's dash was the skull, with the emergency regulator in its mouth. Both were wide-eyed and staring into the abyss.

The underwater laughter was contagious, and the bubbles rising to the surface had doubled. The only one not laughing now was the grouper. He was patiently waiting for more shrimp.

While checking to make sure all the bones had been removed, Stephens noticed a placard on the dash above the instrument panel with the numbers HK778LC on it. He pried the small placard loose and stuck it in his pocket with the weights. Then he pushed his scuba gear out the opening ahead of him, and once outside, got dressed again while Collins secured the body bag and tightened the straps, securing everything in place. The other two divers unfolded the second body bag and draped it over the cockpit opening, once again returning the interior to empty blackness. The bag was secured in place by wrapping the cord around the entire nose of the derelict airplane.

Collins pulled out the package of shrimp and fed the last of it to the grouper, which was becoming braver with each feeding. When all these strange creatures in his territory headed for the surface, Collins thought the creature looked disappointed. The grouper returned to his home under the wing, repossessing his familiar position.

Everyone was back on board the sheriff's patrol boat, and they brought the skeleton aboard as well. The buoy would remain in place as this investigation had now officially become a death investigation and would be handled according to policies and procedures. The buoy had a sheriff's star on it and proclaimed "PINELLAS COUNY SHERIFF'S OFFICE-DO NOT MOORE."

Sergeant Miller had notified his chain of command via the radio and requested that the Medical Examiner and on-call Homicide Detective meet him at the dock in 45 minutes. This was all pretty straightforward standard procedure at this point. The anchor was hoisted, and the return journey to the sheriff's dock began as the afternoon wore on.

Today's afternoon thunderstorms were just beginning to develop as distant thunder became more evident. The contrast between the dark heavy clouds and the penetrating blue sky was always beautiful in the Florida summer.

Six

The Medical Examiner was waiting at the Sheriff's Office Marine Division lobby in front of the dock when the patrol boat returned. Dr. Mujahed got the call earlier and decided to handle this on his way home. It was basically on the way anyhow.

Dr. Mujahed had been sitting in the lobby talking with Detective Rawlerson, the on-call homicide detective, who also was awaiting the patrol boat's arrival. In spite of his thick Pakistani accent, you could understand Dr. Mujahed as long as he didn't talk very fast or use unrecognizable medical terminology. They were chatting about an old case involving another drug deal that had gone wrong and produced a corpse. The victim was suffocated to death by having his entire head rolled in about 8 layers of Saran wrap while he was passed out on a little stronger than usual dose of heroin. The suspect took what heroin was left and some readily available electronics, which he later pawned at the local shop so tracking him down had been easy. Some criminals are so ignorant they leave a trail of clues a deaf, dumb, and blind person could follow. The cops had a universal saying, "If it wasn't for stupid people, the jails would be empty."

The trial for that guy was coming up next week, and the State Attorney's Office was seeking the death penalty. The public defender readily admitted that his client was guilty because the evidence against him was so overwhelming, and he was simply trying to keep his client alive by fighting the death penalty, which he staunchly opposed for personal religious reasons.

After the patrol boat arrived at the dock with practiced precision, the crew securely tied off the vessel without any orders. Everyone knew what needed to be done and immediately went about the tasks at hand. The scuba gear needed to come ashore for a fresh water rinse, and the tanks would be refilled. The bag of bones was placed on the dock for the medical examiner, who was required to sign a chain of custody form prior to opening the bag. The sheriff's office had a form for everything, including a form stating that you had all required forms.

Dr. Mujahed and Detective Rawlerson leaned over the bag and carefully unzipped it, exposing the contents to the first direct sunlight the owner of this set of bones had seen in quite a few years. Both men wore standard issue latex gloves, but in Florida you went through these gloves pretty fast. After about ten minutes, your hands were sweating in the 90 degree heat and 95 percent humidity sufficiently that sweat began to pool in your palms and fingertips. When you got the glove off, your fingertips were pruned from the sweat like you had been in the hot tub way too long.

Dr. Mujahed inspected several specific bones from the pile. He picked and poked and held some of them up to the light. He next lifted the skull to the sunlight and inspected it while turning it completely around. Mujahed told Rawlerson he believed it to be a middle-aged male but said he couldn't tell much more without a detailed examination. Rawlerson was picking through the tattered clothing and came up with a rotted wallet from the skeleton's pants pocket, along with some rusty keys.

The wallet had some sort of identification card in it, possibly a driver's license, but it was difficult to tell what was printed on it, though Rawlerson thought he could make out the outline of the state of California on the left side. Several soggy bills and some other remnants of assorted pieces of paper with the ink long ago faded by the salt water were removed, as was what looked like a photograph of a woman, her image quite faded. Behind that he found an old style social security card that had been laminated. The water had done a lot of damage to the card, but some of the numbers could be made out. A couple of the numbers could be either sevens or nines, but Rawlerson thought this a very good lead.

Across the canal, two old geezers wearing checkered pants and complaining about the government were sipping martinis. They had just returned from a midday round of golf and were sitting on the balcony of a fourth floor condo across from the sheriff's dock. Passing the binoculars back and forth, they were in agreement that this was better than watching that one cop try to catch fish all the time. One guy was holding up a skull, which one of the old men declared, "Too cool!" Then their interest faded, however, but they knew that the story behind where the bones came from should be in the morning paper in the next day or two. They then returned to their favorite post-golf activity: looking at the young ladies in the hotel pool two buildings down.

Detective Rawlerson made a notation on the Chain of Custody log that he was keeping the wallet and its contents for further investigation. He decided that there was no need to do anything special with the keys. They would never work a lock again and had no identifiable marks remaining. The keys were simply chunks of rust. Rawlerson headed back to his patrol car after exchanging pleasantries with a few of the divers and telling the Doc he would see him before the trial for a briefing.

Stephens trotted over to Rawlerson, catching him before he could get in his unmarked car. Stephens was still dripping wet from rinsing himself and his dive gear off with the fresh water hose on the dock. He reached into his pocket and removed the little placard he had pried from the dash of the airplane, then handed it to Rawlerson. He explained that he thought it might be the serial number or registration number of the airplane. The numbers on the tail were not visible, as the entire back half was buried under sand. He also told Rawlerson that the plane was too deep in the sand to float to the surface and not worth the effort. Unless someone thought Jimmy

Hoffa was in the back, the county wouldn't incur the expense of raising the plane.

Sergeant Miller walked up and advised Rawlerson that they would return to the airplane in the morning to document the scene as dictated by the PCSO manual. Until determined otherwise by someone of a higher pay grade, this would be classified as a suspicious death investigation and treated like a crime scene. They would look for additional evidence both inside and outside the aircraft, and they also needed to photograph the scene. There were the further issues of what was in, or behind, the square cargo and the cause of the crash.

Stephens said he would indicate in his Supplemental Case Report that he turned over the data plate to him for retention. Rawlerson thanked him and said he would let him know what he found out about the skeleton and airplane when he knew something. Rawlerson was heading back to the office to get on the computer and get some preliminary work done. The first thing to do was try to ID the skeleton and the aircraft, which he thought was one of the few positive things about the Internet — it really cut down on legwork.

The Doc was zipping up the bag of bones for the coroner's transportation vehicle, which was on its way. The bones would get logged into to the county morgue by the duty driver, and Dr. Mujahed would begin his investigation in the morning, right after he finished the overdose autopsy he was presently working on.

Sergeant Miller called the team together to brief them on tomorrow morning's dive. He wanted the same divers to go down to the wreck in order to maintain the chain of custody and the continuity of the investigation. They discussed additional equipment and supplies they would need, and Collins was put in charge of refilling the drink cooler and getting another batch of frozen shrimp. He didn't have to go far for the shrimp, as he always had some on hand in the freezer in the break room. Stephens would take care of getting the tanks filled at the fire department. The equipment used to fill the Scott packs that the fireman wore met the standards needed to fill scuba gear to the 3,000 PSI working pressure. The fire department was just down the street, which made for quick and easy fills. Phillips was in charge of getting the underwater digital camera charged up and properly sealed for the dive. The strobe lights took the longest to charge up. Dawson, wondering to himself why he kept getting stuck with this particular assignment, coordinated all the paperwork that went along with this investigation. Dawson would rather wax the entire patrol boat by hand than do all the paperwork that was involved. Miller must be pissed at him again, he surmised.

***

Pete had a great sailing day. He could not have asked for better weather and steadier winds. He averaged 6.2 knots and covered the 48 nautical miles in slightly less than 8 hours. He was ahead of schedule and still had a couple of hours until his dinner meeting with Sam.

He turned the Southern Cross easterly when he was abeam of Sanibel Island. He needed to turn north once he passed the southern tip of the island. Passing under the Causeway Boulevard Bridge, he would enter the Caloosahatchee River, which ran through Fort Meyers and into the heart of Central Florida. The river entrance is well marked and easy to navigate with plenty of room for passing vessels.

Pete passed under the third bridge after Causeway Boulevard, which was Highway 41. To the right was Lofton Island, a small uninhabited spit of land and brush, and to his port side was the City of Fort Myers mooring field. Mooring number 12 was where the Southern Cross would remain securely tied for the night. The only thing he did not like about this anchorage was having to listen to truck traffic crossing the Hwy 41 bridge late at night. Pete busied himself with the post-sailing chores. The mainsail had to be tied to the boom to prevent it from unintentionally catching a gust of wind and creating a real disaster. He made ready all the lines, sheets, and blocks for the next sail, ensuring the deck was neat and orderly. He collected the trash from the past two days that needed to go ashore. He didn't want that cocaine bag onboard any longer than necessary, no matter

74

that he had washed any residue away. No sense taking unnecessary chances.

He tossed the garbage bag into the dink that was tied off at the stern rail and had dutifully followed along the entire voyage at a fixed distance of 18 feet. Next he made sure the propane for the stove was turned off at the tank and the automatic bilge pump was powered up. Then Pete climbed into the dink, started the small outboard and headed toward shore, thinking about what he wanted for dinner. The peanut butter sandwich and handful of chips he had for lunch was not staving off his hunger any longer.

Pete tied up to the dinghy dock and walked toward the harbor office, tossing his trash into the large dumpster on the way, and went upstairs to the office. The first level of the building contained several showers with push button combination locks on the doors and two sets of coin operated washers and dryers. He checked in and gave the dock master the number of the mooring ball he was tied to. He paid his fifteen dollars overnight fee and provided all the necessary information on the mooring card, including his cell phone number for emergencies.

The evening was perfect for the short walk to Centennial Park. A block and a half later, he saw that the Philthy Pelican was still open for business. Little businesses had a habit of folding up lately with the property taxes tripling nearly overnight. Numerous small time beach hotel owners had quickly sold out to the condo developers because they couldn't make the tax bill any longer. The money from the developers was more than enough to offset any personal feelings of failure. He was walking upstairs to the second floor open deck overlooking the river when his cell phone rang. "Sam Adams" appeared under the words "Incoming Call" on the screen.

"Hi, Sam, are you on the ground yet?" Pete queried.

"Yeah, we just landed and the plane is taxiing up to the gate now. Where are you at?" Sam replied.

"I'm about to enjoy a frosty mug of cold beer — the Philthy Pelican is still here. I'll get us a table near the rail."

An ice cold mug of draft beer flashed through Sam's thoughts as he told Pete, "I shouldn't be more than a half hour or so. I've just got to grab one bag and hop in a cab."

Pete arrived at the bar and replied, "Roger that. I'll have a cold beer waiting for you."

"You're reading my thoughts again; I'll see you in a few."

Pete flipped his phone closed and replaced it on his belt clip. He could see that the tables at the rail overlooking the river were all taken, and so he sat at an empty barstool. The bartender sidestepped over to Pete and took his order for a draft. The waitress was gathering several drinks from her station at the end of the bar when Pete leaned over and told her he had a friend due to arrive in about half an hour, joining him for dinner, and he wondered if she would be kind enough to let him have the next available table by the rail. She said it would not be a problem. The waitress returned Pete's warm smile while thinking to herself, "Sure thing, handsome. You're getting a table in my section."

Sam arrived at the same time the waitress was guiding Pete to a recently cleaned table next to the rail. The two old friends exchanged hearty handshakes and pats on the back, genuinely glad to see one another again, and then took their chairs, ordering two drafts and menus.

Sam and Pete then caught up on the last year's events while sipping from their frosty mugs. The waitress returned to take their dinner order as they drained the first mug of beer. Pete was having the stuffed crab and Sam ordered the fried shrimp dinner. It was apparent to her that they were catching up on old times and hadn't seen each other in a while.

During dinner, Sam listened intently to the airplane story, extracting every detail out of Pete. Sam injected several times that he wanted to dive on the airplane once the cops finished doing their job and left the wreck to continue its work as an artificial reef. Sam collected airplane clocks along with antique aircraft instruments, but he didn't just grab anything he could find. The artifact had to have a story of consequence associated with it: a military battle, some famous person owned it at one time, some story worth retelling. The clock from the dash of this plane would immediately move to the center of the fireplace mantle. He knew that, once the cops got done with the investigation, the plane's whereabouts would become public record by law. With a little legwork and a couple of phone calls, he would get a copy of that record to go with the clock.

The two sat there for the next three hours, planning their upcoming adventure. For starters, they were going to anchor near the east side of Captiva Island in San Carlos Bay. Pete had planned a couple of days there with the snorkels and underwater metal detectors. Pete fancied himself somewhat of an amateur treasure hunter, and his historical research indicated that the barrier islands tended to shift out toward the Gulf. Pete couldn't back this theory up with any hard data, however; at this point it was *just* a theory he had developed. When a hurricane came ashore, it brought a large storm surge that would quickly wash up and over the barrier island on its way inland, taking part of the sandy island and any manmade structures with it. As the hurricane passed, the waters would recede much more slowly, collecting less sand on the way out than in, thereby depositing remnants of the inhabitants belongings and buildings and so forth on the inside of the island. Over the course of 200 years, his theory went, the barrier islands would have shifted quite a lot. Pete was convinced that Captiva had been one of the islands that had moved eastward before it became home to the rich and famous. He had never hunted this area before, but he thought this would be a great time for some preliminary work. Pete also filled

Sam in on the latest pirate news from his research. As Pete got more animated with his tales, Sam leaned closer, careful to not miss a single word.

Pete related the Juan Gaspar tale, or the highly plausible version of it anyway since no one knew the actual facts, which depended on who you asked. Gasparilla, as he was later known, was supposedly a successful Spanish naval officer who turned to piracy for reasons known only to Juan Gaspar. His reign of terror along the west coast of Florida between 1788 and 1820 was a local legend. The stories credited him and his crew with hundreds of victories in battles in which they lay waste to all who challenged them. Gaspar had sailed to Cuba on many occasions, enjoying his pillaging and the fine women. He was known to have occasionally joined forces with Jean Laffite and Black Caesar while plundering and pillaging Spanish trading vessels and, by one account, he littered Charlotte Harbor with his buried treasures and spoils of battle. Late in 1821, Gasparilla spotted what he believed was a British merchant ship and planned an attack. As he closed into gun range, they discovered that the British ship was in reality the USS Enterprise, an American warship sent to stop Gasparilla and his ship, the Floridablanca. The Floridablanca was pummeled with cannon fire and had begun to sink after losing its main mast. With his dying men around him, the story goes, he tied the anchor chain around his waist and jumped to his death. Gasparilla supposedly shouted that he would die by his own hand, not the enemy's, as he went over the side. Gasparilla and his ship disappeared into the depths off of Florida's west coast, but not before the pirate and his men had buried millions of dollars worth of looted treasure.

Gasparilla was most likely a fictional pirate, but that was unconfirmed. The story originated with a man named John Gomez, who claimed to have sailed with Gasparilla. LaFitte and Black Caesar were well documented as actual pirates during this era, and it was hard to dispute the fact that they hid treasure throughout the region. If not Juan Gaspar's treasure, then there was surely some from the others, especially Black Caesar.

Pete, along with lots of other folks, believed that there was still a lot of undiscovered treasure in the area. Pete thought it was up to him to find it. Sam listened like this was the first time, but he had heard all this before, but the one thing different about this trip was that Pete claimed to be able to actually produce an old map with a clue to the treasure. He leaned really close to Sam and uttered it in a whisper, lending an air of credibility to his statement: "The map is securely stored on the Southern Cross." Pete then winked at his old friend.

Pete went on to tell him that, just two months ago, some treasure had indeed been found, not much but enough to bring a hint of reality to some of the legends. The Charlotte County Commission had hired a dredging company to work on a beach sand replenishment project. Several hurricanes had washed a few hundred thousand metric tons of sand back to sea, depleting the beaches and a large source of tourist dollars. It had been long established that the cost of pumping sand from the sea floor of the Gulf of Mexico back to the beaches was justified as tourist season was soon approaching, and tourism was the lifeblood of many beach communities and competition for their money was fierce.

The dredging machine was a couple of hundred yards off shore in about 14 feet of water, sucking up bottom sand and sending it down a pipe that ran from the deck pumps to the beach. Workers slowly moved the outflow southbound down the beach, pumping hundreds of tons of sand a day back onto the beach. When the new beach sand was sufficiently drained of water, a grader would flatten it out, and like magic, more pristine beach for tourists to lie upon!

One morning after the grader had worked one particular section, an older couple was taking their morning walk down the beach, enjoying the fresh sunrise. The gentleman bent down to investigate a chunk of rounded metal protruding from the sand, which turned out to be a silver Spanish Real. The coin was somewhat worn and abused by the ravages of time and the dredge, but a Spanish coin it was. Channel 6 got wind of the discovery and did a local interest story on the nightly news.

Three days later, the beach looked like it had a terminal case of acne and would be scarred until the end of time, but only 14 more coins were reported, about 1 coin per 200 holes according to one estimate. Once the fever evaporated, the grader erased the scars caused by the digging crowd, but area sales of metal detectors skyrocketed as they always did after this type of news story.

Pete and Sam made their way back to the Southern Cross for the night. Dinner was delicious, and they left the waitress a nice tip. Pete was so intense and utterly focused on his pirate story that he never noticed the waitress's phone number on the bill when she placed it on his side of the table.

Pete had to be careful on the way back as the dink didn't have any of the night navigation lights on it that were required by the Code of Federal Regulations. He didn't have far to go, so he decided that it shouldn't be a problem as long as none of the Florida Fish and Wildlife Commission Officers were working late tonight.

Sam had been on the Southern Cross before and knew his way around well. He stowed his bag in the forward V-berth, so named for the shape it took due to the curvature of the bow. There was an overhead hatch, which Sam opened to allow a rather nice breeze to filter through the cabin. He was tired enough that the noise of the trucks climbing the Highway 41 bridge in the near distance should not be too much of an issue.

***

Detective Rawlerson had completed his preliminary investigation and was locking up his office for the night. He had sent in a request via the teletype in the communications center to the Federal Aviation Administration, as per the new Homeland Security regulations, which required this specific routing to get an answer. If a request was made via any other channel, a subpoena had to be issued for the information. He had requested any information on the serial number HK778LC. The justification for the request included that it was a sunken airplane off of Tampa Bay and the case was likely twenty plus years old. He included that there was a skeleton inside the aircraft and this was a death investigation to help speed up a response. The square cargo had not been confirmed as actually being cannabis yet, and he didn't want to indicate prematurely that the aircraft was possibly an old smuggling plane without being able to offer some proof.

He next had to fill out the briefing report that was distributed agency-wide. The briefing report contained anything and everything that happened after normal business hours, 5 p.m. to 8 a.m., that may be of consequence. The administration needed to be aware of anything that might be newsworthy, or in other words, that might cause them any grief. The briefing report also served to pass along any suspect information or wanted person updates to the midnight and early morning patrol shifts. Stolen cars, missing people, and road closures were reported as well. Each shift completed the form, which was supplied to the briefing supervisors on the oncoming shift. The form was also distributed to all the watch commanders, the Public Information Office, each member of the Senior Staff, Communications Center, Records, Administration Supervisors, the Corrections Center, and probably a janitor or two. "All part of the paperwork reduction act," Rawlerson thought, and he smiled at the strangeness of bureaucracy.

Included in tonight's briefing report were the basic details of the death investigation, the fact that a skeleton was found inside the plane, the serial number HK778LC, and the location of the airplane, which was listed at approximately 5 miles west-southwest from Egmont Key. It was okay to report here that this was possibly an old smuggling plane. It was further noted that the dive team would return to the wreck for further investigation in the morning.

As the lead detective on this case, Rawlerson was going on a boat ride tomorrow. His only thoughts on the subject were to thank God he was getting out of the office for the day. They were having a blood-borne pathogens update training session beginning at 10 a.m. It was tragic, but he had to work on this investigation and wouldn't be able to attend the class. The office door clicked shut for the night, and Rawlerson pulled the keys for the unmarked detective vehicle from his pocket and headed home.

The afternoon's thunderstorms had abated and left a crystal clear night in their wake. The easy evening breeze was a welcome friend. Rawlerson would enjoy his nightly cocktail on the porch tonight.

Seven

Major Leslie Jason Alexander arrived at his office ahead of the rest of the staff as usual. He had worked his way up through the ranks, taking over as the head of the Special Operations Division three years ago. Showing up at the office 45 minutes ahead of everyone else was a strategy he had developed early on in his career. The extra time provided him with little advantages along the way, giving him the extra edge he needed by keeping one step ahead of everyone else. When he was assigned to the burglary unit, he would filter through the in-basket of reports detailing the previous night's crime sprees. Selecting cases that had cogent witness reports, evidence of value, and good suspect leads had served him well — his arrest and conviction statistics were always 25 percent better than the rest of the division. When the sheriff visited the regional office, Alexander always had a properly prepared cup of coffee and banana-nut muffin waiting for him. Alexander had gained the notice of his superiors, who promoted him to sergeant faster than normal. His career path took him into supervisory roles in the Narcotics Division, Robbery/Homicide, Sex Crimes Unit, and then an early promotion to lieutenant landing him back in the Patrol Division.

Years ago, shortly after being promoted to lieutenant, Leslie Alexander had purchased a rather elegant home in a gated community on a golf course. The home was in an exclusive area overlooking Tampa Bay. The usual cop's salary provided for a modest lower middle to middle class lifestyle, depending on how many kids you had, and Alexander made it a point to let everyone know that he was the only surviving relative of an uncle who had passed away in west Texas, the owner of a piece of property with two oil wells on it. The royalties provided a really nice monthly stipend, which afforded him the luxury to live in such a nice community. It also provided for a nicer than usual car and boat. His property backed up directly to Tampa Bay, and the boat was a beautiful addition to the back yard. A short walk past the pool and you were in a 30-foot Bayliner Sport Fisherman, which also frequently provided Alexander a very private audience with the sheriff, who had an open invitation aboard the boat anytime he desired. Leslie Alexander had his fingertip on the pulse of everything important that was happening at the sheriff's office, even more so after the sheriff had a few complimentary beers or cocktails.

His beautiful home was always open to the senior administration as a great place to have their annual private Christmas party. Alexander knew he was living a charmed life, but he also knew that his neighborhood was no place for a mere lieutenant to live. It was more fitting for someone in the upper administration, which Alexander was rapidly approaching.

His reign as captain lasted only the minimum required time as set forth in the *Policy and Procedures Manual.* Captain Alexander began to surround himself with people below him who were properly motivated to get the job done. Part of this motivation included his covey of "yes" men required to run a smooth operation his way. Dissension among the troops could not be tolerated, and the uncooperative usually found themselves transferred to more suitable positions within the sheriff's office. He was expecting absolutely no less out of his subordinates than what he had given when he was in their shoes. He had heard the rumors that, if you were not one of "Leslie's Lovers," you were history. He actually enjoyed the reputation as it kept folks walking the straight and narrow. His private life was his own, and his decision to not be married was nobody else's business.

His role as Major of the Special Operations Division meant that he was in charge of all the interesting departments in the sheriff's office. His people included the aviation unit, mounted posse, marine patrol, crime scene technicians, missing persons, emergency services response unit, disaster response, and a host of other smaller miscellaneous two-or-three person projects.

He only had one more step to complete to achieve his goal, Colonel over the entire Law Enforcement Division. The sheriff's office was divided into three basic segments from that point, the other two being Corrections and Judicial. The sheriff was responsible for the jails and courthouse operations, to include personal judicial security.

Alexander would make colonel as soon as Mike Stewart retired next year. From that position, it would be a logical leap to getting his name on the ballot for the next election. Sheriff Colbert was scheduled to retire precisely one year before his elected term was set to expire. That way he could appoint his replacement, who would then be in office for one full year prior to the actual election, and the voters of the county had shown their desire to keep incumbents in office as long as they didn't do anything outlandishly horrible. He smiled each time he thought his plan through yet one more time. He had plotted a sure path to the office he desired.

One day in the not too distant future, a purchase order would need to be made with the local printing company that had won the bid for the sheriff's office official stationary and report forms. The name would need to be changed to Sheriff L.J. Alexander on everything. It had a really nice ring to it, and Alexander had practiced writing it numerous times while doodling.

Debora Hayes arrived at her desk at precisely 7:55 a.m. She knew better than to be late. It was perfectly acceptable and generally encouraged to be early, as long as your payroll sheet reflected an 8:00 a.m. arrival time. The Major of the Special Operations Division had a personal secretary to handle the mountain of paperwork and scheduling that passed through this office every day, and Debbie was in place when Alexander was promoted to this position. She was comfortable in her job and considered herself to have thick skin. It was just a job and she learned not take anything personal a long time ago, but that was getting more difficult to do as the months wore on.

It was three minutes later when she heard the loud bang and crash in the Major's office. It was not the first time she was a witness to that particular sound. She could envision the coffee mug transiting the distance from behind Major Alexander's desk to the far wall of his office, the mug splintering upon impact, sending the coffee and cream mixture in various directions. It didn't happen very often, but when it did, it was a mess. "Oh joy," she thought, today was going to be one of those that tested her every fiber of self control. Being a single mom required her to keep this job, and she hadn't bothered to put in for a transfer because none of the other secretaries wanted to change desks with her. She was stuck.

Debbie had forced her requisite smile as her boss's door opened and she began her well rehearsed morning greeting. "Good morning, Major. How…"

"Drop it, Debbie. What's on my calendar today?" Alexander demanded while wadding up several sheets of paper and dropping them in her wastebasket.

"You have a 10 o'clock briefing at the Aviation Unit, the monthly awards ceremony with two commendations to hand out.

Then you're scheduled to have lunch with Captain Hodges, and from there..."

"Is there anything important?" Alexander was leaning on her desk now.

"Well sir, the cadets at the training center are expecting you as the guest speaker this afternoon."

Alexander stood straight and told her, "Cancel my appointments. Call everyone and send my regrets. I'll be with the dive team today." Debbie began to say something when the Major closed his left eye halfway and leaned his head lower while using his deepest voice. "Damn it, Debbie. Just do what you're told, and get someone in there to clean up that mess."

Debora Hayes was initially insulted, but then the thought struck her: a couple of phone calls to some disappointed people and the rest of her day would be a breeze. The frown that had recently developed was turning into a slight grin. Looking in the wastebasket, she wondered why the daily briefing report had pissed him off so bad.

***

The treasure hunters were eager to begin their quest, and the Southern Cross had slipped her mooring at daybreak. The Yanmar diesel quietly propelled them under highway 41 as they followed the current down the river toward the Gulf. Pete had the navigation chart on the foldout table in front of the binnacle, and Sam was keeping the vessel in the center of the waterway. Sam enjoyed the feel of the wheel anyway, but Pete needed time for additional planning.

They would not need to cross under the last bridge, Causeway Boulevard, which led directly into open water. They would take a westerly course, and then turn north on the back side of Sanibel Island. The water there was fairly shallow, generally no more than 8 feet deep at its lowest point during low tide. The tide was on its way out now, and by the time he rounded the corner and took the northerly turn, the tide would be at its lowest point. The Southern Cross had a draft of 4 feet 8 inches when fully loaded. Should they run aground at any time, they would just have to wait for the rising tide to float them off. The waters here shifted constantly with passing storms, so much so that the charts only reflected average mean low tide depths. It was up to the Captain of the individual vessel to conduct safe navigation through these waters.

This was a popular fishing area as well. The flats provided the perfect habitat for redfish in the grassy underwater fields. Trout were plentiful as well. Pete knew a full moon was only a few days away, and he was going to show Sam how to catch blue crab one of the next few nights.

They motored toward the last bridge and began navigating outside the marked channel. Pete made his way to the bow with his stainless steel coffee mug and stood perched against the rolled up jib. He hooked his left arm around the sail to steady himself, not so much against the waves, but to keep himself from being tossed over the bow rail should they hit a sandbar and suddenly stop.

Sam was doing a great job moving the boat along at two and a half knots, which provided enough steerage control with the rudder without shoving them hard aground should they find the shifting sands. Pete was watching forward of the bow, looking for changes in the depth, but the water appeared to be about 6 feet deep with some occasional deeper holes. In the process of making forward progress, they spooked several sand sharks, a few sting rays, and some other unidentified underwater critters moving too fast to see clearly. As the boat passed over these creatures, they saw only newly formed clouds of swirling sand created by the rapid departure of a recent occupant.

Pete was quietly keeping a watch out for any bull sharks, an aggressive species that often fed in the shallows. There was no need in alarming Sam if none were hunting in this area. So far they had only passed several small Sand sharks, which were no real threat.

There was one time that Pete directed Sam to the starboard by pointing down to his right at a 45 degree angle. This meant an easy right turn, about 10 degrees on the compass. Pointing straight out meant a hard turn in that direction. Waving his arm up and down meant to come to a full stop by reversing the engine, but so far they didn't have to do that. Once Pete pointed slightly right to miss a sand bar, but the path was not as clear as he thought and even shallower water appeared before them. Pete pointed straight out to his left, and Sam spun the wheel hard over to port. The vessel reacted slowly at first, as she very gently started to kiss the sand. Pete made a fist and pumped his arm up and down, and Sam replied with full throttle. The Southern Cross powered herself over the small sand bar without any problem.

The rest of the way around to the back side of Sanibel Island went easily, and both men enjoyed the beauty around them. To the port side was the Ding Darling National Wildlife Refuge, which is located on the subtropical barrier island of Sanibel and is part of the largest undeveloped mangrove ecosystem in the United States. Pete picked out a good anchorage location and directed Sam to it. They were in about 7 feet of water and the tide was low. The rising tide would only put more water between the keel and the bottom, and Pete was quite pleased with the trek so far. Sam silenced the engine as Pete slipped the plow anchor, which was on the bow rail opposite the Danforth, over the bow. The anchor was so named because it resembled the old-time plow pulled behind mules, and this kind of anchor held better in muddy or grassy bottoms.

"So, this is it, huh?" Sam asked. "Our fame and fortune awaits us below."

"Harrr, me matey. Ye booty rests on the bottom, ye scurvy sea dog." It was the best impression of a pirate Pete could muster. He even used his left hand as an eye patch when he said it.

Sam asked which pirate treasure was at this spot, a question that achieved the desired effect of winding Pete up to full speed. Sam really liked to hear the tales of plundered gold, especially the way Pete told them. Pete jumped right into this tale, becoming more animated as the story progressed.

This particular spot used to belong to Henri Caesar, who was born in the mid 1760s to a Haitian slave owned by a wealthy French landowner named Arnaut. Caesar was enslaved and put to work in a Haitian lumberyard. This assignment was a result of his large muscular physique.

Caesar suffered great mistreatment at the hands of the lumberyard master, but the Haitian slave revolt of 1791 afforded Caesar with his first taste of blood. The master was cut in two with a lumberyard saw, and Caesar got a taste for retribution for his mistreatment. Other former slaves joined with Caesar and attacked French soldiers along the northern coast of Haiti. In 1804, France had given up the fight against the slaves because it was too costly. When a Haitian government began to form, Caesar splintered off and continued his rise to pirate fame. He won a victory over a Spanish ship in early 1805, and he began attacking smaller vessels around Port de Paix on the northern coast. Later that year, he was attacking ships and villages around Cuba and the Bahamas, extending his range. The British warships returned to the area at the conclusion of the 1812 war, too many in number for the pirate, now known simply as Black Caesar, to encounter.

His operation needed to move, and he subsequently found a home on the west coast of Florida. According to legend, Gasparilla had secured Charlotte Harbor as his base of operations, and Black Caesar occupied Sanibel and Pine Island roughly 20 miles to the south. The Caloosahatchee River provided fresh water, and there was plenty of wild game to eat. Black Caesar settled into the area nicely and occasionally joined forces with Gasparilla. Modern day folks had documented markings on old trees of the era that they believed were made by the pirates, but no one to date had been able to decipher the strange tree marks other than noting that one of them pointed toward Sanibel.

So here they were, anchored between Sanibel and Pine Island. If Pete's theory about shifting barrier islands was true, they were in prime hunting grounds for the booty.

Sam was utterly convinced at this point.

***

The dive team had assembled at precisely 0800 hours. Detective Rawlerson was present wearing his PCSO golf shirt with an embroidered sheriff's star over the left breast pocket and his name on the right. He was wearing a pair of quick dry shorts and slip-on docksider shoes. He had greased up well with sunscreen as he had become an office hermit who could easily pass for a Canadian tourist in the winter.

Sergeant Miller had received a unit-to-unit radio message from Major Alexander telling him that he was on his way and wanted a full briefing on this investigation. Sergeant Miller was ordered to standby until his arrival, so standby they would.

Major Alexander pulled into the parking lot of the Marine Patrol Office at 9:15. The patrol boat had been loaded and made ready to go by 8:30, so everything was in place. Half of the team was watching the morning news show in the lobby, and the other half was hanging out on the dock engaged in casual conversation. Major Alexander didn't walk directly toward the dock but instead had opened his trunk and was doing something there. Sergeant Miller was walking to the parking lot when he saw him pull out a dive bag from the trunk. Alexander was dressed similarly to Detective Rawlerson, and so it was clear that he was going on this trip. "Damn," thought Miller, but he smiled all the same.

Sergeant Miller reached out to give Major Alexander a hand with his gear and said, "Good morning, sir. Going diving with us today?"

Alexander replied with one of his trademark direct answers "Make sure I have a full tank on board. You can brief me on the way." Sergeant Miller found himself standing alone with Alexander's larger dive bag. He was certain that it meant that he was supposed to carry it to the boat.

The usual morning cutting up and banter had evaporated as the team pulled away from the dock. Sergeant Miller was at the wheel with Major Alexander standing next to him. The team was keeping busy, getting the gear ready for the dive. They prearranged all the gear. The BCDs were mated with the tanks and the regulators tested.

During the ride out, Miller had briefed Alexander on the previous dive. Major Alexander had questioned him in detail about each item that was removed from the plane and what its status was now. Who had it, that sort of thing. Rawlerson was then called forward to explain his investigation to this point. Rawlerson related that he had received the investigation as a result of the dive team finding the skeleton. Miller then had to elaborate on how Dawson had initially received the information from the Coast Guard, which had received a report from a local boater who had fouled an anchor on the aircraft.

Alexander wanted to know who the boater was. Miller stated he didn't know and received one of Alexander's well known "death to you" stares in reply.

Detective Rawlerson was now trying to explain why he hadn't contacted and interviewed the boater yet. He detailed how he had just gotten the call yesterday morning and submitted an FAA request for the registration information on the serial number. Rawlerson also advised that he may have a possible identification via a social security number, but that was only marginally possible at this point — Rawlerson was not ready to promise anything he was not certain he could deliver. Alexander then instructed Rawlerson to advise him personally if he was able to determine who the skeleton belonged to because, he said, situations like this needed to be handled delicately. Inappropriate notification to the surviving family could give the sheriff's office a black eye and he wanted to make sure everything went smoothly with that process. Rawlerson had made at least fifty such notifications during his career and knew how to be tactful, but orders were orders.

During the remainder of the trip to the wreckage, Dawson and Phillips related the details of their previous dive. They were the first law enforcement personnel at the scene.

"So the windscreen in front of the pilot's head was busted?" asked Alexander at one point.

"Yes sir," responded Collins. "The upper half of the pilot's side of the windscreen was missing when we got there."

"Where was the piece of windscreen? Did you recover it?"

Collins had to think about that a minute.

Stephens heard the question and chimed in. "Major, I saw a busted hunk of Plexiglas on the floor of the plane. One of the rear side windows was broken as well but sealed with incoming sand. I'm sure the Plexiglas is still inside." Stephens added, "We were concerned with recovering the remains before it got too late and we lost daylight."

Sergeant Miller jumped in to protect his men. "They sealed the opening in the windscreen with an extra body bag, and I'm sure everything inside is still there."

Major Alexander replied, "Let's hope so. If we can show that the pilot hit his head on impact that will explain the cause of death. It's up to the FAA to figure out why the plane crashed. We can close our investigation at that point and it would become the Feds' problem."

Alexander knew the FAA would most likely just review the sheriff's office case files and make a determination of pilot error or cause unknown and close the case. This would not be a noteworthy enough case to justify the expense of recovering some old smuggling plane off of the sea floor. After all, the Florida and Bahamian coasts were littered with them. It was a common practice to ditch the plane and destroy any evidence the DEA might try to lay their hands on. The airplanes had usually been stolen, then used for one or two smuggling runs before being scuttled at sea or set alight. Any more than two flights would create a pattern that could be figured out by the cops. The pot would be kicked out while circling a waiting boat. After a nice gentle water landing, the pilot would get out and ride the boat to shore. They tried not to occupy the plane to the bottom, although that was not always the case.

The patrol boat arrived at the sheriff's buoy and tied up. The seas were basically calm, but there were a few thunderheads building out to sea. Today they would probably see Florida's normal afternoon, garden-variety sea-breeze generated thunderstorms; but the team should be done with the dive and headed in well before the storms reached them.

Dawson and Phillips were the first in the water and headed down to the plane carrying mesh bags similar to the kind used during lobster season. They had orders to work the exterior of the aircraft and gather anything that could be part of this investigation as evidence. Collins and Stephens were next to go down. They were supposed to work the interior of the aircraft. Stephens had a mesh bag with him and Collins brought the digital camera.

Upon arriving at the bottom, Collins noticed that the grouper was following Dawson and Phillips. Stephens and Collins removed the empty body bag, exposing the cockpit to the open sea once again, and as Stephens began removing his BCD to go through the procedure that would allow him to reenter the cockpit, Collins got out a couple of pieces of shrimp. He assumed the grouper's one thought could probably be summarized as, "Yee-haw, lunch!" The grouper closed the distance and enjoyed several tasty morsels as Collins shot several pictures of the interior of the aircraft through the missing windscreen.

Dawson's hand was looped into the end of a 20-foot length of rope that had a bowline knot on each end. Phillips had the other end looped around his hand. Dawson stayed within view of the aircraft while Phillips swam away from the wreck to the extension of the rope. Once the rope went taut, he then swam a twenty foot arc that returned him within view of the plane. Then Dawson would move to the next quadrant and they would repeat the procedure until a complete circle of the aircraft had been made.

Once inside the airplane, Collins handed Stephens the camera and the instrument panel was photographed. The camera was handed back to Collins who clipped it to a D-ring on his BCD and allowed it to float alongside. Stephens handed out the two pieces of Plexiglas, which Collins put into the mesh bag. The aluminum center post they had cut away the previous day was recovered as well. On the dashboard, wedged against the copilot's windscreen, was a rusted round object. After brushing away the algae, Collins could tell that it was an old-style wind-up clock, which he added to the collected bits of paraphernalia.

He located a wad of what may have been paper charts at one time and started to hand that out but it disintegrated on contact. Using his dive light, he found a leather bag under the dash on the copilot's side against the foot pedals. The bag was the size of an old-style doctor's bag and snapped closed on the top. Stephens handed this out the opening. Next he removed a small tool bag that was in the back pocket of the pilot's seat. The tools were completely rusted together. Finding nothing further, Stephens exited the cockpit and began getting dressed again. Collins doubted he would be coming back down and so he released the remaining bits of shrimp to a rather grateful grouper.

Dawson and Phillips completed the exterior search and were back at the front of the airplane holding empty mesh bags. They gave Collins the thumb toward the surface sign, indicating that they were going up. Collins replied with the OK sign and then pointed at himself, held up one finger and then gave an upward thumb, indicating they would be up in one minute. Phillips nodded as he and his partner began their ascent to the surface. Less than a minute later, Collins and Stephens were on the surface as well. Stephens got a couple pictures of Collins and the grouper before heading back up. They handed up the gear and evidence bags, then both climbed onto the swim platform and sat with their feet hanging over the end.

Stephens was giving the initial briefing to Major Alexander, telling him which item came from where. Major Alexander was very interested in the medical-style bag and told Rawlerson to open it up. The latch was rusted shut but the rotting top strap gave away easily, allowing sunlight into the contents. Most of the water had leaked from the bottom of the bag. Alexander had maneuvered himself next to the bag for a closer look. Rawlerson began pulling items out of the bag and setting them on the deck: one flashlight, a likely can of shaving cream, regular toiletry items, toothbrush and such, several wads of disintegrated bits of paper, on old magazine of unknown publication, and an old AM/FM transistor radio. "That's it?" Alexander demanded.

"Yes, sir. There's some sludgy stuff on the bottom of the bag, but that's it," Rawlerson responded.

"Well, what say I go down for a look," Alexander announced. "Has anyone probed the pot bales to make sure they don't contain any other evidence?" Looking around and getting silence in return, the Major had his answer. "Sergeant Miller," Alexander commanded, "set me up with a pole spear and put a trident on the end. If there's anything inside the bales, the barbs should grab it."

The spear, a fiberglass pole that was six feet long and about as thick as a hunting arrow on steroids, had a metal tip on the end that allowed you to screw on different style ends to serve whatever task was at hand. The other end had a rubber tube halyard to loop around your wrist. They also had a larger half loop hook that was great for retrieving keys off the end of the dock, and everyone lost a key ring at least once in their Marine Patrol career. The trident tip was a three-pronged fork with barbs on it. This attachment would hook into cloth or other objects allowing them to be easily recovered.

"How long are you planning on going down for?" Miller asked.

"I'm going to take a quick look around and spend a few minutes probing the bales. I shouldn't be down more than 10 minutes."

"How much air you got left, Collins?" Sergeant Miller inquired.

"1700 pounds," Collins informed him.

"OK Collins, you go back down with the Major."

Stephens happily climbed out of the way, making room for the Major on the swim platform.

Collins followed Major Alexander to the bottom. Alexander was an experienced scuba diver but even so, the protocol of never diving alone was strictly adhered to. Major Alexander made two slow passes around the exterior of the airplane, taking note of the left engine nacelle compartment on one of the passes. The right one was partially buried in the sand. This compartment was located directly behind the engine and was commonly used for storage. He made mental note that none of the barnacles had been disturbed and the compartments remained unopened. People unfamiliar with airplanes didn't know this compartment was there, so it was not that unusual that this dive group missed it. Alexander made a slow and steady inspection of the aircraft exterior. Although it was no longer current and he hadn't flown as pilot in command in at least 10 years, he'd had his pilot's license since he was 22 years old.

When they reached the cockpit, Alexander's light illuminated the interior and all appeared to be as described. He noticed that there were no barnacles on the inside of the cockpit area, which meant that the airplane had been sealed until very recently. Even if the pilot had busted his skull on the windscreen, that windscreen had been in place until a few days ago. Water could have seeped in, but sea life was not allowed access, and hence the lack of growth — the windscreen had remained intact post-crash.

Alexander reached into the cockpit with the spear and began prodding into the bales. The trident tip entered the bales easier than he had expected. The vegetation had probably rotted long ago, and it didn't take long to turn the interior of the cockpit into a cloud of disintegrated organic matter of rotted burlap and pot. His light quickly lost the ability to penetrate into the dissipating visibility near the missing windscreen. The tip of the spear had struck a metallic box below the disintegrating bales. "Fuel tank," thought Alexander.

Collins tapped the Major on the shoulder, breaking his concentration. When the Major turned around, Collins was showing him the pressure gauge on his console, which indicated 500 pounds of air remaining in his tank. They had been down longer than planned. Collins gave the Major the thumb toward the surface sign. Alexander gave the OK signal in reply. Collins turned and began the ascent with the Major in tow.

The patrol boat had turned to align with the nose of the wreck as the afternoon breeze shifted, and so Collins surfaced at the back of the swim platform. He pulled his mask off and handed it to Miller, who was leaning over to grab his gear. Collins pulled off his fins and handed them up as well. Fifteen seconds or so had passed when Miller inquired, "What did you do with the Major?"

Collins looked beside himself and said, "He was right behind me. I gave him the mandatory surface signal because I was down to 500 Pounds, and he gave the OK."

About that time, bubbles appeared en masse next to Collins, confirming the Major was only a few feet below. As he broke the surface, Major Alexander heaved a 12 pound grouper onto the deck that was attached to the business end of the spear. The grouper was lanced just behind the gills and gave three final tail flips when it hit the dry deck of the boat.

"I had to stop and pick up dinner," the Major said.

Eight

It was a beautiful day for snorkeling, with light winds and a slight overcast. Pete and Sam had loaded up the dinghy with the day's equipment shortly after arriving at the anchorage. The dinghy now contained a cooler with several cold drinks, two underwater metal detectors, a couple of plastic garden hand spades and the snorkeling gear. They didn't bother to start the motor because the little cove Pete had selected was just a short row away and it felt good to stretch a little and use the oars.

When they reached the potential treasure area, they dropped the pint-sized mushroom anchor made especially for the dinghy, which only needed four feet of line to hit the bottom. This was a nice grassy area mixed with sand and the remains of very old trees. If Pete's calculations were correct, this was the spot where there should have been a shifting of the island over time. Another factor in their favor was that this area had been protected for quite some time. This was a national preserve, which meant that no dredges were allowed and the area was pristine and undisturbed. Mangroves are vital to the ecosystem of Florida's subtropical climate, and there are four types:

the red mangrove, which grows closest to the open water; the black

mangrove, which has a slightly different root system; and the white

mangrove, which grows closest to shore. In the brackish water above

the mangroves grows the stable buttonwood tree. This combination of

trees that sink their roots down to salt water holds a shoreline

together. The mangrove forests can generally survive a hurricane, and

when they don't, the trees quickly regenerate over the altered

shoreline. Some shifting is natural, and this is what Pete was counting

on. The shifting away from the Florida mainland and toward the Gulf

of Mexico should have occurred naturally. If his theory and his

calculations were correct, that would mean this place was high and

dry during the time the land was inhabited by the pirates.

The metal detectors had the center posts removed, making the

entire unit shorter for use in the water. The electronics head was

sealed and rated to 200 feet, nowhere near what they would

approach. Pete had long ago changed out the cumbersome

headphones for small waterproof ear buds that were much more

comfortable and easier to wear. Some park rangers really got

obnoxious when they saw a metal detector, but this was navigable

water, not actually part of the preserve, and so they were allowed to

be here. If you talked to 20 different rangers about where salvage

could be searched for, however, you got 20 different answers, but if

nobody saw the metal detector or earphones, you got left alone. It was

also easier to hear approaching boat traffic with the small ear buds.

Pete had raised the dive flag, a square red rectangle with a white stripe going from the upper left corner to the opposite lower right corner, on the starboard halyard of the Southern Cross. The flag warned passing boaters that divers were in the water nearby and they should give way, which didn't always happen nevertheless and so vigilance was necessary. He also had a small dive flag on a polystyrene float standing up in the dinghy.

They began their sweep working from the very edge of the mangrove toward the east and away from dry land. When the electronic beep was received, the area would be worked back and forth, narrowing the precise spot that contained a piece of metal. After the first hour of searching, they had recovered one fishing reel, several beer cans, and a chunk of unidentified something or other that was so rusted that the origin of this object would never be determined. Silver and gold do not rust, and that is what they were after. Another coating of sunscreen, and back they went to their task.

Searching for treasure is something like fishing, a relaxing activity that allows the brain to wander, that allows strange and miscellaneous thoughts to come and go. Snorkeling for pirate treasure makes for a great mental escape that allows the grey matter to rejuvenate and refresh. The next two hours passed by with minimal results physically but on a scale of one to ten in the chilling out department, this perfect day was somewhere around fifteen.

Pete and Sam decided it would be nice to go to Pine Island for lunch. They could have a light dinner on the boat and a few cold beers tonight as the sun set to the west. If the slight overcast held, it should prove to be a stunning sight. Red sky at night, sailor's delight.

With 135 gallons of fresh water on the Southern Cross, both men were afforded a nice fresh water rinse on deck. Then it was a quick 15-minute run northeast to Pine Island in the dinghy. Pete hadn't been here before, but the street map showed a business area where the main road came into Pine Island about midway, which was between their location and Cape Coral further to the east, the city on the north side of the river near Fort Myers.

The nautical chart showed a place where they should be able to get within a few blocks of the main street running through Pine Island. There was bound to be a restaurant or two near this intersection, or so the odds favored.

Twenty minutes later, the dinghy was tied to a white mangrove tree on the edge of town. After they climbed past a couple of buttonwood trees, they could see the dead end street that would take them to the main highway two and a half blocks further inland. One of the great things about Florida is that everyone is walking around in shorts and flip-flops, at least along the coast: Florida casual, approved everywhere. Most restaurants just required that you not drip saltwater on the cheap furniture as it leaves white salt rings on restaurant-quality simulated leather.

The main intersection appeared as advertised on the local map. Pete was happy to see several small restaurants scattered about the main crossroad, including one in a strip mall on the opposite side of the highway that had several other businesses in it. The proprietor of a photography studio had placed several large portraits in the front window as an advertisement to photograph your wedding or other special event, restoration of old photographs, and a handy service to transfer your old tapes to DVD.

"Hey Sam," Pete asked. "Do you think they might have a Betamax machine?"

"Only one way to find out — let's go in and ask. What do you need one of them for?"

"I'll explain it in a minute," Pete responded.

The automatic door buzzer announced their arrival upon entering. An older gentleman emerged from a back room doorway. "Afternoon. What can I help you gentlemen with?"

Pete took the lead. "Afternoon. I've got an old Betamax tape, and I don't know if it's any good. I was wondering if you have a machine for it?"

"Yasser." The drawl indicated he was a native Southerner. "I don't have one you can rent, not much call for that anymore. I've just got the one I use for processing."

Pete inquired, "Can you process it into a regular DVD?"

"Yassir. It's $45.00 because that equipment is kind of expensive anymore." The proprietor thought to himself that this was probably only the fifth time anyone had asked for the machine since he acquired it, brand new out of the box, 8 years ago.

Sam asked, "Can we watch it while it's being transferred?"

"No sir. I don't have a monitor hooked up to that system because it's rarely used. It will just be a one to one digital transfer."

"That would be fine. When can you do it?" Pete inquired.

"I close at 5 today and open at 9 in the morning. Bring it in anytime."

Pete told him he would be back in 45 minutes or so.

On the trip back to the Southern Cross, Pete told Sam the rest of the story. His plan had been to fill him in during this evening's cocktail hour, but the explanation had been pushed up to now. Sam was mentally adding up the story value to the airplane's clock when he finally got it.

***

The El Paso Intelligence Center, established in 1974 to combat the growing influx of drug trafficking and illegal immigration, is securely located within the confines of Fort Bliss in El Paso, Texas. The Drug Enforcement Administration, along with the U.S. Customs and Border Protection Agency, formed EPIC as a clearing house for centralized information. Any law enforcement officer with the proper clearance and identification had access to the Center's huge database, which in its time exceeded any other joint multi-jurisdictional resource available. The Center has morphed into a culmination of INS, ICE, Department of Homeland Security, and just about any other three letter government organization.

When the FAA enters an aircraft history search or investigative request into their system, the EPIC mainframe is automatically checked without the operator's knowledge. Mitch Jenkins, a 22 year-old data processor at the FAA, had just entered HK778LC into the system. He was new at this job, and consequently he didn't realize right off the bat that the designation HK belongs to Columbia. He did know that it was not a standard US registration, however, which normally begins with an N. When the number HK778LC returned with no record found, it was not unusual, and his training coordinator let him input the information as a learning experience. His instructor then began to show him how to access the international records database along with the flight plan archives, which were held for 15 years. Jenkins received no information on this aircraft whatsoever, but it was a good training scenario for the new hire. He would send Detective Rawlerson a report that indicated his lack of findings.

Without the FAA trainee's knowledge, an alert at EPIC popped up. Anytime a listed drug smuggling airplane was checked, its number run by any governmental agency or a flight plan filed, the EPIC computer captured that information and alerted an attendant. Each flagged aircraft had the basic information, which also came back to the attendant, including the aircraft description, suspected activity, any suspects involved, investigating agency and lead investigator. The standard procedure was for the attendant to then contact the lead investigator and make them aware of the status of whatever had caused the flag to pop up. Sometimes the aircraft would clear customs into the US and the case agent was made aware of its movements upon entering or exiting the US mainland, but at other times, some detective in another jurisdiction would run the aircraft on the local computer system. EPIC would then pair up the different detectives and a joint investigation would begin. On a slow day, narcotics agents nationwide would simply write down all the aircraft registration numbers, foreign and domestic, that were on the flight lines of their regional airports and submit a generic contact report. Scores of airplanes were found by that method, and the Center had enjoyed great successes.

HK778LC was on one of the alert lists, an old one. This aircraft popped up as an investigation conducted by the Florida Department of Law Enforcement, Pinellas County Florida, and the lead investigator was one Special Agent James Wojcik. The case was last active in 1983. The aircraft had been spotted departing the Clearwater

Airpark late one evening by one of the airpark line boys who had been refueling a corporate twin engine airplane. The line boy had reported it to SA Wojcik and was rewarded with a case of beer. The line boy simply had to call the number on a business card telling him exactly when it left. Wojcik had listed the aircraft with EPIC, indicating that it was currently involved in smuggling activities, and he requested any reports of the aircraft's sighting by any law enforcement agency. This notification carried the additional notation that SA Wojcik's investigation needed to be kept strictly confidential, indicating that his request for information would not be released to anyone, including law enforcement, without his personal prior authorization.

The aircraft was never spotted or reported again, and the flag had been idle ever since. The attendant glanced at the request from the FAA, which indicated that the Pinellas County Sheriff's Office had made the initial contact for information from the FAA. Pinellas County was now reporting that the aircraft had been located underwater near Tampa Bay. This was now a death investigation, which explained why it had not been spotted since. The attendant sent a contact request to the new Florida Department of Law Enforcement Office in St. Petersburg via secure encrypted email to the listed electronic address in the EPIC database. The message traffic indicated they had a report for Wojcik pertaining to a 1982 case and required an updated phone number for contact. Wojcik simply had to give his EPIC 6 digit identifier code and the attendant would tell him everything he had received about the case.

***

SAC, or Special Agent in Charge, John Hollis received this message upon returning from lunch, along with a host of other routine messages. John had known Wojcik, but only very briefly. When Hollis was assigned to this office from Tallahassee he recalled meeting Wojcik once. Wojcik was nearing his retirement, which was then several months away, if he recalled correctly. Whether it was a few too many doughnuts, the high blood pressure, or some combination of the two that had caused the fatal heart attack had been long forgotten. Wojcik went home one evening and never returned. He was pronounced dead at the hospital late one night.

There had been some question as to his death and possible suspicious circumstances, but Hollis couldn't recall anything specific. Wojcik's active pending case files were reassigned to other agents for follow-up. What could not be followed up on, for one reason or the other, was a decision made by the SAC at that time. Special Agent Wojcik's caseload history and field notes, along with his desk calendar, Rolodex, and entire desk contents, were archived at the main records warehouse for the State of Florida in Tallahassee.

When SA Janet Cantu returned to the office after testifying in court that afternoon, she found a note on her desk. Her presence was requested in the office of SAC Hollis, where she promptly reported.

"If your caseload isn't too big, I need you to look into an old archived case," Hollis requested.

"Not too big," Janet said. "I've got an active bank fraud case and a couple of local agency assists. The trial is over, my portion of it anyway. What do you have for me?"

Hollis handed Janet the message from EPIC requesting contact with SA Wojcik. "This is before your time here, but Wojcik worked out of the old office until 1984 or so, when he died of a heart attack. Seems that something with his name on it just cropped up, although I can't imagine what. The request Wojcik put in to EPIC is from the early eighties." Hollis explained. He went on to tell Janet what he recalled about Wojcik, which wasn't much. Janet had never had a reason to deal with EPIC directly, but she knew the procedure. Hollis instructed Janet to follow up on the matter and to let him know what it was all about when she had some answers.

Janet Cantu had been assigned to the St. Petersburg office for the past 18 months after a two year assignment to the Gainesville field office. Janet had initially followed in her father's footsteps by signing on with the Tampa Police Department, which was eager to hire her when she completed her Criminal Justice Degree. A Cuban father-daughter combination made for a great public relations image with the large Cuban community. Janet's father, Jorge Cantu, had been promoted to Captain after working his way up from a foot beat in the Cuban community of Ybor City on the outskirts of Tampa. Margarita, Janet's mother, had immigrated with her husband to Tampa many years earlier and worked in the cigar industry that was making Tampa famous. The Cuban missile crisis and ensuing economic blockades had increased the demand for local "Cuban-made" cigars.

Their only child, Janet, was born 35 years ago when her father was just a rookie. Janet gave her father the highest compliment possible when she announced her intention to become a police officer. Janet had always held her father in the highest regard and wanted to make him proud. The local community college provided her with the necessary degree in Criminal Justice as it was simply all her parents could afford. The Tampa Police Department then hired her and sponsored her in the police academy as soon as she applied for the position.

Her mom and dad were equally proud when she decided to expand her Law Enforcement career by joining the Florida Department of Law Enforcement. Being a Cuban female applicant with eight years experience with the Tampa PD had put her application on the top of the FDLE recruitment list. Janet didn't deny that her ethnicity and sex had played a major role in opening doors for her — she did not intend to waste the opportunities. Janet had a long record of proving her worth, always continued her education

119

with selective college courses, and was just a damn fine police officer. When she was first assigned to the St. Pete FDLE office, a couple of the local agents knew why a good looking Cuban female was hired, and they had quietly mumbled amongst themselves, "Quotas." There was also no mistaking her strict policy of not dating anyone in the office. Sexual innuendos or inappropriate comments were part of her zero tolerance work ethic, a line her peers learned early on not to cross.

It was always interesting to see how the mood of the ignorant changed as they scrambled to keep up with her. She had more than proven her worth on several investigations that had been at a standstill before she came on board. Janet once went undercover and moved into a migrant trailer park. She picked strawberries for 3 weeks while documenting the abuse perpetuated upon the migrant community by some local slum lord. The migrants were living in squalor and being blatantly stolen from. After all, who would they call or report him to? Any contact with the local police would get them thrown out of the country they loved so much. The opportunities were better than they had ever known previously, so long as *Mal de Señor* could be tolerated.

That jackass landlord is still serving prison time as a result of Janet's arrest and court testimony. Janet then gained the complete support of the Cuban community and was presented with several awards at banquets and luncheons, and she became a well respected agent among her peers.

Janet returned to her desk and booted up her computer. She initiated a message to the computer ID number that generated this particular missive. Part of the security at EPIC was that none of the attendants was ever identified by name. Only the computer terminal ID number was ever sent in electronic messages. The terminal ID that corresponded to a specific individual was known only inside the compound. Janet explained the death of SA Wojcik and that she was assigned to follow up on any investigation. She then supplied her contact information and sent the message.

The next message to go out was to FDLE records and archives requesting that Wojcik's archived case history files be sent to her via FedEx. "ASAP Case Sensitive" was added to the request. If you didn't specify that on your request, it might find its way continuously to the bottom of the in-basket and take a month to be answered.

***

Pete and Sam had enjoyed a leisurely lunch while the Betamax tape was being converted into ones and zeros that would be morphed into a format able to be played out on a DVD disk. Pete enjoyed a grouper sandwich while Sam found happiness with a fried shrimp basket. Sharon, Sam's wife, would not have approved of the fried food, and so he especially enjoyed such a feast on this fine afternoon.

The photography studio owner had told Pete that the tape itself seemed okay, but the internal metal parts had suffered damage. The internal rollers and bearings had a fine layer of rust on them and didn't want to move freely. The tape had transferred some of the content, about the first ten minutes, before a loud squealing sound had notified him of the problem. The machine had shut down automatically when the take-up reel would no longer turn, a safety measure built into the machine that kept it from eating the tape. There had been some transfer, according to the digital read out. About 18 gigabytes of information had made it to the DVD. He went on to explain that, if it was an important tape, he could strip out a good Betamax cassette and rewind this tape onto it and try it again, assuming the oxidation hadn't destroyed the magnetic properties of the tape itself. The problem was that he didn't know where he could get a good Betamax tape. "I could probably order one off the Internet and have it in a week or so, but I don't know what it will cost you."

"No thanks," Pete let him know. "Let's see how this turned out first, and if I think the rest is worth the trouble, I'll let you know." Pete paid the man and headed toward the dinghy.

Sam suggested they stop at the small supermarket on the opposite street corner on the way. They could always use a couple more beers, maybe a steak for dinner, and a bag of ice.

Back on the Southern Cross, the ice was put in the cooler on top of the newly acquired Coronas. The temp would be perfect by the time the steaks were cooked later this evening. Pete was thinking that a late dinner, about 8:00, would work out fine, since lunch was delayed this afternoon. The moon was scheduled to be near the full, and an incoming tide would begin to fill the bay around 10 p.m. Pete thought this might be the perfect time to show Sam how to catch blue crabs.

They were sitting in the cockpit enjoying the evening with a cold beer when Pete snapped the DVD into his laptop computer. He had brought it up to the cockpit and set it between them on the foldout table. You could hear the DVD begin to spin up as his media player program kicked in and started with the options screen. Pete moved the cursor to the play button, and with a gentle tap, the images began.

***

Major Alexander notified his secretary on the way out of his office that he would not be in until after noon the next day. He had a dentist appointment in the morning and would be unavailable. Debora acknowledged the schedule change and inwardly smiled — tomorrow morning would be nice and quiet.

Leslie Alexander found his evening peaceful and somewhat refreshed after the expected daily afternoon rain shower. He had loaded all the necessary equipment on his boat and secured it below.

Adding fishing poles sticking up from the deck rod holders sent the message he wanted conveyed to any onlookers. With everything in place, he untied his vessel and headed out into Tampa Bay.

***

The first image on the computer screen aboard the Southern Cross was that of an office setting. The camera angle was strange to the two viewers watching silently. It appeared that the camera was on a table of some sort, possibly in a corner. There was something blocking the right edge of the screen, a vertical bar or something like that. The camera was obviously concealed within something. The center of the room had a coffee table with a couple of photographs hanging on the far wall, though it was difficult to tell what was inside the frames. The left side of the screen showed the wall with a couch extending along the wall from the table the camera was on. There was a light on inside the room from an unseen overhead bulb. Either the room was very poorly lit or the camera was behind dark glass.

The scene popped on and stayed like that for a minute or so. Nothing was changing or moving, so Pete checked the digital readout and saw that it was still advancing, indicating that the DVD was indeed advancing. The scene remained unchanged for another minute or so.

124

Then someone entered through a doorway on the right side of the room, partially blocked by whatever held the camera. When the doorway opened, you could hear a noise, a motor of some sort. Pete thought it sounded like an airplane engine. Looking closer at the picture hanging on the far wall Sam thought he could see an aviation theme to it, but he decided that could be a subconscious suggestion initiated by the sound. The door clicked shut and someone approached the camera, walking straight to it. The man obviously knew it was there, and he bent down, looking directly into the face of the camera. He then grasped both sides of the unknown container that held the camera and adjusted the view by turning the container an inch or so to the right. As the unidentified man stood and exited the room, Sam and Pete could clearly see the doorway now, and this was obviously an aircraft hangar. An airplane came into view as the stranger stepped clear of the closing door.

The scene remained the same for another two minutes or so, and then the door finally opened and three new people came into the room and the recording revealed its first glitch. The screen popped up with some odd static looking lines that made the image appear to stretch lengthways across the screen. The image popped back into focus and right out again. Several flickers later, however, and one man could be seen sitting in the chair with his left shoulder to the camera. He kept leaning forward to sip, no, not sip, but spit into a cup. Pete knew he must be chewing tobacco. He was a white male, youngish with close-cut hair. The second fellow was sitting on the couch to the left. He was leaning forward on the cushion, and his demeanor indicated that he obviously was not comfortable. The third man who had entered the room was a victim of the stretchy static that began on the top of the screen and worked its way down. His upper torso was cut off and unrecognizable, but what was clearly visible was a gold star attached to the front of his belt on the right side. There was a gun perched on his belt next to the metal star, which quickly disappeared behind the distorted screen.

When the picture cleared up once again, the man seated in the chair leaned forward and set his cup on the table. Pete could easily see the leather strap of a shoulder holster running under his left arm. The third guy had stepped outside the field of view and was somewhere to the far right when the image cleared again.

The guy on the couch was looking generally agitated, and he fidgeted with a balled-up piece of paper he had in his hands. He looked like he was going to jump out of his skin when the shoulder holster guy said, "You were supposed to simply follow orders. What made you think we wouldn't hear about it?"

The nervous guy appeared to be Hispanic and had the accent to match. He replied, "Señor, you know I will not steal from you. I swear by Jesus' name I would not steal from you. It is what I was given, and that is all!"

The shoulder holster said, "You do not wish any harm to come to you or…" and the static started again. When the picture popped back into focus, a leather bag had thudded onto the coffee table, obviously dropped there by the unknown guy to the right. Only his protruding belly was visible as he wavered in and out of camera view. The man who had adjusted the camera previously had not yet reappeared.

The shoulder holster leaned forward and opened the leather bag. He lifted up a pack of cash and waved it in the face of the Hispanic, who flinched backward. "Is this worth dying over? Is it?"

"Please, please, Señor. You must believe me. I would never take ~static~ mine, I swear..." came part of an emotional plea.

The picture blinked out again, this time going to a black screen with some white fuzz developing along the vertical lines. The picture reappeared as the Hispanic guy was leaning all the way back on the couch. His arms were crossed in front of his face in an automatic defensive posture. The shoulder holster had picked up his cup of tobacco spit and thrown it into the face of the Hispanic fellow. There was more static, five seconds of black screen, and then several more flickers.

When the image reappeared, the Hispanic was screaming "Noooo, please! I beg..." His words became muffled as the view was blocked by the backside of the shoulder holster guy. It was clear by the movement that the Hispanic fellow was presently having his head bashed onto the coffee table, the money, or both, by the other two. In between the thuds, thumps, and bangs, one of them was barking through clinched teeth, "Don't you ever, ever, ever think you can..." when the tape went blank permanently.

Nine

Leslie Alexander dropped his anchor on the southeast side of Egmont Key in the mouth of Tampa Bay. The sun was setting and the passing thunderstorms had ended. Leslie sat on a deck chair on the stern of his vessel with a fishing pole in hand waiting for time to pass. There wasn't any bait on the other end so he wouldn't have to contend with throwing anything back. Leslie's mind was trapping him in emotions and fears that he had repressed years ago. It was not an easy climb to the top, and he was damn close to being there. The past needed to remain buried, or submerged, as the case might be. Things were done long ago that needed to be done, and that's all there was to it. Moral standards had to be adjustable as the situation dictated.

Darkness was setting in, but there was too much boat traffic to make the necessary journey right now. Leslie was about as agnostic as they come, but not tonight. Tonight he prayed to some unknown being above that the Betamax tape was in the wing locker of the sunken plane. How the hell had Vince been able to get so close to shore? Leslie thought there was about a 10 percent chance of finding the tape tonight and a 90 percent chance that the sailboat guy took it. He must be sure, however. There could be no guessing. As soon as the evening boat traffic slowed enough that he could get to the sheriff's buoy without being seen, he would have his answer.

Egmont Key was a great place to wait while deep in thought as the minutes ticked by. It was an island that had been the site of an early Spanish-era fort and was now a tourist destination, like so much of Florida had become. There was a lighthouse sweeping the darkness with a beam of light to warn of the shallow waters, and on the north side of the island were the Tampa Bay shipping lanes, which would also grow quiet as the evening grew older. The lighthouse provided enough light sweeping by to count the mosquitoes hovering about looking for a free meal. Leslie was getting more and more agitated as the evening twilight faded and the mosquitoes took over. "It has to be in the airplane, damn it! It just has to be." Leslie's blood pressure was rising at the thought of losing everything he had worked for. This simply added to the blackened mood aboard the fishing vessel. Leslie now stomped back and forth on the small rear deck of the boat. Leslies' fury was escalating into a full-blown tantrum as his thoughts carried him to the possible undesirable conclusions looming in his future. Would he be able to personally kill someone to get the tape back? Rage was growing exponentially as his thoughts went in directions he didn't like, as long-repressed memories gave rise to evil emotions. Blood vessels on the side of his head and neck began to stick out "Goddamn it! If that stupid son of a...," Leslie screamed into the growing night Then, *swoosh, swoosh, swoosh, splash* and the rod and reel landed 15 yards to the stern of the boat and immediately sank into the bay. "Why couldn't that stupid, worthless Mexican follow orders?" he thought while kicking the transom of the boat. The past was returning and it was leaving a very bad taste in his mouth.

***

Vince was sure of it—1982 *was* going to be a better year for him. He was known in the local community as a treetop flyer. Stephen Stills had even written a song immortalizing the smuggling pilots of the era, an easygoing group of folks who quite simply found a nonstandard way of making a pretty good living. The penalties were not too terrible if you got caught by the Feds. You might spend a few years in a nice cushy federal prison somewhere, which was much better than any local lockup, and so it was worth the risk. Vince was flying cargo out of Fort Lauderdale early in his aviation career when his life began to take on new meaning. The cargo flights didn't pay very well, but at least he was flying. One night in an airport bar after a flight, he was approached by two men, and the offer was simply too easy to accept: take a nice boat ride to the Bahamas and enjoy a couple of days in Nassau. He would then be delivered to an airstrip on an island a little further out. They had a twin engine Piper Aztec they needed flown back to the US via a specific route at a particular time.

He was to land the airplane at an airstrip on the southeast side of Lake Okeechobee. He would then be given money, $25,000 cash, and he would walk away.

He was not supposed to get friendly with anyone, just take the final payment and leave. Vince wanted to know why he should believe they wouldn't just kill him after he made the flight and how could he be sure he would be paid. Vince was then handed an envelope with $5,000 in it, all crisp new hundreds. "Keep this as a down payment," he was told. "You'll get the rest when you get to Okeechobee."

"It's in our best interest to be fair with you. I may need your services again one day," the second man had told him.

"Are you saying that I have to fly for you again after this one?" Vince questioned.

"Only if you want to. It's your choice," the first man replied.

"How do I find you?" Vince queried.

"You won't," the man said. "We will *always* find you."

This was more money than Vince had ever had in his hands at one time, and his brain quickly reasoned that he needed to only make one quick flight. They got all the details worked out, and yeah, one flight, and that would be all. "Okay. When do I go?" Vince chimed in.

"We'll let you know," the first man stated as he and the other man got up and vanished out the door.

Two weeks later, Vince had returned from another mindless midnight cargo run hauling bank transfer slips and paperwork to Atlanta from Miami. The return flight had found him with a load of Wall Street Journal's and the Atlanta Constitution newspaper for the morning newsstands. By 4:30 a.m. he had unloaded all the papers and was closing up the hangar that held the boss's airplane.

"Good morning Vince," came a voice approaching from the side of the building.

Startled, Vince turned to see one of the men from the bar a couple of weeks earlier.

"You need to find your way to Nassau this Thursday," the man told him. "Go hang out at Rasta Rick's near the waterfront and enjoy a few beers. It's time to earn the rest of your money."

"Okay, how do I get to Nassau?" Vince inquired.

"You've got five grand. Buy a plane ticket or rent a canoe. I don't care, just be there Thursday night at 10." The man then vanished as quickly as he had appeared. Vince had understood by the man's tone that the time schedule was nonnegotiable.

Vince only had $1,300 left. The past two weeks had been a blast. Vince could feel a nervous twinge building in his stomach as he thought about what he was getting into. "What the hell," Vince thought, "only one flight."

His boss was a little pissed that he was going to have to fly the route himself for a few days, but he didn't have much of a choice. Vince had told him he needed to go to Kansas to his Aunt's funeral, and Vince explained, she had always been a big influence in his life. He said he just had to go and would get back as soon as he could. He had explained all this twice.

Rasta Rick's, as it turns out, was a cheesy broken-down waterfront bar outside of Nassau where the patrons were comfortable enough to light up a joint to go along with the Bahamian produced beer, Kalik. Bob Marley music was playing in the background on a cassette tape player that had seen one too many decibels forced through the speaker. Vince was seated at a corner table with a Kalik while being watched cautiously by the other patrons. Vince felt like a real outsider.

But that had been a few years ago. He was a regular now. The first run was so easy he decided to do it just one more time, which led to another and another flight. The cash was flowing and the good times were phenomenal. The beaches, booze, and constant flow of one night stands was an expensive lifestyle, but as long as he kept flying, the high life was his.

But before he realized what happened, he was standing on the taxiway of the Clearwater Airpark at 2 a.m. wearing a pair of handcuffs. The DEA had conducted a sting operation and Vince was caught up in it. He had simply delivered an airplane to a customer, nothing more. The problem for Vince this evening was that the aircraft had an illegal fuel system in it. The State of Florida had a law making any non-FAA approved fuel system a third degree felony, a law enacted in an attempt to stem the ever increasing flow of illegal narcotics pouring into the State via privately owned aircraft.

Vince was handed over to the narcotics detective in the local sheriff's office, which was assisting in the sting. The other three people in custody were the actual targets of the sting and would be prosecuted federally. The Feds didn't have anything on Vince Vorsino other than the state charges, and subsequently, they had no further interest in him.

Sergeant Leslie Alexander drove the handcuffed prisoner to the satellite substation office in Clearwater. This time of the morning, they were the only two people present, which was what Alexander expected, and what he needed. Vince looked at the Affidavit of Criminal Charges being prepared by Sergeant Alexander and could see his life draining away with each throw of a typewriter key. If that wasn't bad enough, the damn handcuffs were beginning to hurt. He had mentally surrendered and given over all his identification information without fuss. He always knew this might happen, but he kept thinking, "Just one more run, then I'll quit." He didn't reveal anything about the load of primo reefer he flew in the previous week, but nevertheless, the sergeant was typing his life into a new direction. Blank spaces on official documents were rapidly filling in and sealing his doom. Vince had visions of becoming some big man's lover in a six-by-eight cell. The mere thought caused him to shiver. He was getting sick to his stomach and could feel the bile creeping up his windpipe. If he could just get his hands on a joint right now…

Sergeant Alexander opened the Florida Statute book and began reading out loud: "Blah, Blah, Blah… Second degree felony, punishable by 15 years in prison and a twenty-five thousand dollar fine," adding, "never been to jail before, huh?"

"No sir, my first time." Vince sat there with his shoulders slouched, his head hung low, and he was ready to break into tears any second.

"Now," Alexander thought to himself. "He's ready." Alexander leaned closer to Vince and looked directly into his eyes. He put his right hand on the defeated criminal's shoulder and took a deep breath while feigning a look of intense concentration. In the softest and least threatening voice Alexander could muster, he told Vince, "I can get you out of this."

Vince Vorsino walked out of the substation a little after 4 a.m. It was up to him to find his own ride home. He inhaled the night air trying to unscramble the torrents of emotions twisting and turning inside him. Sorting the facts out as clearly as he could right now left him with the only words he could come up with: snitch, rat, stool pigeon. Sergeant Alexander had turned him into a confidential informant. One thing was becoming perfectly clear in his confused state — Alexander owned him

It started slowly at first, and he provided just snippets of information here and there. Then a couple of his loads got taken down, after Vince was allowed to escape on foot, of course. He was also required to hand over exactly half of what he made on each load. It was either that or he got to listen to Alexander threaten him again with the big horny cellmate story again. If that wasn't bad enough, Alexander had his ace in the hole ready to be played. Either Vince worked exclusively for Alexander and paid everything he demanded, or Alexander would play the ace. Alexander explained to him one evening that he had a video tape of "Vince the Snitch" taking a cash payment from an undercover narcotics officer while an airplane full of pot sat in the background. Releasing that tape into the circle of smugglers would seal his fate and probably get him killed. If he was lucky enough to stay alive, Vince would have to make a living working at McDonald's.

Vince was making bringing in more loads than most of the other pilots he knew in the business. He outwardly appeared to be gifted and have a knack for getting loads through at just the right time, with only a few confiscations here and there, which were to be expected. Vorsino was lucky as hell, according to the other treetop flyers drinking at Rasta Rick's.

Vince was becoming sick of taking all the chances and handing over way too much money to Alexander. The thought of Leslie releasing the tape convinced him that he would be killed and left to rot on some foreign airstrip, but Vince had managed to secretly develop a side business and bring in some extra cash, making a couple of reefer runs on the QT. If he got caught, he planned to say he tried to call ahead of time and blah, blah, blah. He would worry about the particulars when the time came. He knew, or at least firmly believed, that Alexander was watching his bank account and other movements. So Vince had found a great place in the Bahamas to use as his personal bank, keeping the extra funds somewhat available while out of view. His master plan was beginning to take shape. The extra cash would afford him the opportunity to finally sever all ties with his owner and get back out on his own.

Vince was at the Clearwater Airpark late one evening, where the Pinellas County Sheriff's Office maintained an undercover hangar. Vince knew that he wasn't the only person supporting Sergeant Alexander with drug profits. He was inside the hangar when he overheard Alexander talking to someone on the office phone about the next payment coming in late that night. The opportunity Vince needed seemed to be about to present itself, he thought. Vince made an excuse about needing to get the airplane ready for the next run. He said he needed to replace a magneto on the left engine. Alexander waved him off, telling him to fix the plane and stay out of sight, that he was not to disturb him or anyone else in the office this evening.

Vince had busied himself long enough with the fictitious repair to get one step closer to completing the master plan. Timing was going to be critical, but the risk was worth it. Two hours later, Alexander stepped outside the office and told Vince he would be

138

right back, he had to go to the front gate to let someone in. Vince took that opportunity to turn on the hidden camera in the little office. The cops recorded select meetings for one reason or the other all the time. The Betamax recorder was concealed inside a locked toolbox on a workbench along the outside wall of the office near the airplanes. The cables were well concealed, the camera hidden inside the base of a lamp on the end table. Vince had seen Alexander switch it on once when Alexander thought he was otherwise occupied.

The lock was easy to work open without any telltale marks giving away his entry. He had practiced this before when nobody was around. Once the camera was turned on and adjusted inside the office, Vince was satisfied his plan was taking shape and returned to the fictional engine repairs. "Two can play an ace card," Vince thought. If an incriminating tape was good enough to hold him hostage, then another incriminating tape should be good enough to release him. Vince would hold onto his tape as long as Alexander held onto his. Alexander would have no choice but to keep his mouth shut and let Vince return to Rasta Rick's a free man.

Several minutes later, Alexander returned to the office with two other people. A third person, who he didn't get a very good look at, stood outside the hangar door smoking a cigarette. Not too long after the meeting began, Vince could hear the muffled disturbance inside the office. Someone was getting a beating in there, and he doubted it was the cops. Not wanting to tip his hand, he disappeared a little deeper into his engine work.

Not long after the sounds of the beating subsided, Alexander and the other guy helped the bloody faced man out the front of the hangar. They met with the third guy out front, who did some more talking to the bloody guy. They carried the conversation around back, out of the light that was escaping the front of the hangar. Vince took this time to retrieve some tools off of the workbench, or at least that was his excuse for being at that precise spot if he got caught. He opened two toolboxes while nervously listening for footsteps on the painted hangar floor. Should someone approach, he would close the fake toolbox and simply hope for another shot at getting the tape out before he was discovered.

Vince was able to slip the tape out of the recorder unnoticed and put it inside his shirt, in the small of his back. Pulling his loose tee shirt over the back and feeling it to make sure it wasn't sticking out reassured him that he might get away with this.

Alexander returned alone a few minutes later and told Vince to finish up for the night; he needed to lock up the hangar. Vince told him he could finish the repair the next afternoon and that he was just about done. Alexander went into the office, locking the door behind him.

Vince felt like he could breathe normally again once he was outside the hangar with his tape. He got in his car and left the airport, and a smile began to appear on his face. The master plan was coming together.

It was almost three weeks later before Vince managed to stash his accumulated wealth, almost two hundred thousand dollars, and a copy of one Betamax tape on a small island in the Bahamas. He would return when it was safe to retrieve his private retirement fund, but for now, the final smuggling run to release him from Alexander had to be made. Nobody in Rasta Rick's really cared about what Vince was celebrating, as long as the liquor was free and the reefer didn't run out. It was a hell of a party, at least what Vince could remember of it. As the party wore on late into the night, somebody passed Vince a joint sprinkled with angel dust to increase the good times, which he inhaled deeply. The PCP, or phencyclidine, served to severely loosen Vince's tongue.

Almost a month after the party, Vince found himself sitting on an airstrip located on the tip of the Yucatan Peninsula. He had not been back to the States since that party. A commercial airliner had delivered him to Bogotá, Columbia, where he picked up HK778LC from a private airstrip. Two kilos of cocaine, something Vince had never hauled before, were along for the ride. They were not so well wrapped that Vince had trouble shaking out "his cut" into a smaller plastic baggie. Vince knew some girls who would be extra appreciative of the cocaine, and he stashed the coke in a PVC tube of cash he was supposed to bring to Leslie from the Columbians. Leslie wasn't going to get most of this cash, which had become Vince's self awarded bonus. He did write Leslie's initials on one of the packs of fifties, which would be more of an insult to Alexander than anything else. Vince envisioned throwing the cash in Leslie's face and telling him that was the last of any money he would ever see from him. Vince also had the coordinates to his secret bank account written down as well. He didn't trust his memory for something that important.

His flight took him directly from the strip in Columbia to the airstrip in Mexico. This particular slice of nowhere was an established cannabis shipping point that Vince had used a dozen times already, and he was familiar with the folks running the strip.

Juan had invited Vince into the small shack for a hot meal and a shot of tequila, which had become customary. The other workers were experienced in their tasks and were left to it. They would stuff the airplane with the bales of cannabis, allowing just enough room for the pilot to get in. The refueling was accomplished out of 55 gallon drums using a hand pump. The normal wing tanks were filled to the caps along with the added internal tank, except for this trip. Juan and his crew had direct orders from Alexander that, if carefully followed, would net them a generous bonus for their loyalty. The illegal internal fuel tank, which was on the cabin floor, normally held 70 gallons of aviation gasoline. Tonight it only had 10. Bales of reefer were stacked on top, blocking access to the fill cap that contained a fuel gauge Vince was not supposed to see.

Vince was done with his tamale dinner and sipping on the tequila when one of the workers came bursting into the shack, knocking a glass off a table. "Federales! Federales! You must leave now! They will be here in minutes!"

"My plane," shouted Vince as he jumped up. "I need it fueled, quickly!"

"It is, señor. The gas it is full and your cargo it is on, but you must hurry. The Federales, they come now!"

Vince ran to the plane as the other workers scattered into the surrounding jungle. Vince got the engines running in record time and forced the heavy plane off the dirt strip. He stayed low in the fading day as twilight set in. "Treetop flyers! What a way to earn a living," Vince said out loud to himself. Vince quickly put enough miles between him and the Federales to feel safe. He was out over the Gulf of Mexico heading for Florida as he leisurely climbed to his cruising altitude of 11,000 feet. With the autopilot engaged, Vince settled in for the long quiet flight. Nobody else was out here, so he had a wind up alarm clock on the dash to wake him up in a half hour just in case he fell asleep. Every half hour it went off, prompting him to advance the time another thirty minutes and activate the alarm.

***

The gringo was long gone and would not dare return, thinking that the Federales would be at the airstrip. Juan had told Pedro to go to the jungle and get the pilot's bag and the two kilos of cocaine he took earlier from the airplane. "Fetch it my friend, and bring it here into the light," he instructed Juan.

Two minutes later, Juan returned to the shack with the suitcase and cocaine. Alexander would get the video tape, and Juan and his crew would get the cocaine and tube of money. "We are rich now, no?" Pedro asked.

"Si Pedro, we are rich!" Juan told him as he opened the pilot's suitcase.

***

Vince had managed to stay awake the entire flight. It was so peaceful, dark, and cool that he had to take great care to not fall asleep without setting the alarm clock. It was about time to transfer the fuel from the auxiliary tank on the cabin floor up into the wing tanks. A small electric motor would suck the fuel from the auxiliary tank and back feed it through the fuel crossover system to fill the main tanks. The mains would then gravity-feed into the engines. There was also a small hand pump as a backup.

Vince reached behind his seat to get a fresh pack of smokes from the side pocket of his suitcase. He would enjoy a smoke first and then transfer fuel. As he reached around behind him, he couldn't feel the suitcase where he had left it. He lit up the cabin behind him with his red lens flashlight to protect his night vision, but he still couldn't see his suitcase. The suitcase was obviously gone. "Goofy friggin' Mexicans will steal anything that isn't nailed down," he thought. He would just have to buy new clothes when he got back to Florida. He would be able to afford them now that he could keep all the money he was earning. The bag that contained his freedom from Alexander sat out of view on the floor in front of the copilot's seat, right next to his toiletries and flight bag. The PVC tube of cash he had would keep him, and several young women, very happy until he got to the main stash in the Bahamas.

Vince flipped the switch to energize the fuel pump. He could hear it spin up and then slow down as it had to work a little harder to gain its prime and start moving fuel. In less than two minutes, the pump sped up as it no longer had the prime and ran dry. "Damn it," he thought. "Now I have to hand pump the gas into the main tanks." He adjusted the autopilot to maintain heading and altitude, then twisted around into the aisle and manipulated the crossover valves to accept the hand pump configuration. This pump refused to pick up a prime as well, however, and the shot of adrenalin at the thought of running out of gas in the middle of the Gulf of Mexico hit him with such a jolt that he knew he wouldn't sleep for a month. He climbed

145

onto the marijuana bales and pushed them aside to see the gauge on the cap. *"EMPTY! GODDAMN EMPTY!"* His worst nightmare had become a horrible reality. He began tapping on the side of the tank after shoving two bales out into the small path the loaders had left him. The tapping returned empty hollow sounds from the top to the bottom. The gas hadn't leaked out of the tank — he would have smelled it. It was simply empty.

His first reaction was to pull the mixtures as far back on the engines as he dared, sparing every drop of fuel that was being consumed by the thirsty Lycomings. Both engine temperature gauges responded to the choked fuel supply by rising to the red line. It was the only way to extend his range and conserve fuel. The engines would be ruined, but that didn't matter right now. The engines needed to stay alive long enough to get him to shore, or at least close enough to swim.

The next hour and a half was pure torture. Vince went over the last couple of weeks in his mind, every detail he could recall. After a great deal of thought, he was left with the obvious. The night at Rasta Rick's with the laced pot and too much to drink must have been his downfall. He remembered now being a little too free talking about the details of his master plan to another treetop flyer. Nat, Nate, something like that, not that it mattered now. The fellow was quite obviously on Alexander's payroll. Every stinking detail of the conversation must have been repeated to Alexander. Vince didn't know how right he was. Nate got a hefty bonus by ratting on the rat.

146

Nate didn't know where the tape was, or what specifically was on it, but he knew it was very important to Leslie Alexander. Vince said it contained Alexander, a couple of other cops, a load of pot, and some payoffs. Vince wouldn't reveal where it was, just that on his next trip home, he would take it with him. "Then we'll see who pushes who around," a very stoned Vince had bragged.

The Mexican load was an obvious setup, and now that he gave it some thought, it was starting to make sense. The Mexicans were supposed to steal the money and Betamax tape, and *THEN* send him to his watery grave. Vince would simply vanish into the waters forever with his secret lost to the depths. Alexander needed that tape now that he knew about it. His curiosity had the best of him. Besides, he could only be absolutely certain of where the tape was if he was the one that had it. And what the hell, he might have to use it one day against his partner. In this business, you can never be prepared enough for how people turn on each other. A little insurance policy in the form of a Betamax tape couldn't hurt.

"What a freaking loser I am," Vince thought to himself. Well, at least neither one of them got the damn money. With a glimmer of hope surfacing, Vince thought that, if he could swim to shore, the game was still on. Alexander was going to pay extra for the tape now. The price to be in this poker game had just gone up considerably. Getting to shore was the key, and that was beginning to look like a possibility.

Way off in the distance was a light. Vince thought it might be a boat, which would be just fine. He could ditch the plane near the boat, get rescued, and pay the captain to take him to shore. "Things are looking up!" The light flicked on and off at a very steady and predictable rate and stayed at the same spot on his windscreen. Taking a quick look at his navigation chart, Vince was now beginning to believe this might be the Egmont Key lighthouse. The evening coastal thunderstorms had died out, leaving a high overcast, and as Vince began his descent to stay off of the Tampa Airport radar screen, he could tell the waves were up. He thought for a moment about just staying up high, but he knew Customs or DEA would bust him as he got near the coastline. Altitude meant he could coast further, about one foot forward for every seven feet of altitude he started the glide from. The money would do him no good if it was in the hands of the Feds. Getting caught would mean he would be alive but in prison the rest of his life. "Some choice," he thought. He was hauling cocaine this trip, which meant the rules had changed. "Well, one must take chances in this business," he thought.

The first cold front of the season had headed south thereby causing a ruckus with the water. His descent to 1,000 feet caused him to momentarily lose the blinking light over the horizon. When he saw the light return again, he would have to drop to 200 feet above the water to avoid detection. Vince knew that, if he held his course, he would see the light soon; and if his navigation was correct, that blinking light would in fact be the Egmont Key lighthouse. He would

148

then pop up looking like he came out of the little airport south of Egmont Key, appearing to the radar screen watchers as just another local flight along the coast.

His hopes were soaring as the pulsing light house reappeared on the horizon. Then things got quiet, *very, very* quiet.

Everything was a reaction now as it was less than 200 feet to the angry seas below. Vince understood the theory of ditching at sea, although he had never actually done it. Just about every airplane would make a good seaplane, once.

The airspeed had bled off to just above the stall speed of the wings. The stall warning horn had been rising in intensity, filling the cabin with the eerie screeching sound the designers intentionally built to be annoying. Vince had already flipped on the landing light to better gauge his touch down. Keeping the nose high, he could ease the belly of the airplane onto the sea. Keeping the landing gear up would create a smooth rounded surface for the airplane to settle in on. The propellers were windmilling, turning from the forward airspeed. Normally the pilot would feather the props to increase the forward glide ratio, but there was no need to do that here — there simply wasn't time anyway. Vince was now busy envisioning himself swimming the last few miles to shore toward the lighthouse.

As the last of the lift evaporated from the wings, the airplane settled the final few feet toward the sea. Everything was looking fine until a six-foot swell filled the windscreen with water and the nose of the airplane hit the wave head on. The crests of the waves were not exceptionally thick, but water doesn't compress. The airplane's forward momentum helped it plow through the wall of water, slowing it down considerably. Vince's seatbelt and shoulder harness did their jobs by keeping the pilot securely restrained in the seat. His head was another issue altogether. The sudden deceleration when passing through the first wave caused Vince's head to snap forward once, then all the way back, bouncing off of the head rest and breaking it off, then forward again with the second wave. Vince heard a loud wet crack and a pop somewhere between and just behind his ears. His neck broke with wave impact.

Quite suddenly nothing seemed to matter. The airplane rapidly lost every ounce of forward momentum against the unrelenting water as Vince noticed that he no longer had any feeling in his body. He was completely and utterly numb. For some really stupid reason that he couldn't comprehend at the moment, he felt euphoric. His brain still worked quite well and he was very alert. His vision was clear and everything in focus. His thoughts were lucid. The landing light provided enough illumination for Vince to see his reflection in the front windscreen while the airplane gradually filled up with water and sank.

Securely strapped into the pilot's seat, Vince waited patiently as the water crept increasingly higher in the cabin of the airplane. He watched his reflection in the windscreen and saw the water rising until it covered his mouth, and then slowly sealed his nostrils cutting off all oxygen. His last memory was of a very wet and salty taste in his throat. Vince Vorsino, treetop flyer, beach bum, and party animal, got to watch himself slowly drown five miles from Egmont Key, Florida.

Ten

It was 2 a.m. before Alexander felt sufficiently comfortable
that he would not be seen to tie up to the sheriff's buoy. It was now
too late for last night's fishermen to be about and too early for today's
fishermen to arrive. He left the anchor light on anyway. Preparing all
his dive gear while he was waiting at Egmont Key made him ready
for this dive when he arrived. The less time he spent tied here, the less
chance he took at being noticed. Monitoring his police-issued walkie-
talkie, which included the Special Investigations Nets, had confirmed
that none of his people were working out here tonight. He couldn't be
quite so sure of the Coast Guard or the Florida Wildlife Commission,
so he needed to make this dive quickly and get out of here.

Slipping quietly into the night water, Leslie swam to the buoy
and turned on his dive light. He began his scuba descent into the
blackness that was pierced by one lone ray of light. Night dives
always presented a different set of emotions. You know all the fish are
still out there; you just can't see them. Sharks still move about in the
utter darkness, barracuda still hunt and jelly fish continue to float on
the currents. The stingrays like to move about as well. The darkness

cloaked Leslie in the unknown and unseen. Turning his head to see what he was sure was watching him in the blackness only elevated his fears. The black water held mysteries at night that were not there during the daylight. The only thing that accepted artificial light now was the buoy line leading him straight to the past, which possibly held the key that could destroy everything he had worked so hard for.

Arriving at the engine, he caught the movement of something from under the wing. It had bolted from the newly arrived nighttime intruder, leaving a swirl of sand in its wake that diffused the foreign beam of light. Alexander was trying to calm his fears by believing that what just swam away was more afraid of him than he was of it, probably just a small stingray, or so he rationalized.

The empty blackness had a way of bringing out primal fear, which Alexander pushed aside when he located the wing locker and started to pick away at the barnacles covering the latch. The small flathead screwdriver was just big enough to get the barnacles off without leaving too much noticeable damage. Once the latch was pried open, he had to work the door in small increments, breaking free the barnacles covering the seams and two forward hinges. The door finally opened, releasing a small amount of stale air in one bubble that grew in size as it raced upward.

He opened the door and watched as two quart-sized engine oil cans floated leisurely away — the old style round metal cans were empty and rusty. The compartment contained a few spare parts, a fuel sampler cup to check for water in the fuel tanks, some rags and a small wooden folding step stool. There was no Betamax tape and no PVC tube of money, and Leslie Alexander was left with not much hope. He swam to the buried wing and saw that the engine locker was deep in the sand. He knew better than to get his hopes back up. He could use a couple more tanks of air and dig it out, but he already knew what he wouldn't find in that side as well. The first wing locker was on the same side of the airplane as the cabin door. The other locker was usually empty when it didn't have spare engine parts in it. Leslie could dig until the sun came up and the only thing he would accomplish was to see the sunrise while being very disappointed. This dive was his last hope for an easy conclusion, and that last hope had just drifted away into the night with the oil cans. There was only one place the tape and money could be now, only one logical spot left. If you removed all possibilities, then what remained was usually the answer. The Mexicans from the airstrip years ago didn't have it; it wasn't in the airplane; the dive team didn't have it; it didn't float off on its own; and he certainly didn't have it. That only left one possibility, the diver who found the wreck, and in that one person was the answer to this very annoying situation.

***

Pete and Sam, stunned by what they saw on the videotape, spent their evening aboard the Southern Cross. They talked about the images that had played on the computer screen and the implications they possessed. They broke the recording down to its basic elements. Two of the men were obviously cops. The guy on the couch was not. The guy on the couch took a beating. The camera was well concealed and the cops more than likely didn't know they were being recorded. There was a lot of money involved, and probably drugs. This was bad, very bad, karma for someone. They agreed that, if this tape was part of an official investigation, the tape would be in an evidence room somewhere and not with a dead guy and a load of dope in an airplane on the bottom of the Gulf. There was nothing good on that tape. The pilot had the answers, but he wasn't talking. Sam had wanted a good story to go with his airplane clock, and it looked like he was going to get one.

Pete brought out the bundles of cash and showed Sam the numbers that were written on the piece of paper. Sam looked at all that cash and studied the assortment before him. "Who do you suppose LA is," Sam wondered aloud. "The pilot maybe?"

"I don't know. It could be anybody, but if the cops are dirty, which is a strong possibility at this point, who do we trust?" Pete answered.

"I know a guy with the FBI we can talk to. He flies on the counterterrorist missions with our group occasionally. I'm pretty sure that he can give us the name of someone we can talk to."

Pete had developed a very serious expression now. "We certainly can't trust any local cops until we know more. I know the tape has been down a long time, but that doesn't mean that all the participants have gone away."

"I'm sure the FBI will want to start an investigation. I'll call my office tomorrow and have someone get my contact's number from my card file so I can give him a call," Sam said.

Sam was studying the unknown string of numbers, trying to make some sense of them. He was writing and rewriting them with different spacing, backward, split in half; nothing was making sense so far. They were not phone numbers and didn't appear to be a normal bank account number, not that he could tell, but they were quite obviously important. "It's probably in some kind of doper code," he thought. "The FBI should be able to figure it out," Sam then said out loud. "You really need to keep this stuff well hidden for now."

Pete agreed. "Nobody knows where we are right now, or that we have this, so everything should be fine until we turn it over to the Feds." Pete stashed the money and the tape back over the drawer where it would be secure for the time being.

"So what's on the agenda for tomorrow?" Sam inquired.

Handing Sam a cold bottle of beer, Pete turned on that cheap pirate accent and covered his left eye with his hand again. "Pirate gold me matey. Harrr, pirate gold…"

***

The night had been a pleasant one onboard the Southern Cross as a gentle cool breeze kissed the bow, and once again, the morning was visually stunning. The colors grew into full bloom as the sun crested the shoreline. Fish started feeding and birds got at the daily business of flying while men searched for treasure. Pete and Sam headed out in the dinghy to resume their quest for the lost booty. Sam had gotten the FBI agent's number from his office before they took off. When he called, however, he was advised that the agent was presently unavailable and would get the message as soon as he returned to the office. Sam left his cell phone number.

***

Major Alexander was on his way to his office shortly after noon. He was returning from his dentist appointment and had planned on stopping in at the Support Services Division. This entire

157

department was directly linked to him via the organizational flow chart. Maggie Jones, Missing Persons Investigator, worked indirectly for him. Ms. Jones had a special talent for finding the missing, and a gift of gab to match, a major component to her success. She had the ability to keep someone on the phone until they realized that the only way to get rid of her was to tell her what she wanted to know. She was as polite and pleasant as could be, but she was also as tenacious as a pit bull on a t-bone. Alexander needed her to find someone, and he had no doubt she would be successful. Ms. Jones was at her desk with the telephone imbedded in her ear as usual.

Alexander simply had to look directly at her for Ms. Jones to understand that he was now the most important person in the room. She made her apologies to the person on the other end and hung up. "Good Afternoon, Major. What a nice surprise!" She was always this consistently perky and delightful. "It's always good to see you. You should drop in more often, and next Tuesday we're having a birthday party for..."

Major Alexander held up the palm of his hand, silencing her. "I need someone found. He's not a missing person, just a witness we have to locate. Do you think you could help?"

"Yes, sir. I'll find whoever you're looking for. Yesterday I was able to track down two..."

"Maggie. Maggie," Alexander interrupted. "I have faith in you. All I have is a cell phone number and I need you to tell me where he is so we can interview him."

Maggie explained that, if the cell phone was a newer one with GPS tracking installed and activated, then she would be able to put him within ten feet of it. If however, it was an older phone or the owner had that function disabled, she could only tell him which cell towers it was pinging off of and give a general three block location. The GPS track would require a court order as the phone companies didn't like to give out that information. However, she told Alexander, she was friends with one of the loss prevention specialists at Sprint. He would be able to give her the basic tower information right away, assuming it was available. "Everything's on a computer these days," she announced.

"Okay, find out what you can this afternoon and give me a call at my office," Alexander instructed. He pulled a small note pad from his breast pocket and copied the number down on her desk blotter, then turned and walked out. Maggie just shrugged her shoulders and picked up the phone.

Twenty-two minutes later, Alexander was walking into his office. Among the other pending messages was an inter-office fax with "Maggie Jones/Missing Persons Unit" written across the top. "Damn, that was quick," he thought. Maggie ran her usual checks at her computer terminal, which revealed that Mr. Pete Mitchell had no criminal history. She also had full access to the NCIC (National Crime Information Center) and the FCIC (Florida Crime Information Center) databases. She could get a pretty good read on someone from these two initial sources, and another resource she used was the DAVID system, an acronym for a high-tech government computer program that showed all properties, vehicles, and vessels owned by an individual. The system was also linked to the Homeland Security Database as a cross reference. All of the information was at her fingertips via the keyboard within three minutes — four minutes if the computers were running slow. The amount of immediately accessible information to someone with the right computer connection and password was staggering. If misused, that fact was downright terrifying.

She had faxed over her own investigative history form that she made on the computer to help her keep track of a case's progress. The phone number belonged to a man named Peter James Mitchell, 43 years of age, who had a valid Florida driver's license listing the St. Pete Beach Municipal Marina as his home address. He owned a 38-foot Endeavour sailboat, and he had never had a traffic ticket. But then, he didn't have a car registered. He had the standard credit cards, did not have a State of Florida Marriage Certificate, and owned no taxable property in Florida. No tax liens or court ordered wage garnishments were known to exist, and he possessed a valid passport. He had also received an honorable discharge from the U.S. Army. He was also listed as the sole owner of a private dive and salvage company, "Shallow Water Recovery" of the same address.

She further advised that the phone number in question had been hitting two towers. She could locate the phone precisely as it was GPS enabled, but she said she needed a subpoena. One tower was on Sanibel and the other on Pine Island. She scribbled a note on the bottom: "Please call me if you need more information."

Alexander looked at the wall map of the state of Florida and tapped his finger on a piece of water between the two islands, San Carlos Bay. "A perfect place for a sailboat," he remarked to no one in particular.

That same afternoon found Janet Cantu in her office. She had received a call from Operator 114 at the El Paso Intelligence Center, who explained to her that they had verified the death of Special Agent James Wojcik. The request for verification was emailed on the secure net to FDLE Tallahassee requesting release of the deceased agent's record. The request was officially approved, authorizing Janet as a single point of contact to take over all of Wojcik's investigations with regards to EPIC.

The gentleman on the other end of the phone then explained what his case file contained. On October 2nd 1982, EPIC received an RFI (Request for Information) from Special Agent Wojcik, Florida Department of Law Enforcement, St. Petersburg Florida Regional Office. The request was for any information on an aircraft with the identification number HK778LC, which also included a confidential BOLO stipulation, to "Be on the Lookout" and report any sightings of this aircraft to the investigating authority. The confidentiality had to be justified as EPIC would only acknowledge receipt of incoming intelligence concerning this aircraft to SA Wojcik. The justification block stated "LEO Corruption Investigation."

Janet sat a little straighter in her chair as the thought bounced around her head: law enforcement officer, corruption... Operator 114 went on to explain that the records at the time showed only that the aircraft's registration was Columbian. They were unable to get any further identification information from Columbia as their government was very uncooperative with the United States due to its anti-drug policies. The aircraft was believed to be in Bogotá as reported by a confidential informant to SA Wojcik. HK778LC was never reported in the system again, until a couple of days ago, 25 years later.

Operator 114 continued, telling Janet that Detective Rawlerson, Pinellas County Sheriff's Office, had made the initial RFI through the FAA. The aircraft inquiry had caused the alert to surface in the EPIC system. The message traffic to the FAA indicated that this was a death investigation and advised that the originating case report was from the Coast Guard, Petty Officer Thompson, Salt Creek Marine District Office, St. Petersburg, Florida. He advised that a report had been received giving the location of an old sunken airplane from a private boater, one Mr. Pete Mitchell of St. Pete Beach, Florida.

There was no additional information to pass along. "Do you want to keep this BOLO active?" 114 inquired.

"Let's keep it status quo for now. If I confirm that this is the airplane on the bottom of the ocean, I'll let you know. You can archive it or suspend it at that time," Janet told him.

Operator 114 gave Janet her new security pass-code to access the case file again in the future and politely terminated the call.

Janet made a call to the FDLE records warehouse and inquired as to the status of Wojcik's archived files. The clerk had told her it was being processed and should be sent out tomorrow morning by Federal Express. Janet thanked her and dialed another number.

"Pinellas County Sheriff's Office. If you have an emergency please hang up and dial 911. Otherwise, the next available operator will be with you shortly," mimed the canned computer lady. Janet got to listen to some sheriff's office safety message about the Neighborhood Watch program for a minute or so. "Nonemergency, how may I direct your call?" a human finally answered.

"I would like to speak with Detective Rawlerson please."

The operator told her, "One moment please. I'll have to look that up." She then sent Janet to another safety message, this one about drinking and driving. "Please hold while I transfer you."

"Homicide, Detective Edwards."

"Good, another human," Janet thought. "Hi, I'm Special Agent Cantu, FDLE St. Petersburg. I need to speak with Detective Rawlerson, please."

"He's out on a case right now. If you give me your number, I'll make sure he gets the message as soon as he returns," Edwards told her.

Janet supplied her cell phone and office number, thanked the detective, and hung up. Janet next went two offices down to the analyst's cubicle and talked to Tim Reece, who was responsible for all the basic intel that went through the office. Janet gave him Pete Mitchells' name and told the analyst that he was a boater from St. Pete Beach. She requested any I&I (Intel and Information) on the subject. She also asked him to research the records to see if there were any Law Enforcement Corruption Investigations initiated by this office between 1979 and 1984. Reece said he would get right on it and asked Janet to go to dinner with him again. "Standard answer, Tim — you know the rules." Janet smiled.

"I'll light another candle at church on Sunday. I can always hope!" Tim chuckled.

Janet tracked down the number for the St. Petersburg Coast Guard station at Salt Creek and dialed the phone. She was able to get in touch with Petty Officer Thompson on the first try. He told her that he didn't have any other information about the airplane other then what he received from the D.C. office. He had called Deputy Sheriff

164

Dawson at the PCSO Marine Patrol Division and passed along the report to him. "This must have turned into something important," stated Thompson.

"Why do you say that?" Janet inquired.

"I just got off the phone with a Major at the sheriff's office a little while ago, and he told me to keep any information on this wreck confidential. I'm sure it's OK to talk to you about it, right?"

"Yes, it's okay," Janet told him. "Do you remember the Major's name?"

"No ma'am. I'm sorry but I don't." Janet thanked Thompson for his help. "Odd," she thought to herself.

Janet began to build a case file for this investigation, which would only officially exist once it got an FDLE case number and was entered into the system. The file was listed for now as an historical corruption investigation, and the primary suspect was FNU/LNU, which stood for First Name Unknown/Last Name Unknown. Janet tidied up and locked her desk, as it was time to leave for the day.

She was going to enjoy some family time tonight at dinner with her parents. It had been a couple of weeks since she had taken the time to stop in, which her father had reminded her of twice this week already.

Leslie Alexander hadn't had occasion to use that particular phone number for a while, so he had to dig it out of his old address book. With caller ID and the electronic telephone records-keeping system so available, he decided to call from a pay phone on his way home from the office. "What?" a voice answered on the third ring.

"Carlos, remember me? We need to talk," Leslie said.

"Yeah, I remember. Every time I talk to you, I have to argue for more money. It's been a few years since we have done any business together. Times have changed — it's more expensive now." Carlos tried to sound disinterested.

Leslie encouraged him. "Not this time, *mi amigo*. This job will be very, very good for you. Can you meet me tonight?"

"Okay, after 8 o'clock, but only if the payment will be sufficient this time."

"It will be," Leslie assured him. "Meet me at Veterans Park, by the statue at 9 p.m., and don't keep me waiting," Leslie commanded. He hung up the phone without giving Carlos any time to object or negotiate.

***

"Pete! Pete! Get over here!" Sam was yelling. The first thing Pete thought was that Sam must have stepped on a stingray. That would cause anyone to jump and yell. Pete knew it hurt like hell too. He pitched his metal detector into the dinghy and swam over to Sam 30 yards away. The water here was only four feet deep but swimming was still quicker than wading.

Sam had the metal detector in his right hand and was holding something in his left clenched fist. "Whatcha got, buddy boy?" Pete asked. "Treasure, Pete, treasure!" Sam said as he opened his palm in front of Pete's face. If he would have had any bigger grin, his ears would be touching on the back of his head.

"Well I'll be damned," Pete said. He reached out and took a dull silver coin from Sam's open hand.

***

Alexander was five minutes late for his scheduled meeting. He had stopped at Wal-Mart and purchased a prepaid cell phone with 60 minutes of talk time on the card. The phone was basically disposable and would be discarded after this job, which rendered it untraceable. The phone was paid for in cash and a fictitious name was used for the activation.

Carlos Rivera won the waiting game by being 10 minutes late. He had worked for Alexander before and knew all about the little ways you showed someone who was in control. He had waited some distance away where he could see the statue without revealing his presence when his old acquaintance arrived. When Alexander began pacing back and forth while constantly looking at his watch, Carlos knew the time was right. He knew that, if Alexander needed his services bad enough, he would wait, and he would keep waiting as long as Carlos made him. Carlos Rivera was a go-to man Alexander met many years before. Theirs was a professional relationship secured by cash and limited trust. Carlos had proven his ability to keep his mouth shut, with the proper payment of course, in past times. Carlos knew Alexander was connected with one of the local police departments somehow, but he didn't know which one or exactly how. This was information Leslie kept guarded from Carlos because he didn't want this relationship ever used against him. Leslie had adamantly refused Carlos's request many years ago to help him out of a legal situation with the Tampa Police Department. Leslie would not cross that line to reveal how he was connected with the cops, not to Carlos anyway.

When you needed someone to get something done that you couldn't, or wouldn't, do yourself, you made a call. When you needed someone who possessed the right connections and wrong moral values, that was what Carlos was for.

Before he even began to tell Carlos the job he needed done, Leslie handed him one thousand dollars in fifties. Carlos looked at the money and said, "This thing you need done must not be very important."

"It's important, Carlos, and this is only the beginning. There is much more money if you do this thing for me."

"How much more? My interest is not yet very strong."

"Ten grand, minus the thousand you're holding. You pay your own expenses," Alexander stated.

"Okay, boss. Tell me about the job you need done, and then I'll decide." Carlos folded the cash and shoved it in his front pocket.

"You'll need to go to Cape Coral or Fort Myers, which one doesn't matter. Rent a boat if you need to, or use your own if you have one, but either way, that expense comes out of your payment. You'll need to look for a sailboat in a bay and then search it for me. There are two things you need to bring back. It's that simple. I'll pay you the rest on delivery."

"Nothing is that easy, not with you. What are you looking for that is so valuable?" Carlos was becoming more interested and wanted to know more. "You'll be looking for a very specific video tape that belongs to me. It's an old tape, a Betamax. There should only be one on this boat. There will also be a sealed four or five inch piece of PVC pipe along with the video tape. Wait for the owner to leave or go to sleep, but just get on board and get my property back."

"Okay," Carlos said. "You need to have the rest of the cash when I deliver the items. Give me the details and I'll start to work on getting some of my friends together."

Alexander firmly interjected, "No one else is to know about this, only you. I don't want anyone else involved, no exceptions. Is that clear?"

"Do you have any other little details you're leaving out? You seem a little more agitated than usual, and I am really not in any mood to get my brains blown out, *amigo*."

"Your ten grand is the payment if you deliver within 48 hours. Each day you fail to deliver, the price goes down two thousand. After you're down to a thousand and haven't delivered my items, you can do it for free if you like. If you can't get the job done, let me know now and I'll hire someone else. Further, you must let me know when you're going to the boat to get my property. I'll have the money waiting for you when you get back to shore."

Carlos had a few questions of his own. "What about the owner of the boat? What if he should get hurt?"

"Not my problem what happens to anyone on the boat. There should only be one guy there, and he's your problem."

"What if I find other interesting things on the boat: jewelry, radios, stuff like that? Can I have them?"

"Fine by me. Make it look like a burglary or a fire or whatever you want. I don't care. Take whatever you want — just don't let it slow you down. Time is important for me. You will be paid well, if you do well," Alexander said.

Carlos nodded. "I'll have your property in 48 hours, but there will be a five thousand dollar bonus. I must cover the cost of inflation, and secrecy is certainly worth a bonus." Carlos made it clear that this part was non-negotiable.

Alexander nodded in agreement. "Okay, where exactly is this boat I need to go to?"

Eleven

Sam woke Pete an hour before sunrise with the smell of percolating coffee. While Pete was getting dressed, he could hear Sam go up the companionway ladder to the cockpit. Several minutes later, Pete joined him in the cockpit for the daily sunrise show. "Up a little early today," Pete said.

This time it was Sam's turn to hold his hand over his eye. "Harr, me matey. 'Tis pirate treasure be here, ye scurvy sea dog."

The previous evening, Sam had insisted on standing in the exact spot he found the coin until Pete could return with the portable GPS. Pete then marked the spot with the coordinates and saved it to the internal memory. They made it back to the Southern Cross as the sun was setting, and they ate their evening meal while researching the coin that was recovered from the silt. Pete had plenty of reference books on hand, and they leafed through them until a possible match was made. This particular coin appeared to be a silver Spanish cob.

Due to the discovery of new silver deposits in the colonial territories, Spain had demanded that the silver get exported as quickly as possible. To do this, Philip II had the mints produce irregular coinage called cobs around 1570. The silver bar was simply cut into chunks of silver of the appropriate weight. The chunks were then hammer-stamped between crude dies. The procedure was quick and easy while verifying the weight of the silver for documentation and transportation back to Spain. If the weight was a little high, the minter would simply clip off a piece, correcting the weight.

The cobs were portable and could be sent to Spain en masse, and when the crude coins arrived in Spain, they were melted down to produce fine jewelry, finished coins, and other negotiable items. The obverse of a cob shows the crowned Hapsburg shield with the mintmark and assayer initial on the left side. The denomination to the right of the shield indicated the weight. The legend in one variation or another had the name of the king and the word *DEI GRATIA*, By the Grace of God, stamped within. The reverse displayed the arms of Castile and Leon within a quatrefoil design. The arms are similar to those on the Charles and Johanna pre-cob silver coins. The two intersecting lines divided the shield into quadrants. They subsequently represent the very recognizable cross in the center of the shield with the castle and lion images in the corners. The legend appearing on some, *REX HISPANIARUM ET INDAIRUM*, which meant Of the Spain and Indies, was also prevalent on some coins. It was not until the seventeenth century that the cobs were dated on the obverse side. Due to the hammer-stamping process, the date was not always visible, if it appeared at all. Dating and locating the mint for the cob can be particularly difficult due to the crude methods used and the stamp being worn or illegible.

The particular cob that Sam had found was likely struck in Peru in the late 1600s. The obverse was similar to the earlier cob reverse, which consisted of a cross that incorporated the heraldic

173

symbols of Leon and Castile. The reverse was based on the design used for the pre-cob coins by depicting the Straits of Gibraltar with the Pillars of Hercules. The two vertical pillars intersected three horizontal lines of text, which gave the appearance of the tic-tac-toe design most people are familiar with. The top line was stamped L 2 N, which meant that it was struck in Lima, the value was 2 reals, and the assayer was N. The middle line contained the letters PVA, which stood for *PLVS VLTRA*, More Beyond. The final line gave the assayer's initial along with the last two numerals of the date and the mintmark. That line was unreadable on this coin. They would have to research the king's mark to try to narrow it down further.

Sam was busy inspecting the coin again as the sun crested the horizon, bringing about a new day of treasure hunting. They would go back to the same spot and begin a regular search pattern. Pete had designed a grid pattern on paper, showing the dinghy in the middle. He would use a couple of pelican markers to separate the two largest areas. The tackle box provided several fishing bobbers that would be weighted with sinkers on about 7 feet of fishing line to complete the grid. They would work their respective areas and try to map out which location might hold more coins. Where there is one, they reasoned, there are probably more. That theory would be put to the test today.

***

Janet Cantu arrived at her office a few minutes late. The traffic across the bay bridges was only getting worse month by month. So many people were moving into Florida that construction companies couldn't keep up with the demand. Highway 19 was once a pleasant drive with some of Florida's natural beauty still intact, but it was now an endless string of billboards and strip malls. Anything and everything you could want was here, but there was also unbelievable traffic and all the other stressors that went with fast growth.

She had just sat down at her desk with the usual morning cup of coffee when Tim Reece came in with several sheets of paper. He had completed her request early the previous evening. Tim sat in one of the two office chairs in front of her desk. They exchanged the standard morning greetings, and then Tim began to relate his findings.

He had located three possible law enforcement corruption cases during the timeframe in question. In 1980, a street cop was taking bribes for fixing traffic tickets; and in 1981, a Pinellas County Corrections Officer was smuggling small amounts of marijuana and cocaine into the women's correctional facility, not only taking cash payments from the ladies but allegedly accepting sexual favors as well. The last one was another drug case. A jilted girlfriend turned in her deputy sheriff boyfriend after she caught him cheating on her with a female deputy. The girlfriend had alleged that he was removing captured narcotics from the evidence room and selling it. The deputy had failed two drug tests and the polygraph, but the sheriff decided not to prosecute because it was an election year and the negative publicity would have been catastrophic for his campaign. The deputy's employment had been terminated very quietly and his Police Officer Standards Certificate revoked.

Tim had been unable to find anything that would have involved FDLE or Special Agent Wojcik with a major case. The previous cases were handled by their respective Internal Affairs Divisions, and FDLE was only notified if they pulled the officer's accreditation to ensure they would never work in law enforcement in Florida again. There was nothing official in the timeframe that Janet specified that could be linked to the aircraft investigation or to Wojcik's case file.

Tim then supplied Janet with all the printouts concerning the fellow that found the aircraft in the first place, Mr. Pete Mitchell. This information included the only phone number listed, a local cell phone. Janet thanked him for his efforts and picked up the phone as Tim walked out.

After six rings, the standardized electronic message greeting lady spoke up: "If you would like to leave a message...beep."

"Mr. Mitchell, this is Special Agent Janet Cantu with the Florida Department of Law Enforcement, St. Petersburg Office. I would like to speak with you concerning a local investigation. Please call me at..."

Janet needed to talk to the deputies involved with the airplane, and so she called the Sheriff's Office Marine Patrol Division. Deputy Collins answered the phone, and Janet identified herself and requested to speak with one of the deputies who investigated the sunken airplane. "We're all here for another half hour or so this morning, ma'am. We're heading back out to the plane and should be back by three if you want to stop by after that," Collins told her.

Janet gave it a quick thought. "Mind if I go with you? We can talk on the way."

"No problem. Can you be here in less than thirty minutes?"

"On my way," she said.

Just over twenty minutes later, Janet arrived at the Marine Patrol Division office as the patrol boat was warming up. Sergeant Miller met her in the parking lot and introduced himself. Janet briefly explained that she had gotten a request for assistance from the FAA to follow up on the downed aircraft. She told him she would file the official report with the FAA, which in turn would dictate which way they would go with the case. Janet had made it all up as she went along. She couldn't reveal the true nature of her investigation once the corrupt cop label got attached. Sergeant Miller told her to grab a cup of coffee from the office if she wanted one and to meet them on the boat.

During the ride to the scene, Janet spoke with each of the divers that had been to the airplane. All of them related basically the same story like they were under oath on the witness stand. "Does anybody have a guess as to why this plane crashed?" Janet asked everyone. She received a bunch of headshakes indicating a negative. "So what are you looking for today?" She directed the last question at Miller.

"We're not looking for anything. Major Alexander told us to recover the buoy, so I guess our part of this investigation is closed."

"Then I don't understand why your men are getting ready to dive?" Janet nodded her head at Collins and Phillips who were suiting up.

Miller responded, "The Major told us to just unhook the buoy and drop the rope. He said it's not worth the dive, but I know our supply department. It'll be six weeks before they cut a purchase order for another buoy line." Miller added, "Besides, it will only take a few minutes to go down and get it."

When they arrived at the buoy, Collins and Phillips slipped over the stern as soon as the engine was silenced and swam to the buoy. They disappeared into a flurry of bubbles as they made their descent down the line.

The divers surfaced about eight minutes later without unhooking the chain from the propeller. "You girls need a wrench? Ah, no offense intended ma'am," Miller said.

Collins spoke up. "We found a compartment behind the engine that we didn't know about before."

178

"Did you open it?"

"Didn't have to, Sarge. It was already opened. Nothing worth a damn is in there now, but someone went to the trouble to scrape the barnacles from the seams and hinges to get it open."

Miller thought about it a moment and asked Janet, "You need us to photograph it or anything?"

"If you have the camera, a couple of pictures wouldn't hurt, and take anything that might look like evidence.

Was anything else taken or disturbed since yesterday?"Janet inquired."No, nothing from inside the cockpit," Collins said. "Just the wing compartment."

"Is there the same kind of compartment on the other wing?" Janet inquired.

Collins answered up, "Don't know. Probably, but it's buried under too much sand. We could dig it up but it would take a day or two."

"No, let's not start digging yet," Janet told them. "We can always come back if we need to." Since the unknown intruder didn't go through the effort to dig it open, whatever the diver was after had probably been discovered in the wing locker and removed.

"Okay boys, you heard the lady. Back down you go. When you're done, bring the chain back up this time."

Stephens handed Phillips the camera and they disappeared below once again.

***

Detective Rawlerson was at the Medical Examiner's office with Dr. Mujahed getting the preliminary report on the cause of death for the pilot.

"You didn't have to come down here for the report. I was going to send it to you via internal mail this afternoon."

"Thanks Doc, but the Major is on my ass to close this case. He said it's just an old drug smuggler who got what he deserved and to close this one and move on."

"Well, the preliminary findings indicate that your pilot broke his neck. You can copy the fancy medical lingo from the report," the doctor said, handing the report to Rawlerson.

"How could he break his neck? It didn't look like he hit another airplane or a boat or nothing." The Doc's handwriting was a little tough to read.

"Remember that guy, the race car driver? A quick high speed impact with little damage can be enough to cause your head to snap forward and then immediately back again. It's enough to cause sufficient nerve and tissue damage to be fatal, especially in a sinking airplane. There are still more tests to run, but I'm only working with a skeleton here and so a little guess work is needed to fill in the blanks."

"Okay, Doc. We'll probably just write the guy off as a dope smuggler who crashed into the Gulf for unknown reasons, cause of death a probable broken neck on impact. I'll NFL, no further leads, this one and just close it out. If you come up with anything different, give me a call."

"Have you been able to identify the pilot yet," the Doc asked.

"No, nothing so far. The numbers and papers are a dead end. Smugglers don't usually carry valid ID with them. Just keep him listed as John Doe for now."

Rawlerson still had to interview the guy who found the plane in the first place. He used his PCSO-issued cell phone to call Mr. Mitchell and received the standard electronic message service. He hung up without leaving a message and would try again later.

***

During the boat ride back to the dock, Janet had a seat opposite Sergeant Miller, who was driving. She sat quietly and listened to the conversations going back and forth between the deputies. Sometimes you got more information by not asking questions. It was a method that lots of cops never mastered, the art of listening. It was clear that they didn't know about the wing compartment during the previous dives. Someone else knew about it though. The compartment had been opened and searched last night or early this morning. The prevailing theory was that some local divers had simply wanted to see what the sheriff had marked with the buoy and stumbled on the compartment.

Several things started to eat at Janet as she thought about this turn of events. Why had the unknown divers not taken anything from inside the plane, something from the cockpit for a souvenir? Who would risk tying to the sheriff's buoy in the first place? Who else knew the plane was here? If the sheriff's divers didn't see the compartment, how could the mystery diver, especially at night? There was also a timing issue. The whereabouts of this wreck had only been known for several days, and none of the local media outlets had reported it yet. If not the cops, then did the guy who found the wreck in the first place come back for a second look? Next on her list was to talk to Rawlerson and then to find Mr. Mitchell.

***

Rawlerson had made it back to his office and was working on the death investigation report, adding the ME's findings, when Janet called. They exchanged the basic pleasantries, and Janet gave him the same FAA investigation story she had given to Collins. Rawlerson told her the steps in his investigation to date and the lack of leads he was coming up with. He suggested that he might NFL this case as he was hitting nothing but a series of old dead ends.

When the conversation ended, Rawlerson included in his supplement report that Special Agent Cantu, St. Petersburg FDLE Office, was conducting a separate investigation at the request of the FAA.

Janet then called Tim Reece at his office and asked him to track down Mr. Mitchell. She told him to use her name on the blank State Attorney's Office Investigative Subpoena form if he required one, but she needed to find him. Tim said he would get to work on it right away, and he told her, "You have a box. It came from Records in Tallahassee via FedEx."Janet had missed lunch and was starving, and so she grabbed something to eat at a drive-through. When she got back to the office, she closed her door and looked for something to open the FedEx box with.

***

Major Alexander had recently arrived at the training division, and he was preparing to give an afternoon pep talk to the class of new recruits when his *other* cell phone rang. The recruits were here completing firearms training, one of the final courses of instruction prior to graduation. Alexander pressed the talk button and simply said, "Wait." He walked outside where he had some privacy and said to the only caller with this number, "Talk."

"Yeah, real nice to talk to you too," Carlos said with a slightly sarcastic tone. "I've got a boat and I'm going out this afternoon to find your friend."

"Where are you putting in at?"

"There's a boat ramp on the Fort Myers side of College Parkway. It's the exit right before the toll booth, north side of the highway. It's a small public boat ramp — you'll see my truck."

"What time will you get there?" Alexander was looking at his watch.

"I'll be there in a half hour." Carlos had a slight grin on his face. He knew it would drive Alexander nuts that he did not call earlier.

"Don't piss me off, especially if you want full payment."

"Don't worry. I won't be back at the ramp before ten tonight. You have plenty of time to get there with my bonus." Carlos hung up before he got a response. His grin broadened, knowing he had just caused about a ten point rise in Alexander's blood pressure.

***

This afternoon's dive had gone extremely well. Pete was getting waterlogged, and there seemed to be no stopping Sam, who had the fever. Sam started to get multiple hits in an area of the grid north of the dinghy and toward the shore. Both men started to work the area with the metal detectors once the additional bobbers had been set up. This particular grid area had been further sectioned off, giving each man a smaller work area to allow for more concentration and slower scanning. When you were working an area, you needed to make two sweeps over the same spot before advancing one foot forward. When working this slowly, it became easier to work standing up in the water. They had abandoned their fins in the dinghy, opting for the added stability of standing. The current had less effect that way, and you wouldn't keep drifting off your work area, but the downside was that you really muddied up the water. Their feet shuffling across the bottom and kicking up the silt kept the visibility at exactly zero, and so they couldn't look at the bottom any longer to see what they were grabbing at.

The most productive spot yielded what appeared to be small rusty spikes about an inch and a half long, tapered on one end and a beveled head on the other. They appeared to be an early type of nail that was often used on ships and homes in the 16th and 17th century. The nails were a possible indication that there was some form of manmade construction at this site a long time ago. The local Indian tribes had used nails as well, sometimes trading with the Spanish. The nails were not grouped together, which would have indicated that they were contained in a single lost box, but scattered about like they came from something that was constructed using them but was no longer in one piece.

"You know, Sam, if there was a building here at one time, that would help support my shifting sand theory."

Sam reminded him, "Yeah, but you know a hurricane could shove a building out here — the tidal surge is enough to move a house."

"I don't know exactly what structure was here before, but I know there is another coin!"

Sam held up a coin remarkably similar to the one he found the day before. He swished it back and forth in the water to get the muck off of it. The coin appeared to be another cob. He would have to get it back on the boat and start comparing it to Pete's books to find out more about it. Pete found the next two coins, and Sam found one more. Finding the additional coins after spending the entire day in the water made every hour worth it. The afternoon shadows were growing long and evening was approaching, when they decided to call it quits for the afternoon. They left the bobbers in place. They would begin fresh after breakfast. Back on the Southern Cross, the coins were rinsed and scrubbed clean. One coin was a two real piece and the other three were half real pieces. Two of the coins had large cracks and were disfigured, and two of the coins each had a clipped edge.

186

Pete explained that a planchet was the blank used to make the coin. The coin would naturally split along the edge when it was originally struck and many of the cobs were cracked. The minter clipped off pieces of silver to bring the cob down to its proper weight, and underweight coins were clipped down to the next lower denomination. Sam was having a great time. "When do we find the gold coins, the doubloons?"

Pete explained that there was generally a ratio of forty cobs to one gold coin. The gold coins of the seventeenth century were full-sized finished coins called royal or presentation strikes, and they were highly valued. The cob was a mass-produced coin for transportation only, which made them easier to find. Interestingly enough, a lot of the clipped and lightweight Spanish cobs made their way to Boston and were turned into the Massachusetts silver coinage used early in America's history. Pete told Sam that, if they were lucky, very lucky, there was a gold coin or two in their future.

Pete ran the Yanmar diesel engine for half an hour to fully charge the bank of house batteries and to bring the water heater up to temperature. Sam had proposed that they take the dinghy back to Pine Island for a steak dinner. After all, a bit of celebration was in order. They would get to shore while there was enough ambient light available to find the road again. They had both noticed a family type restaurant that advertised steaks when they were at the photography studio with the Betamax tape.

Pete turned on the Southern Cross's anchor light according to the Code of Federal Regulation rule. The white anchor light was 54 feet high on the top of the mast and was visible for 360 degrees. The guys then headed out in the dinghy for a nice dinner ashore.

***

Carlos leaned a fishing rod against the side of the Hewes flats fishing boat, which was 18 feet long and powered by a Yamaha 150 HP outboard engine. The boat and motor were ten years old and it was obvious the rig had led a hard life of fishing the flats. Everything still worked, which served Carlos well this evening. He had rented the boat from an acquaintance for $150.00 cash for the evening. All of his acquaintances operated with the same business ethics as Carlos: anything, anytime, anywhere, just as long as the price was right, and more importantly, there were never any questions asked. This was his boat for the next twenty-four hours.

Carlos Rivera had launched the boat and followed the marked channel to the south side of Pine Island. He had been told that the sailboat should be between Pine Island and Sanibel somewhere in the bay. Alexander had provided Carlos with the name of the boat he got from the Coast Guard guy that reported the original incident. It wasn't difficult to find the only sailboat there. Binoculars confirmed the identity of his evening's prey. Further to the north were two other boats, but they were cabin cruisers and he ignored them. When the wind was just right, he could hear the fluctuating tunes of rock and roll emanating from one of the other boats. Carlos had taken up a station with the fishing pole and binoculars far enough away to be dismissed as some guy fishing after work. He wouldn't attract so much as a second glance.

Shortly before dark, he watched as two guys got into a small rubber boat and motored toward the land marked on the map as Pine Island. Alexander had said there should be only one, but Carlos didn't care, as long as they were gone and these two didn't look like they would be back soon. The sun was setting and Carlos left his navigation lights off. He didn't want anyone seeing him idling over to the sailboat as darkness set in.

Twelve

The small restaurant had that charming relaxed atmosphere you immediately noticed the moment you walked in. It was obviously a family business, as most of the folks seemed to know each other. The steak was pretty darn good, too. The dinner conversation was centered on the coins and future plans for the search. Pete had picked up a stray cob here and there during his amateur treasure hunting career, but he had never seen five come from the same area like this. He had only read about such finds. His time may have finally come, and he couldn't think of anyone better to share it with than Sam.

The conversation drifted away from the dreams of pirate booty for a short time, and Sam gave Pete a reality check when he asked when he was going to call the two cops back. Pete had received a message from some lady at the Florida Department of Law Enforcement who left her name and number. He also saw a Pinellas County Sheriff's Office phone number on the caller ID panel, twice, but there was no message.

"It's a sure thing that all of the cops know I reported the airplane and got my cell number," Pete said. "Maybe you should try to give your FBI friend a call again tomorrow. I don't know how long I can ignore the local cops without pissing them off." Pete added, "I just don't know who to trust right now."

Sam agreed. "If I don't hear from the FBI guy I left a message with in the morning, I'll make a couple more calls. I'll see if we can get a contact number for a local FBI agent. We need to turn the tape and cash over and get this into official channels."

"Yeah, that would probably a good idea, and the sooner the better," Pete said. "Just so their investigation doesn't interfere with our search." Pete raised his glass in a mock toast. "We still have a couple of other areas I want to look at. Besides, we haven't done any open water sailing yet, and you're going to forget how if we don't do some this trip."

Plans were formulated to continue the search in the morning by starting in the same area and branching outward toward the shore, a strategy that seemed to be producing the best results so far. The men had hopes that this was not some passing scrap of luck, but would lead to one of the main caches of cobs stolen centuries ago by any number of pirates who frequented this area.

Dinghies don't have night navigation lights as a rule. They are too small and impossible to wire up. Pete kept a small flashlight in his tote bag, however, which would be sufficient to shine at another boat if one approached in the dark. Tonight's return trip to the sailboat shouldn't be a problem because there didn't appear to be anyone moving on the water except them, unless of course there was another dinghy without lights out here too. In that case, two rubber inflated boats bouncing off each other shouldn't create too much havoc on the bay waters.

Pete was in the process of convincing Sam that tonight would be a good time to get a few blue crabs. They would stay out long enough to put fifteen or so in the cooler for lunch tomorrow. That would make for a great noontime break as they got out of the hot sun for a while. Sunscreen and t-shirts had kept them from getting burnt, but it still heated up after noon. They needed to return to the Southern Cross for the portable spotlight and a cooler first, then on to the crabs.

Pete slowed the dinghy to an idle and suddenly grew very serious. Sam saw the expression change on Pete's face as he was looking in the general direction of the Southern Cross.

"What's the matter, Pete?" Sam asked.

"Look at the anchor light on the mast." Pete nodded in that direction. "Does it look like it's moving to you?"

"Yeah, a little," Sam replied. "It's a boat, and boats move around in the waves."

"There are no waves, and just a little breeze, not enough to rock the boat. I don't see any passing boats creating a wake either." Pete had a slightly concerned tone in his voice.

The white anchor light on top of the mast magnified any hull movement tenfold. With a little rocking back and forth, the top of the mast would sway proportionately to the height of the light above the deck. When you were in a crowded anchorage, you could tell when a power boat had passed the anchorage by the boats' movement. The outer mast lights would start to sway back and forth while the ones closer remained still until arrival of the wave. The boat lights moved systematically like the people in a baseball stadium when they did the wave, for which it was appropriately named. There was no reason for his light to be swinging this evening.

There was not enough ambient light to see the Southern Cross, with the exception of the mast light from this distance. Pete's small motor was quiet enough to get relatively close to his sailboat before he cut the engine, and the forward momentum of the dinghy helped carry it a little further but the paddles would still be needed to complete the journey in silence. As they closed the distance, both men could clearly see that the mast light was rocking back and forth for no reason other than the only logical explanation — they had been boarded.

The full moon was coming up and beginning to provide some ambient light, not a tremendous amount but enough to start seeing things clearly. When they were about 15 yards from the Southern Cross, they could see the engine and small platform on the stern of the flats fishing boat concealed around the port side of the Southern Cross. This type of boat has a flat fiberglass platform supported over the top of the outboard engine by four stainless steel corner stanchions where someone would stand while using a long fiberglass pole to push the boat along the shallow water. The added height was sufficient to give the fishermen an advantage in spotting game fish. The trespassers had tied to the port side amidships cleat. Whoever was on the boat had used the platform to step over the lifelines and onto the sailboat.

Pete silently eased up to the stern of his sailboat with the oars. Sam held the side of the ladder, which was already extended into the water. Pete could see that the trespasser had tied his boat to the middle port side because it faced the uninhabited nature preserve. No passing or approaching boats would see it on that side as it was hidden from view by the sailboat. Sam gave a cautious look around the hull to the power boat to ensure nobody was sitting in it. The boat appeared to be empty.

With rehearsed precision, Pete stepped up onto the ladder and then onto the main deck without making a sound. Sam quietly tied the dink to the ladder. Pete had crouched low and remained completely still while looking and listening, just as his ranger training

194

had taught him. Sam silently slipped up next to Pete. The training never went away. It was practiced to the point that things started to happen automatically once engaged in an operation. Pete took the lead by giving Sam silent hand signals. Sam was to go up the port side halfway and stop. Pete would go up the starboard. He pointed two fingers at his eyes and then one finger down in the companionway hatch through the cockpit, which meant they would take a look see at who was below. The one minute sign was given and then they would return to this spot. Sam completely understood that this was just a quiet sneak and peek. They needed to know how many intruders there were, and they needed to see if they had any visible weapons. Once they knew who, and what firepower, they were up against, the decision would then be made as to how to handle the intruders.

A face to face confrontation would work well on a couple of petty thieves. The surprise factor by two big guys suddenly arriving in the main salon would be enough to get the edge and control the situation, but if they were facing a couple of well armed thugs, that would certainly change things. One plan would be to slip into the dinghy and move over to the fishing boat. They could then sever the fuel line from the engine on the flats boat and wait nearby in the darkness. The carburetors would have enough fuel to get the bad guys cleanly away from the Southern Cross but not to shore. Pete and Sam would then get back on board and at the radio, and the intruders would be in Coast Guard custody in short order. It was the beginning of a plan, Pete thought.

Sam headed up the port side as Pete went up the starboard. Neither one could hear any talking, just things being moved about down below. Pete and Sam progressed halfway along the 38-foot boat evenly so as to not alert the intruders by rocking the boat themselves.

Carlos was busy checking the cabinets situated over the settee on the port side of the main salon. He had already been through the drawers, under the mattress, and in all the little cubby holes he could find in the master stateroom. There was a bathroom back there too. "Pretty nice setup," Carlos thought to himself, very comfortable. As he worked his way up the starboard side passageway next to the engine room, he checked the storage spaces under the bench. What he found clearly caught his full and undivided attention.

The 4-inch end cap of a PVC pipe had been cut off of a larger pipe, and the glued end of the original pipe was still attached to the inside of the cap. Digging a bit further, he found the rest of the PVC pipe, about 30 inches long with the other end still capped off. "Well then, whatever was in the pipe is probably around here somewhere. I'll bet when I find the Betamax I find what was in the pipe," Carlos thought.

He continued the search with renewed vigor. It would have helped if Alexander had told him what was in the pipe, but obviously he didn't think it would have been opened. Carlos had visions of large sums of cash or dope, which could be the only reason he wasn't told what was in the pipe, because it would be something he wanted to keep. It was certainly worth a lot more than what his bonus was supposed to be, he reasoned. Well that, as with all things, was subject to change.

Carlos was checking behind the books in a recessed case above the settee when the moon disappeared from view through the porthole. As it had come up low on the horizon, he thought it would make the perfect amount of light to slip away in after he completed his task. Now the moon had been replaced by an ankle. This was not good. Carlos had not been aboard very long, at least he had not thought so. He was sure he would have heard the dinghy approaching. He intended to slip over the side, get into his rented boat, and then disappear into darkness prior to the two men returning. The Hewes could easily outdistance the little dinghy. "Too late to worry about that now," he thought.

Carlos reached around behind him to the small of his back without taking his eyes off of the ankle. Tucked neatly into the back of his shorts was a .9mm semi-auto Walther pistol with seven rounds — six in the magazine and one in the chamber. The gun was traded one night a long time ago in a small drug transaction, so it was probably stolen, not that it really mattered. When the time came to use it, he could ditch it easily and it wouldn't be tied to him in any way. He saw all the CSI TV shows and knew he had to wipe it clean before tossing it into the bay.

It's amazing how fast the human brain processes information. In less than two seconds, Carlos went from being startled by the ankle in the porthole to making a life altering decision. The portholes were 24 inches wide and 11 inches tall, and there were eight of them in the main salon, four on each side. They were near the overhead if you were standing in the salon and just above the deck at your feet if you were outside. If you lifted the Plexiglas window inward, a screen covering the opening to the outside was revealed. With no threat of rain, Pete had left all the ports open so he and Sam could really enjoy the nice evening breeze. It made for great sleeping weather.

The ankle in the porthole had not moved. Carlos had rationalized in the two seconds that had just passed that he didn't know if one, or both, of the men had returned to the boat — he assumed both. He had not heard any talking, and there was absolutely no movement for the past few seconds. He firmly believed that he was outnumbered. He didn't know if anyone other than himself had a gun, and so it was best to act as if they did. He told himself, however, that Alexander said earlier that he didn't care what happened to the occupants of the boat. Carlos was now trapped below with no discernable path of escape, which narrowed his options considerably. It was a busy few seconds in Carlos's head.

The little firearm was raised to within inches of the porthole and pointed slightly above the ankle. Such close range eliminated the need to look down the sights to aim the weapon. Carlos decided that he had to take the advantage and take it quickly. His index finger wrapped around the trigger and began to give the trigger the five and a half pounds of pull needed to activate the firing pin. A split second before the silence of the night was horribly interrupted, Carlos heard someone shout, "GUN!" The voice was obviously behind him and up on deck. His brain processed this as a confirmation of the second person returning to the boat as well.

A small flame spat from the end of the barrel, melting the nylon screen. With very little distance to travel, the bullet, along with splatters of expended gunpowder, struck Sam three inches above the ankle, hitting the center of his leg bone. Sam felt his bone shatter as the added weight of his body helped collapse the remaining bone that was still in place. What remained was wholly insufficient to support his weight as his muscles released all tension in a reflexive action to save his leg from further damage.

Sam crumpled to the deck in front of the portholes.

Pete began to move aft from this position, and as he did he could see the shooter's backside in the main salon. Pete had never felt more inadequate in his life. His best friend had just been shot and the shooter was lining up for another one. "Roll, Sam, roll!" Pete yelled.

Sam was flat on the deck. His military training had taught him to seek cover, to get low and stay low, but his face was directly in front of a porthole, and what he saw was very disturbing. The shooter had sidestepped and a gun was coming up to within inches of this opening. In a matter of milliseconds, he was going to be looking directly into the barrel of the gun that had already done so much damage. Sam heard Pete's shouts and rolled away from the porthole. He felt the bottom strand of the lifeline try to contain him on the deck where he would get himself killed. Sam sucked in his breath and pushed between two of the portholes with his good leg, forcing himself under the lifeline and away from the gunman. The second bullet missed his head by only fractions of an inch. It clipped the lifeline stanchion and changed direction, causing it to tumble harmlessly off into to the night.

Pete had been working his way around the stern to grab Sam when the second shot rang out. His only plan to this point was to grab Sam and get over the side. The darkness would provide them with the path they needed for an escape. When Pete had made it halfway around the stern, Sam disappeared over the port side. Pete heard a very loud and uncomfortable thud along with the sound of breaking glass. "Sam must have landed in the fishing boat," was Pete's first thought. "No splash."

Pete had to come up with a plan and come up with one quick. He immediately thought about getting to the fishing boat and making his escape but rejected that plan as too time consuming. He could not get to the fishing boat, untie it, get the unfamiliar boat started, and make good his escape before the gunman made it up on deck.

He was looking at the aft stateroom deck hatch, which was three quarters of the way open, providing a nice evening breeze down below like the portholes. The hatch was 30 inches by 30 inches and supported by an aluminum position rod. The hatch itself was 5/8ths of an inch thick and made of smoked Plexiglas within an aluminum frame. He could hear the gunman taking a new position in the main salon as he knocked the small portable TV off the shelf next to the V-berth hatch. "He must have been all the way forward," Pete reasoned.

The hatch came all the way open after Pete unscrewed the retaining knob that held it in place. A screen was on a light wooden hinged frame on the inside, but that easily, and very quietly, pushed out of the way. Pete silently dropped feet first onto the main salon mattress. The room was dark, for which he was appreciative. He knew every inch of his boat and didn't require a light. As he was lying on the bed, he reached toward the aft bulkhead. The natural curve of the aft bulkhead separated it from the flat edge of the bed and formed a shelf. No space on a sailboat was wasted, and on this shelf were various sailing books, novels, and instruction manuals. Mounted over the books was a spear gun on hooks. The spear gun was just less than five feet long when loaded. It had two very powerful rubber surgical-type tubes attached to the front below the spear. This particular model had 15 feet of line attached to a slide spring on the shaft of the spear, and the other end was attached to the front of the weapon. When fired into a fish, this lead would keep the wounded prey from swimming off. Pete quietly unclipped the line from the slide on the shaft. The bands were slack, which meant the weapon was not ready to fire, not yet anyway.

Pete silently slid off the edge of the bed and was standing on the deck that led through the companionway to the main salon. He braced the butt of the weapon against his right hip and grabbed the tension bands, pulling them hard to the rear one at a time. The bands' stainless steel end clips were set into the shaft's indentation, putting a great amount of forward tension on the spear. Pete had to be careful with the weapon as it was good for one shot only. Once fired, the gun would simply become just another stick with big rubber bands on it.

Crouching low, Pete peered around the corner and down the companionway. The navigation station had a clear Plexiglas plate covering the circuit breaker panel that enclosed various switches. The reflection in the glass showed an out-of-focus image of a man with his back against the closed V-berth door. He was standing in a semi-crouched position with both hands on a dark handgun thrust out ahead of him, and he was looking up through the main hatch, which was identical to the one in the aft stateroom with the exception that this one opened with the hatch facing forward. The one in the main stateroom opened aft. This allowed the front hatches to act like wind scoops and the aft one as an exhaust port, a very efficient ventilation system. The intruder was peeking cautiously up at the hatch and through the portholes.

Carlos knew there was a second man up there somewhere, but exactly where was his problem right now. He was fairly certain that, due to the lack of return gunfire, the boat's owners were not armed. Carlos began to move cautiously toward the ladder leading up to the cockpit.

As he neared the ladder he started edging up one step at a time. Carlos would peek quickly, looking like a frightened gopher. He would poke his head up, take a quick scared look, and pull his head back down onto his shoulders. Carlos repeated the process for five steps until his shoulders were above the main deck. He could not see anyone standing anywhere on deck. He got braver and finally stepped all the way into the center cockpit.

Pete saw the stranger begin to work his way up the ladder very cautiously. There was absolutely no reason at this point to believe there were two intruders. Pete could lean over far enough to clearly see the intruder's torso and legs through the openings between the steps of the companionway ladder. He was easing the spear gun tip into a good firing position but recognized this as useless early on. The ladder provided the shooter with some great cover. Pete's .45 with a full magazine would have done the trick nicely at this range, if he had it. One or two hits to the torso or legs and the man would be on the deck of the main salon. It would then be his choice as to how this ended from that point, but it was not to be. He had to make his one shot count. The gunman finally disappeared upward into the cockpit.

Carlos had assumed a crouching position, trying not to make himself stand out until he could locate the other guy who had come on board. Swinging around with his gun always pointing the direction he was looking, Carlos completed a full circle and saw no one. He didn't see the one he shot on deck either. Carlos was facing forward and stepped out from under the bimini top that covered the cockpit, and then he stepped to the port side deck, where he found blood.

Pete kneeled on the bed and very quickly and cautiously stuck just enough of his head through the hatch to locate the bad guy. The smoked Plexiglas concealed his movement. The bad guy was now stepping out onto the port side deck where the fishing boat was tied.

Carlos gave another 360 degree glance around the boat and still didn't see anything. He leaned over the side and saw the man he shot lying crumpled in a heap in the fishing boat. The other guy must be over the side hiding along the sailboat in the water. He would have to slowly walk around the boat watching for any waves or bubbles, any telltale sign emanating from his next victim. He might be back in the little rubber boat as well, which was probably tied up at the back of the sailboat. A quick search along the waterline would turn him up. Carlos thought he saw something move next to the fishing boat and reached over the side with the handgun pointing down.

Pete knew a window of opportunity when he saw one. Everything happened at warp speed as he stood up in the hatch opening. The spear gun was brought up ahead of his body so that, when he was standing erect on the bed, his shoulders crested the top of the open hatch. It wasn't much, but it was something of a shield. As the spear gun was brought to a level aim, thoughts of Sam being shot again flashed in his consciousness as he saw the pistol being pointed down over the side.

"*HEY ASSHOLE!*" Pete yelled.

Carlos instinctively turned toward the loud voice while raising his gun and squeezing off rounds one after the other. Carlos had never learned that the single most dangerous thing on any battlefield was that one well-aimed bullet. He was firing wildly and firing often.

The first bullet whizzed past Pete's head and off into in the direction of the mainland. The next bullet was a little better aimed and hit the smoked Plexiglas where it was fixed to the thick aluminum frame. This projectile shattered and caused damage to the frame only. The third hit the opposite side of the hatch two inches from the frame, stripping the metal jacket from the lead and fragmenting it. Several of the shards peppered Pete's chest cutting into his skin. The airborne spear had passed the fourth bullet over the center of the cockpit in midflight. Time seemed to stand still while the forth bullet entered Pete's right shoulder. The well-aimed spear found the center mass of Carlos's chest. The spear tip was a razor sharp point with two barbs on hinged pins. The weight of the shaft carried by forward momentum proved quite sufficient to slice through

Carlos's sternum, splitting flesh and bone as the spear penetrated deeper into his body. The barbs expanded once inside the chest cavity, which prevented him from pulling the spear out.

The pistol fell from Carlos's hand and clattered on the deck. He stumbled backward several steps with his arms flailing about, and then he grasped at the spear sticking from his chest. As he stumbled backward the artery next to his heart began pumping blood into his body cavity. The artery had been completely severed, robbing the rest of his body of any hope of life. Carlos stumbled one last time as he fell backward over the top life line. The spear pointed momentarily skyward as Carlos took his last breath, and then his lifeless body hit the water face down. The three foot spear sticking out of Carlos and pointing toward the sea floor would ensure his body didn't drift too far away.

Pete dropped the spear gun and jumped up on deck through the hatch, taking three large strides over to where the fishing boat was tied. He saw Sam lying in a mangled heap across the steering quadrant. He had landed on the center console windshield and shattered it. His head was in an odd position on the seat, which was mounted in front of the console, his legs falling off to either side. The growing full moon revealed a pool of blood on the deck of the boat under one leg.

Pete jumped down the companionway ladder and grabbed the underway first aid kit, a pretty comprehensive package designed to perform most minor surgeries when far from shore. He made it quickly over the side and onto the platform over the outboard motor, then down into the boat. Pete opened the pack and grabbed a large square sterile gauze pad. He immediately placed it on the bleeding bullet hole in Sam's leg. As Special Forces had taught all of its members about battle condition first aid and trauma management, controlling bleeding was first, and he tied the bandage tight enough to provide pressure to the wound. Sam's breathing was shallow and not very even.

Pete knew that Sam could have a broken back by the way he was lying over the console, or it could be that his position, along with internal injuries, were causing his labored breathing. Life decisions would have to be made, and made now. There was no time to wait for outside medical assistance — any rescue was at least 30 minutes away.

Pete decided he had no choice but to move Sam. His breathing was becoming slower and shallower. He moved Sam as carefully and as slowly as he could, reaching up under him and supporting his shoulders and upper body with his arms. Sam's head rested on Pete's left shoulder, the one without the bullet hole in it. Pete gently slid Sam off the console to the side and cautiously laid him on the deck. There was some minor bleeding on his back that appeared to be from the busted windscreen. "Deal with that a little later," he thought.

Sam appeared to be breathing a bit easier now that he was lying flat on the deck. He didn't look very good, however, but for that matter, Pete assumed that neither did he. His right shoulder had a bullet in it, although it had stopped bleeding for the most part. He had been hit in the chest too, but that didn't look too bad. He had to keep Sam alive. Pete lifted the bullet-torn leg placing it on his lap where he could keep pressure on the bandage. Pete was now sitting in a pool of blood, some of it his, most of it Sam's.

Pete saw a bloodstained white waterproof marine radio mounted on the center console above the steering wheel. He reached it with his free hand and turned it on. The little LCD screen lit up confirming that it had power. Pete spun the channel dial to 16, the channel constantly monitored by the U.S. Coast Guard.

"Mayday! Mayday! Mayday! This is the Southern Cross in San Carlos Bay with a medical emergency. Mayday! Mayday! Mayday!"

Thirteen

Alexander was parked at the boat ramp where he could see Carlos's truck and trailer. The ramp was fairly quiet because this was a weeknight. During the weekend though, parking was at a premium. Alexander had arrived by 8:45 p.m. to make sure Carlos didn't get back early and sneak off with something he didn't know about.

The siren of the rescue boat racing past him down the river toward the bay caused Alexander to silently wonder. He didn't have any of the local police or rescue frequencies, and so he was out of the loop as regards to official activity in this county. Not too much after the rescue craft went by, he watched a sheriff's office patrol boat head the same way. Emergency lights were flashing but no siren. Now the helicopter that he had seen a bit ago made sense — it was probably law enforcement as well. He didn't see any police cars running code toward the west, which meant the emergency call was not on dry land. Whatever happened out there was drawing some major attention. "Carlos must have really screwed this one up," Leslie thought.

Shortly after 10 p.m., the rescue boat was heading up river past the boat ramp with its lights and siren on. The rear deck lights illuminated the aft portion of the rescue boat, making the activity visible from shore. Alexander stood at the end of the pier as the rescue boat passed, clearly seeing two stretchers on the deck with the occupants being tended to. "Not good. Not good at all," Leslie thought.

There had not been one pleasant thought in Leslie Alexander's mind for the last two hours. He waited until midnight, keeping a small shred of hope that Carlos would appear with his items. The helicopter had returned inland over an hour ago, and two more official-looking boats had headed down the river during the past hour as well. The local marine towing service, TowBoat US, was westbound now heading into the bay. It was time to get some answers.

Alexander opened his map of Fort Myers, which he had picked up at a convenience store on his way down because he was not familiar with the town. He followed the river inland from the bay with his finger. He was looking for the closest hospital to the water. There were three in town that were near the water. One was on the north side in Cape Coral, and the other two on the south. Directory assistance connected him to Cape Coral General. He identified himself as Captain Torrance, Sheriff's Office, and inquired as to the boating accident victims. "Sorry sir, we've not admitted anyone like that tonight," the receptionist advised.

210

The second call went to Fort Myers Regional Hospital. The receptionist told him that she was not allowed to give any information concerning the shooting patients over the phone; he would need to appear in person. He thanked her and disconnected the call.

Following the map to Fort Myers General, Alexander found himself in the emergency entrance parking lot with a view of the admissions desk through the double glass doors. There was the normal late night activity one always sees at the emergency room. Once Alexander was certain no local deputies or police officers were hanging around the admissions desk, he walked inside.

Flipping open his badge and ID case to the middle-aged admissions clerk, he said, "Good morning. Major Alexander, sheriff's office." He had to use his correct name as it was clearly printed on his custom-engraved star. Below that was an ID card with his photo, another standard State of Florida Sheriff's star, and his information. His fingertip just happened to cover the word Pinellas before the words County Sheriff.

Completely disinterested and unimpressed, the clerk casually glance at his ID and said, "What can I do for you, Major?"

"The two gentlemen that were admitted a few hours ago, the ones from the boat, do you have their information?"

"Just a minute. I'll look them up and see if they were updated," she replied. The emergency room admissions clerk took a few minutes to cross reference information to make sure she had the right two men.

"Here is all I have so far," she told the Major. "Peter Mitchell from St. Petersburg, no date of birth yet, W/M, mid 40s, one gunshot wound, noncritical; and a Mr. Samuel Adams, W/M, mid 40s, active duty U.S. Army, serious condition, emergency surgery. If you go to the nurses' station on the 4th floor, they may have more information that's not in the computer system yet."

"What about the third man? Any word on him?" Alexander queried.

"No, no one came in with them. We've just had a few walk-ins and one traffic crash." She was scanning the evening's logs.

"He's dead."

Alexander turned around to see the nighttime security guard standing there.

"Who's dead?" Leslie asked.

"I heard two EMTs from the rescue boat talking earlier," the guard stated. "They said he had a spear right through the heart and was floating in the water. That's not the same thing you know about?"

"Ah, no. I was called out for this and haven't been to the scene yet," Leslie told him.

"Oh, well the dead guy should be going to the morgue," the guard responded. "I'll take you to the 4th floor nurses' station if you don't know where it is."

"Ah, no thanks. I've got to go outside and make some calls. I'll see you in a little while." Alexander turned and walked out through the double glass doors.

The admissions clerk looked at the security guard and shrugged her shoulders. Due to the new laws regarding patient confidentiality, she made a notation in her computer record to comply with hospital policy and procedure: Major Alexander from the sheriff's office was given information concerning patients Adams and Mitchell...

***

Janet arrived in her office as usual. She needed to continue her review of Wojcik's archived records and try to make some sense of the situation so far. There was not one specific case file or report alluding to a law enforcement corruption case, so far only handwritten notes. She was in possession of the large desk calendar for the timeframe she needed, upon which the agent had penciled in court dates, several first names with phone numbers, and the odd doodle here and there.

One doodle had a five point star with a dollar sign in the middle. Next to it was the name "Nate" with a slash behind it, and then "motive?" There was also a crude five point leaf drawing that resembled marijuana. Wojcik apparently did not possess enough drawing talent to pass the TV art school talent test by correctly drawing the turtle head. PCSO was written in bold letters, and an airplane drawing was nearby. The doodles and words gave her no clear direction — they were just hints that needed deciphering.

Janet had serious doubts that any of the phone numbers would lead anywhere. New area codes had been added to the county phone listings over the years. She would give them to Tim to research anyway, however. After all, Janet's parents had the same phone number for the past 20 years or so, but they were in a zone where the area code had stayed the same. It took a while for the phone company to straighten out where it wasn't a toll call just because area codes were different. They couldn't call their friends five miles away without being charged for long distance because of the new number. Progress wasn't always a good thing, she thought.

Janet picked up her phone on the third ring. "Good morning, Special Agent Cantu," she said.

"Good morning. This is Detective Rawlerson, Pinellas County homicide. You asked me to give you a call if I came up with any information."

"Yes, I remember. What do you have?"

"Dr. Mujahed thinks the pilot probably got a broken neck on impact with the water. That's his finding so far. No luck getting an ID on the body yet. Have you had any luck?"

Janet paused a second. "No, nothing from the FAA. I'm going through some old records, looking for reports of plane crashes or missing pilots, but so far, nothing."

"Were you able to ID the guy that found the plane?" Rawlerson inquired.

"No, not yet," Janet said. "It's on my list of things to do though."

"You might have missed your opportunity." Rawlerson explained, "My buddy at the Coast Guard told me about an emergency call in Fort Myers last night. It seems as though the guy that found the airplane might have gone and got himself killed."

"What's the story?" Janet sat up.

Rawlerson told her that he had received a call from his Coast Guard buddy this morning when he got into the office. The Coast Guard unit that handles the Fort Myers area had intercepted a mayday call via the marine radio last night. The morning pass-along report indicated that they responded to an anchored sailing vessel, the Southern Cross, which was in San Carlos Bay, and that was the name of the boat owned by the original reporting civilian who found the plane.

The incident was listed as a medical emergency in which three adult males were involved. Upon arrival, the Coast Guard found one subject floating face down in the water with a fishing spear in his chest, deceased. Two other men were in a fishing boat tied alongside the sailboat, and both subjects had been shot. One was in critical condition, the other in fair. The report didn't indicate any names. The injured were transported to Fort Myers Regional. The Charlotte County Sheriff's office had responded to conduct the investigation.

Rawlerson told her that was all the information he had for now and asked her to return the favor if she found out anything new. "Major Alexander is pushing me for information on this case," Rawlerson advised. Janet assured him she would call with any updates.

Janet told her boss she was heading to Fort Myers this morning. She gave him a short synopsis but none of the actual details.

**

Pete woke up wishing the damn nurse would leave him alone and let him sleep. If he was dying, he would accommodate her and push the call button first. He tried to roll over and was reminded of why he was here in the first place as pain shot through his shoulder, negating the effects of the medication that was steadily wearing off anyway, which was the reason the nurse was waking him up in the first place.

"And how are we this morning, Mr. Mitchell?" the RN asked.

"We are lying here with a hole in us," Pete quipped. "Groggy as hell too. What are you sticking in my IV?"

"It will ease the pain. You're scheduled for surgery in a little while. It shouldn't take long to get the bullet out."

"How's my friend, Sam Adams. He came in with me last night?"

The RN let him know that Sam went into surgery right after he came in. "He's in recovery now and should be alright — his prognosis is for a full recovery." The nurse was busy messing with the IV as she talked. "He was in bad shape when he got here last night, but some great surgeons worked on him."

Last night's events began to creep back into Pete's thoughts, filling the foggy void. Then the newly administered medicine began to take effect, which served to muddle Pete's thoughts once more. He remembered signing some forms last night giving permission for his surgery. He also gave someone Sam's home phone number. Nope, no relatives for himself, Pete remembered explaining, nobody they needed to call. He couldn't understand what the nurse was saying now anyhow.

"Good morning, Mr. Mitchell. How are we this morning?" the nurse asked.

Pete blinked his eyes a few times to try to clear them up, and his mouth really tasted terrible. "We are lying here with a hole in us," Pete said. "Didn't you hear me the first time?"

"Yes I did, but that was three hours ago. You've been in surgery, and by the way, you no longer have an unauthorized hole in you," Mr. Mitchell. "How do you feel?"

"My God, I'm thirsty."

The nurse held a small straw between his lips. "Here's a little water while you wake up."

Two detectives from the Lee County Sheriff's Office were patiently waiting outside the room as the nurse was attending to her duties with the guy that had a bullet hole in him. They had lots of questions and were anxious to speak with the man as soon as they could.

When she came out, she told them, "He's awake, but still kind of groggy. Don't count on anything he says as 100 percent accurate for the next couple of hours."

The detectives went inside and introduced themselves to Pete. One of them asked all the questions while the other younger detective did the note taking. The questions were pretty standard at first: who are you, where do you live, work, DOB, phone number, who owns the boat, and so forth.

Pete explained as much as he could, surprising the detectives at how lucid he was having just come out of surgery. No, he didn't know the guy with the spear in the chest. Yes, he was the one that shot him. Adams was his friend and they were staying on the boat in the bay. Yes, they were on vacation. No, they don't know why the dead guy was on their boat. No, he didn't know the fishing boat was stolen. Yes, the dead guy shot Adams, but no, he does not know why. Yes, the dead guy shot him, and that's why he got a spear in the chest. No, he didn't owe anybody any money he and Sam aren't drug dealers. When asked for motive, Pete said he thought this was just a crime of opportunity, a simple robbery gone bad.

The detective doing all the talking told Pete that Mr. Adams was stable but not well. The U.S. Army had been contacted because of Mr. Adams's active duty Army ID card in his wallet. The Army would be sending investigators to interview Pete as well. He further related that, once Adams was stable, he would be transferred to a military hospital, he didn't know which one.

Pete asked about his boat, which the older detective explained had been towed to the Fort Myers municipal marina. The sheriff's office tied it up to the last slip on the end, which was used for short term transient boat traffic. A 30-foot sailboat that was in the spot was moved to a different slip. The sheriff's office wanted to restrict access to the end of the dock with the standard yellow "Police Line — Do Not Cross" tape.

The sailboat was simply too large to go to the sheriff's dock, which was where the Hewes flats boat had been taken. Additionally, the sailboat was being processed for evidence by the crime scene unit. Should the investigation clear Mitchell of any wrongdoing, he would be allowed to have his boat back in a day or two. The detective was quick to point out that, as soon as the sheriff released the boat back into Mr. Mitchell's custody, he would be responsible for the slip fee's beginning at that point.

The interview went on for an additional 45 minutes. Pete did not mention the sunken airplane, the Betamax tape, cocaine, cash, or crooked cops. Not knowing which cops were crooked made all of them suspect, more so since they all had the same badge that the unknown dirty cop was wearing in the video tape. That fact by no means meant all cops were crooked, but figuring out which few were dirty was the trick.

Pete thought it was amazing how many different ways the cops can ask the same question trying to get a different answer. Pete knew that the process had become completely redundant once the younger detective put the notebook away. Pete was wondering what the difference was between an interview and an interrogation.

"Maybe it's an interrogation when they use the bright lights and rubber hoses…"

***

The drive had taken Janet a couple of hours. Traffic was backed up on I-75 southbound for miles because of an overturned semi off the side of the interstate. He had apparently pulled a bit too far off the shoulder into the tall grass, which had covered the unseen ditch that caused the truck to fall on its right side. Everyone needed to creep by to maximize their opportunity to see a bloody crash and bodies lying everywhere. The drivers were disappointed at the lack of carnage, however, and the traffic sped back up immediately after the wreck. The delay did provide Janet some time to work through the minor details of her investigation so far. She needed to start putting the puzzle pieces mentally together and get the bigger picture to form. One of her investigative talents was to never get ahead of the facts with an inaccurate conclusion, and there were some odd shaped puzzle pieces so far that were not quite fitting into the bigger picture.

Janet parked in the posted "police cars only" spot near the front of the hospital parking lot. She put the magnet mounted blue light on the dash of her unmarked FDLE Crown Victoria and headed into Fort Myers Regional Hospital.

After identifying herself to the woman at the information desk, she was directed to speak with the admissions supervisor. Information could give you directions to rooms, floors, and offices, but not patients due to the new patient confidentiality laws.

"Mrs. Sanderson-Admissions Supervisor" was clearly marked on the office door, which the information lady happily gave directions to because that news was on the approved list of what she could say.

Mrs. Sanderson carefully inspecting Janet's ID. Janet requested a printout with all the information concerning the identification of the two boating victims. Identification information was okay to give her, but medical records would require a court order, the administrator explained to Janet. After a bit of typing, the forms were printed and handed to her.

While Janet was waiting for the elevator to take her up to Mr. Mitchell's room, she scanned the printout. The patient identification information was fairly complete. Adams had an N/A next to his insurance information with the notation U.S. Military, active duty next to it. Down toward the bottom of the form was a section titled "Request for Patient Information." She immediately saw her name on the bottom with today's date. Above her name were five others. Three were listed as earlier today and indicated Detective so and so. The one above that was from the U.S. Coast Guard Rescue Boat Commander and dated last night. The first one on the list ahead of him was a Major Alexander, sheriff's office, but which sheriff's office was omitted, and this name sent a shiver of recognition down her spine. Janet still had that tingly feeling on the back of her neck when she went into Pete's room. She thought of Major Leslie Alexander with the Pinellas sheriff's office, but what the heck would he be doing down here?

She had already stopped by the nurses' station and talked to the nightshift RN. Mr. Mitchell was listed in good condition and was staying overnight for observation. If everything looked good during tomorrow afternoon's rounds, the doctor would release Mitchell. Mr. Adams was in serious/guarded condition but expected to recover. He had not been awake since the surgery. His wife had called and would be here sometime late tonight.

Janet stood in the doorway for a moment as she saw a nurse helping Mr. Mitchell with his hospital gown. Her brain seemed to be stuck on the first name on the list that she was holding. It could be a coincidence she told herself, but she didn't believe it.

When appropriate, Janet entered and introduced herself. The nurse had completed changing Mitchell's bandage and was fiddling with the IV. The nurse told Janet that Mr. Mitchell had received his evening medication and would need to be getting some rest soon. "Please don't be too long."

Janet began with all the standard questions, the same ones that Pete had heard several times today. He gave the lady all the same answers. The conversation continued for the next 15 minutes or so, during which time Pete thought that this was more chit-chat than it was an interview. It certainly wasn't an interrogation; this detective was much too nice. Pete did not know if she had lowered his guard by turning the conversation to something very casual or if she was genuinely interested in sailing.

"Did you make a second dive on the airplane?" She cocked her head to one side. This was the first time the word dive and airplane had been used in this conversation. This had the desired effect and caught Pete completely off balance. She could see it in his eyes now — there was much more to the story than he was telling. Pete had not mentioned the airplane to anyone so far, not any of the cops here anyway. His thoughts were bouncing off all the likely scenarios and trying to come up with a logical reason she had asked that specific question. The medicine wasn't helping.

"You look confused, Mr. Mitchell. You know the airplane I'm talking about? I want to know if you made a second dive on it." Janet leaned a little closer and scrunched her eyebrows together.

Pete yawned. "No, only the first time to get my anchor free." Okay, he was thinking, she knows more than the rest. "I wonder how much she actually knows and how much she is fishing."

"What did you take?" Janet queried.

"Nothing, just my anchor."

"I need you to be sure, Mr. Mitchell. It's very important." Janet could see that the medication was beginning to take effect and she was losing her edge. She was indeed fishing and had no solid answers yet.

"Listen, I only got my anchor loose." Pete was beginning to slur his speech a little. "That's it, just my anchor. Why do you care about an old airplane anyhow?"

Janet needed to play her card, and it was now or never. "I'm conducting a Law Enforcement Corruption investigation — I'm looking for a dirty cop."

Pete looked at her for a minute. She looked a little too young to have been around when the tape was made. She didn't work for the sheriff, and she seemed to know more than the rest. "How do I know you're not one of the dirty cops?"

Janet keyed in on the plural usage. "He truly does know more than he is telling," she thought. "I don't know how to get you to trust me. Any suggestions?" she asked.

"Let me give it some thought," Pete told her.

Janet knew when not to push. Forcing an issue too early could erase all the little commonalities and bonds a good interviewer made with the subject. "Okay, Mr. Mitchell. Sleep well and get better. I'll see you tomorrow afternoon, if it's alright with you. Maybe you can tell me then what I need to do to gain your trust."

"Pete. Call me Pete."

Janet smiled. "Good night Pete," she said and walked out.

Sitting in her car, Janet was pleased at the progress she just made. Pete absolutely knew more about her case, and now she knew she was chasing a corrupt cop, correction she thought, *cops.* He had confirmed many suspicions in their short amount of time together. The questions were racing through her head at light speed. She needed to find some answers and find them quickly.

She dialed the Lee County Sheriff's Office and was told that they did not know a Major Alexander. The only Alexander employed in that office was a corrections officer on the nightshift. Her next call was to Tim, who answered his cell phone on the second ring while looking at the caller ID. "Hi Janet, stopping by for dinner?"

"Only if it's at the office. You know I wouldn't ask this favor if it wasn't important." Janet had a serious tone to her voice. "Can you meet me there in an hour and a half? We have something urgent to talk about."

Tim glanced at his watch; it was going to be a late night, he surmised. "See you there. I'll bring the coffee and burgers."

"No onions please," Janet said, disconnecting the call. That cold shiver on the nape of her neck returned as she thought about Major Leslie Alexander, the Pinellas County sheriff's official "Golden Boy." His intended path was no secret within the law enforcement community.

Fourteen

In this business, you have to eventually trust someone, Janet thought. That's why last night she talked to Tim at length. She explained what she had so far and included her suspicions. The problem was that she didn't know what kind of corruption she was looking into, which meant she really didn't know what to look for specifically. She was on a wide-ranging fishing expedition, searching for anything out of place.

So far she had found lots of small indicators but nothing concrete. She related what she actually had so far to Tim, which wasn't much. The EPIC information was a solid lead, confirming that Wojcik was dealing with some sort of law enforcement corruption. Wojcik's notes and doodles supported that theory but did not provide anything specific, including a suspect. There was an aircraft with a skeleton on the bottom of the Gulf that had been searched by unknown persons some time during the night. What, if anything, had been removed was anyone's guess. There was now a dead guy and two men in the hospital who were somehow connected to all of this. One of the men in the hospital possibly knows something about the old law enforcement corruption case, and Major Alexander has been way too involved in this case and keeps popping up in unexpected places. At the very least, Alexander appears to be operating outside the scope of his authority with regards to the Lee County shootings.

The puzzle pieces were beginning to present some sort of a picture, not a very clear one yet but the pieces were beginning to mesh together. Tim was instructed to start digging and to dig quickly. FDLE could justify asking Lee County for information due to the multiple jurisdictions involved, and Janet needed to know more about the dead guy with the spear in his chest. She told Tim to run down all leads he could find, and "Don't forget the boat he showed up in. And Tim," asked Janet, "very, very quietly, see if you can find out where Major Alexander was yesterday evening."

"What about our boss? How much do I tell him?" Tim asked.

After a bit of thought, she said, "As little as you can for now. He started out as a deputy with the Pinellas County Sheriff's Office before coming over to FDLE. I don't know what his connection might be with Alexander, and so we must move with a bit of caution. Let's keep everything very quiet for now, at least until I know which direction this is going to take."

After a few short hours of restless sleep, Janet was back in the office going through Wojcik's files one by one, looking for any clue that might help. The small TV in the corner of her office was on the local news station. They were running a story about last night's shooting in San Carlos Bay. The news stations were reporting it as a robbery in which the suspect had been killed while in the commission of the crime and reporting that the owners of the boat were in the hospital with gunshot wounds but expected to live. There was a live news helicopter shot of the sailboat, and the reporter was talking about how the boat was now in custody of the sheriff for crime scene processing. As the camera zoomed in from 1,000 feet above, you could see blood on the portside deck.

Janet knew she needed to have a look around that boat. She also needed to talk to the crime scene technicians and learn what they had found. The only relevant thing she found in Wojcik's material was in last notation, which happened to be a Thursday: "Nate 2100 park re POS LA." At some time after he made this note, not long apparently, Wojcik had his reported heart attack.

***

Debora Hayes answered the office phone, "Special Operations Division, Major Alexander's office. May I help you?"

"Debora, I've got a bad infection with my tooth and the dentist has me on pills. I won't be in for a couple of days. Please handle any appointments I may have and let the Deputy Commander know I'm out." Alexander, spoke softly, and his tone was missing his usual pissy attitude, Debora thought.

"Yes sir. I'll take care of it. If there is anything I can…" The other end of the line went dead.

***

Janet was using the time while driving down to Lee County to think things through. She was heading to the crime scene unit offices, and after that she was going to go back to the hospital to try to pick up where she left off in the interview. What happened after that depended on the answers she got from Mr. Mitchell. She needed to interview Adams before the military moved him as well.

The drive down was easy, and with no delays, she arrived at the crime scene unit before noon. She met with the supervisor and was directed to the technician's office who had just returned from the sailboat. The tech advised her that the marine patrol unit had hauled the smaller boat out of the water and brought it to the impound lot for processing this afternoon, time allowing. They also had found the deceased person's truck and trailer at a local boat ramp. That, too, was in the impound yard.

Janet got a rundown from the tech on all the evidence collected so far from the sailboat. They had lifted over one hundred latent prints from various places on the boat. The spear gun and one handgun were also in custody. They were being processed for latents in the glue box now. This is where the heated superglue process was used. The glue would vaporize inside the box and stick to any of the residual oil from hands and fingers on the pistol and spear gun. The print would become permanently etched into the metal due to a chemical reaction with the vaporized glue. It did little for the resale value of the item but gave great prints that could be photographed.

CSU had also taken blood samples from several places on the boat, removed one screen with a bullet hole in it, and several bullet fragments from around the deck, the rear hatch, and the decedent's cell phone, which was lying on the floor of the sailboat. The tech handed Janet a list of numbers from both incoming and outgoing calls to the cell phone over the last few days. The tech said that there was surprisingly little evidence on the sailboat, but they had photographed everything digitally and were processing them into prints.

The tech told Janet that she could ride along to the impound lot, but Janet opted to take her own car and called Tim on the way. She related the telephone numbers and the other information she had received so far. Tim told Janet that he had talked to a friend at the sheriff's office and found out that Major Alexander had been out sick the past couple of days, something to do with dental work. That damn shiver returned to the nape of her neck again upon hearing that bit of news.

Janet watched the tech begin to process the Hewes flats boat. She noticed blood on the VHF marine radio and microphone, blood on the deck, a first aid kit and a broken windshield. When the tech lifted the wide bench seat behind the console, they both noticed all the other gear: two small radios, obviously marine type, binoculars, a marine navigation accessory pack, another larger radio with clipped wires, and a very nice three instrument-gauge wall mount display. This display contained a brass temperature gauge, relative humidity gauge, and a seven day clock. A small brass plaque on the bottom said "Southern Cross" with a line underneath proclaiming "Pete Mitchell, Captain."

The tech explained that they had found a small stack of items on the couch opposite the companionway ladder. There was a clock radio, two small power tools, a laptop computer, and an underwater dive watch. The items were stacked on top of a large beach towel and wrapped in a plastic garbage bag. They looked like they were being gathered up to take off the sailboat. Apparently, the tech surmised, the dead guy had only gotten one load of stolen property into the smaller boat when he was interrupted by the owners. All of the items were being processed for latents and photographed.

The decedent's truck had not been processed yet, the tech relayed. "It will probably be tomorrow morning before we can get to it," she said.

The tech advised that they had completed processing of the sailboat and it was being returned to the custody of the owner. The two exchanged contact information before Janet left. She found a Wal-Mart and picked up a few things, then headed to the hospital.

Arriving at Sam's room an hour later, Janet introduced herself to Sam and his wife, Amy. Once again, she made the interview seem more like casual chit-chat than an official investigation. Sam was stable and able to talk just fine. He wasn't getting up and going out for a walk anytime soon though. Sam told her that he had already talked to the local detectives this morning and didn't remember anything more than he had relayed to them.

Sam then described how he had crept up along the main deck to try to get a look at who was on the boat. He remembered being shot in the leg and then pushing himself off the boat, but he could recall absolutely nothing after that until he woke up and to see his wife sitting next to this bed. She'd had to explain most things to him. Well, what she knew anyway. She tried to get Pete to tell her more, but he only gave her a sanitized version. It seemed as though Sam and Amy had more questions for Janet than she had for them. Amy related that she had received most of her information from the local morning news show.

Once again, Sam explained that he had no idea why that guy was on the boat. He didn't know anything about an airplane on the bottom of the Gulf either. He had simply arrived here a few days ago to spend some time on the sailboat with his friend. They knew each other in the Army, he told Janet. Pete was severely injured in an aircraft accident years ago during a classified mission. Sam had nothing but friendly categorical praise for his pal but would give nothing specific.

Janet's intuition assured her that there was more to Pete. She couldn't put her finger on exactly what made her feel this way, but she was a good judge of character. She walked into Pete's room. "Good afternoon, Mr. Mitchell."

"Pete, please," he said.

"I brought you some things. The nurse said they had to dispose of your clothes because of the blood." Janet set a t-shirt, a pair of swim shorts, and flip-flops on the table next to the bed.

Pete picked up the t-shirt and let it fall open. There was a parrot dressed like a pirate with a martini in his feathered hand, the caption read "It's drink thirty!"

"I like your taste in clothes," Pete said.

"We couldn't let you walk out of here naked, now could we?"

The conversation began as casual chit-chat once again, which was not surprising to Pete. He had expected their conversation to get back to being an interview somewhere along the line. The clothes were a nice touch, he thought, for it was generally a reason for concern when a woman bought you clothes. That usually meant she

234

was taking the first steps in molding you into the man she always dreamed of. This was not the case, of course, but it was nevertheless reason to keep one's guard up. Pete thought she was rather attractive but more than likely spoken for.

Janet skillfully guided the conversation back to where they left off yesterday. "You told me you needed time to think about trusting me."

"Yeah, I do need to get some things cleared up. I would like to talk to Sam first, if you don't mind," Pete told her.

"Okay, but I hope you don't delay too much — there are some timing issues with my investigation. I'm working on a couple of leads and I don't want anything to get stale." Janet pushed just a little. "If you have any information that might help me, I would appreciate your cooperation — before anyone else gets hurt," she added.

"Do you have a business card?" Pete queried.

Janet handed a card to him after adding her private cell phone number. "Use the cell phone to get hold of me. I'm not in the office much lately."

"Are you busy this evening?" Pete asked.

"I'll make sure I'm not."

"I'm told I can have my boat back and I'm being released this afternoon. How about meeting me at my boat later, and then we can talk privately."

Janet stood. "I'm looking forward to it, and can I give you a ride to the boat?"

"No thanks. The city marina is only a couple of blocks away, or so I'm told. I could use a short walk to clear my head a bit anyway. I'll call you when I'm on the way."

"I've got a couple more local people to talk to. I'll see you later at the boat then." Janet gave him a warm smile as she was leaving and got one in return. She was pleased with her progress and was sure Pete would open up to her this evening. She was looking forward to getting some solid answers, which she was certain Pete had. Janet started to dial the phone again...

Pete completed the sign-out process and went directly to Sam's room. The clothes fit nicely and the flip-flops were only a half size off. "Good guess Janet," he thought.

The conversation with Sam and Amy lasted about 45 minutes, a combination of trying to sort out the previous night's events and catching up on old news with Amy. The boys were doing great and everything was fine, until this. Amy had that worried worn-out loving wife look of having missed a lot of sleep the past day or so. Pete suggested she go get a cup of coffee and a sandwich at the cafeteria. He would keep Sam company for a little while.

Once alone, Pete told Sam, "It's got something to do with the Betamax tape. I'm sure that Janet, the FDLE Agent, is investigating something that is somehow connected to that tape."

"Do you think you can trust her?" Sam asked.

"I made a call, and I'm having her checked out. I should hear something in an hour or so. But I think we can skip your FBI contact and work with her."

"Does this decision have anything to do with the fact that she is a single beautiful woman?" Sam questioned.

"How do you know she's single?"

"Amy found out — she really likes her. She was in here for an hour or so this afternoon. I couldn't tell her much, and I didn't say anything about the plane or the tape." Sam looked like crap. "If you're going to change my story with her, let me know. I'll blame my forgetfulness on the pain medicine."

"I'm meeting with her this evening," Pete said. "If she checks out, I'll give her the tape." Sam knew this meant that Pete was still talking to the folks in the National Intelligence circles, who would have that kind of information readily available. They had both been involved with the agencies to varying degrees over the years.

The rest of the conversation centered around what had actually happened after the shooting, and Pete informed Sam that he was planning to head back to St. Petersburg in a few days once his shoulder healed. If he wasn't able to work the sails he would just motor home. Sam told him that he would probably be going to the Army hospital in Maryland to finish his recovery. He was scheduled to be transferred to MacDill Air Force Base by military ambulance the next morning, and then he would be on a medical transport flight to the base in Maryland. Amy would fly up commercially out of Tampa after he left MacDill.

The afternoon thunderstorms had ended, making for a nice evening walk. Pete was following the pretty simple instructions the gal at the information desk had given him to get to the marina, which was actually about 10 blocks.

The nurse had wiped down Pete's cell phone with some hospital disinfectant before turning it off and putting it in the desk drawer next to his bed. She couldn't save the clothes, just the phone she had told him. When Pete had turned the phone back on before going to Sam's room, he saw there had been another call from the Pinellas County Sheriff's Office but there was again no message. His phone rang about halfway back to the boat, the caller ID indicated the call was out of area.

"Pete, Mike here," the voice said. "Your friend, Janet Cantu checks clean." Mike then gave Pete a full rundown, including who her parents were, her high school and college years, her stint with Tampa PD — just about everything except her favorite perfume.

"Thanks pal, I appreciate it," Pete said. Brief goodbyes were exchanged and he snapped the phone closed.

Pete found the marina office, which was locked. There was a number for after hours emergencies posted on the door. Boats arriving late in the day were directed to contact the office after 8 a.m. the next morning and arrange payment. There was also a list of rules concerning noise, trash disposal, holding tank pump-out and related items below it. Pete decided he would come back in the morning. He had called Janet's cell phone a couple of blocks ago and got the answering machine. He left a message that he was now heading back to the boat and would like to meet up with her. He had some things to discuss. The low battery alarm beeped twice.

The Southern Cross was down at the end, her bow pointed toward the river. The tow company had backed her in allowing access to the starboard side amidships from the dock. There were remnants of yellow police tape on the pilings along the dock next to his boat, and as he approached the boat, he could see that none of the dock services were in use. He would have to break out his 30 amp shore power cord and plug in. It would be nice to run the A/C since there wasn't much of a breeze. "Probably ought to fill up the fresh water tanks while I'm here and pump out the holding tanks in the morning," he thought.

As Pete stepped onto the boat, he glanced at the dock lines and noted that someone only used two lines to tie her up, one fore and one aft. He would do a proper job before going to bed tonight. Stepping into the center cockpit, he noticed the aft hatch cover had been removed. He recalled that it was no good anyway. It had bullet holes in it and was shattered. An old piece of sailcloth would fix that for the time being. There was still a lot of blood on the port side deck where Sam was shot. He would clean that off when he filled the tanks in the morning.

As Pete came down the companionway ladder, his thoughts attempted to rationalize what he was looking at. The scene materializing in front of him just didn't make sense. The crime scene people should all be gone and there was no reason for a woman to be lying on the salon floor. When he got to the bottom of the ladder, he could see her head near the main mast support that ran from the overhead to the deck. Her hands were handcuffed around the main mast, securing her to the mast below the table. A large matted and blood-stained area covered the side of her face. She was partially wedged up under the salon dining table. The sides of the table were hinged and hanging down, which provided more room in the salon when not in use.

In order for Pete to reach her head, he had to squeeze between the table and settee cushion. When he brushed her hair aside, he was stunned to see that it was Janet. It was then that he heard the very familiar and instantly recognizable sound caused by the slide of a semi-auto handgun charging the chamber coming from directly behind him, the passageway that led to the master stateroom. Pete froze in place. He knew he was at the immediate disadvantage.

"Good evening, Mr. Mitchell," came an unknown voice. "Would you like to die today?"

"Not particularly," Pete responded. "How about you?" He slowly began to stand while displaying his hands at his side. "What do you want?"

"I want you to turn around and remain very still," the voice said. "We have some business to conduct."

As Pete turned, he saw a man about the same age as himself who was dressed Florida-casual style and standing in the passageway. He was holding a brushed stainless steel semi-auto a Smith & Wesson .45 pointed directly at his chest. The barrel was absolutely huge when seen from this end of it.

Pete was looking the intruder in the eyes, which was not a good sign. When someone like this let you see them, that generally meant that you wouldn't live long enough to identify them later. There was something very familiar about the man. He couldn't quite place his face, but he had seen it before.

"You have some property of mine, and returning it is not open for discussion or debate, Mr. Mitchell."

"Okay," Pete said aloud. Then he thought to himself, "The guy knows who I am." He told the intruder, "I don't know what property you could be talking about."

Without moving his gun hand or breaking eye contact, the man reached under his right arm with his left hand and picked something up off the workbench below the navigation station panel. He had to bend slightly at the knees and twist and reach it without disturbing his aim point.

Pete caught the PVC end cap the man tossed to him and was careful not to make any other movements while suspending the end cap in front of him. Pete was watching the intruder carefully and noticed that his gun hand was very steady and sure. This guy was used to handling high stress situations and was very much in control. Pete's training kicked in and he was very aware of every movement while looking for that split second of opportunity to present itself.

"I want my video tape."

Pete instantly knew it would do no good to play dumb or argue with the man. That was not the opportunity he was looking for. "Okay, it's in the galley." Pete gestured toward the small galley on the port side of the companionway ladder and dropped the PVC cap on the cushion.

"Be very, very careful while you get it. I'm just not in the mood to be toyed with today." The barrel of the gun was waved in two short ticks toward the galley, indicating Pete was allowed to move.

Pete stepped in front of the ladder and then into the one person galley. As he moved, the man with the gun repositioned himself in one very fluid movement, never getting too close to Pete. He kept the gun out of Pete's immediate strike zone. There would be no kicking the gun or grabbing it from this man. He had been trained well, Pete thought. The gunman was now standing with his back to the V-berth where he could clearly see all of Pete's movements.

"I need to take out this drawer," Pete said while cautiously grasping the handle.

"Very carefully and no mistakes, I only want to see the tape come out after the drawer."

Pete slid the drawer out and set it on the countertop to the right. He slowly reached in with one hand while lifting the panel up slightly. He used his other hand to steady himself while he grabbed something up in the space. Pete initially felt for the grip of his own .45. He was unable to grab it easily. This was apparently not going to be the time either, and he slowly pulled the Betamax tape from the hiding spot.

"Toss it on the cushion, here." The man nodded to his lower right and Pete complied.

"Out, over there." The man motioned to the passage way back on the starboard side.

Pete didn't like the way this was going. He had been racing through his options as each scene was quickly played out in his mind's eye. He was busy working out possible scenarios in his mind, trying to formulate a plan as he made his way into the companionway where the workbench was located. "There should be some tools lying there that could be used as a weapon," he thought. If the man was going to make him go to the master stateroom, he would have to make his move when he stepped into the aft stateroom. The gunman would still be in the confines of the passageway and unable to move quickly. There was a fire extinguisher attached to the bulkhead just to the right of the door in the stateroom, another possible weapon.

This is the only place he could think of when he wouldn't be directly in front of the .45. His one advantage was that the gunman, although he appeared to be very willing to shoot, was apparently refraining from firing the weapon in the marina. The wound on Janet's head didn't appear to be from a bullet, and Pete wasn't killed as soon as he retrieved the tape. These hesitations could be used to his advantage to turn this situation around.

Pete stepped out of the galley and in front of the companionway ladder. He began to step toward the passageway while formulating his plan when his world went suddenly black.

Fifteen

Alexander had never driven a sailboat before, but it couldn't be too much different under engine power than his boat. "Just one hell of a lot slower," he thought. The engine controls were easy to find. He energized the start battery by flipping the "engine on" switch, which was conveniently located, and clearly marked, on the circuit panel. He also turned on the navigation lights to comply with the law — he didn't want to do anything to draw any unnecessary attention.

The key was already in the ignition panel in the cockpit, and the Yanmar diesel engine started easily with just a tap of the key. He assumed that, since Mitchell had been living on the boat recently, all the proper cooling inlet valves were open and the engine would operate properly. He didn't have the time to trace down cooling lines and check their positions.

The evening darkness had descended upon the marina and all was quiet. Nobody was paying any attention to him or to this boat. Leslie slipped the dock lines off the bow and stern, freeing the Southern Cross, and then turned the rudder fully to the right then left, counting revolutions of the wheel. There was one and a half turns each way. He counted one and a half turns, bringing the rudder back to the center position. He didn't want to smack into another boat or pier as he was getting underway but to slip away from the dock and head down the river just quietly and without any fanfare.

The moon was bright enough to provide sufficient light in order to navigate the well-marked river. As he eased away from the marina, he twisted the wheel to the left, turning into the center of the river. Leslie would simply need to keep the red day markers on the left as he was heading out to sea. The markers would keep him in the channel until open water was reached. Leslie was passed by the occasional fishing boat here and there, but there was no indication that he should be concerned. He was quite anonymously making his way out to sea.

Leslie thought about the contents of the tape and was elated to finally have it back. He rationalized his actions, especially considering the two people down below. The woman simply should not have shown up. The result was simply her misfortune and bad timing. Alexander had used her own handcuffs from her purse to lock her to the mast. The only reason he could think of for an FDLE agent to be involved at this stage was the fact that this investigation crossed jurisdictional boundaries between Lee County and the Coast Guard. The CG did not have an investigative law enforcement branch like the other services did, so they would use the local state agencies when a crime had been committed.

Mr. Mitchell simply had to be disposed of. He had seen Leslie's face, which made the man's death a certainty, but as importantly, he more than likely viewed the contents of the tape. He could be very problematic in the future. Mitchell's demise was also simply his misfortune for sticking his nose where it didn't belong. "Sucks to be him," Leslie thought. They would have to disappear at sea where they would remain in a watery grave, hopefully longer than that damn airplane. The airplane itself would have posed no problem for him had it not been for the Betamax tape. He got pissed again at the Mexicans for not doing their job 25 years ago. If the idiots would have taken the right suitcase from Vince in the first place, none of this would be necessary.

The trip down the river to the open Gulf went without hearing from the two occupants below. The FDLE agent was handcuffed to the mast and Mitchell was flex-cuffed to the companionway ladder. Leslie didn't have a pair of handcuffs with him, and the agent had only one set in her purse, but after pistol whipping Pete in the back of the head, Leslie found some heavy duty plastic tie wraps on the workbench in a small overhead cabinet. The cable ties were about the same size the police used. The only difference was that the official flex cuffs that the cops used had several thin wire inserts imbedded into the plastic for extra security. The large black cable ties would work just as well for a few hours. Pete had crumpled on the deck below the ladder after having his skull cracked. Leslie simply had to cuff Pete to the side of the ladder with his hands between two steps. He wouldn't be going anywhere, if he woke up at all. Looking below revealed that both future drowning victims were still unconscious. "Just as well," he thought. He didn't want to listen to them sniveling anyhow.

When the Southern Cross passed the last day marker, she entered the Gulf of Mexico heading due west. "This is as good a course as any," Leslie thought. He pushed the button on the instrument console that turned on the autopilot. The small red light illuminated, indicating power had been applied to the system. There was a course button next to that. This appeared to be a simple heading only autopilot without GPS course guidance. It would basically maintain a magnetic heading. When Leslie pressed the course button, he felt the hydraulics immediately take control of the wheel. Watching the compass for a minute or so, he decided that the autopilot was holding a course due west, and another instrument indicated they were maintaining a steady six knots.

Leslie went below while the Southern Cross motored along, found the circuit breaker he was looking for on the instrument panel, and found the switch that was selected to auto on the bilge pump. When the sensor became wet, the pump would automatically come on, discharging the water over the side. Leslie then opened the side hinges, allowing the entire panel to swing open to reveal all the wiring behind that was connected to the breakers before going on to specific tasks. Checking the front and counting the breakers, he
248

double checked that he was cutting the correct wires. He didn't want to interfere with the west-bound progress of the boat.

Next he saw a circuit breaker simply listed as "Bilge Pump" on the top left side. All boats should have several powered pumps and a couple of manual ones as backups. When out at sea, you could never have too many ways to get water out of your boat. He cut the wires to this pump breaker as well. Checking the panel again, he saw no more bilge pumps. Next he needed to find the correct size seawater inlet hose.

There were several flashlights conveniently hanging in wall mounts near the engine room, galley, and aft stateroom. The one by the engine room was providing enough light to check the bilges for the hose he was after.

The engine cooling intake could not be used as he needed the engine to run for a bit longer without overheating. There were several inch-and-a-half hoses that ran from the floor of the center cockpit through hull fittings on the bottom of the bilge to keep the cockpit drained in stormy weather. These were easily accessible but too large to suit his needs. The forward half of the engine room had a 110 volt A/C heating system for use at the dock. The cooling pump was on the port side of the unit and had a cooling water intake hose attached through hull fitting, a half inch hose. "Perfect," Leslie thought.

The hose had double stainless steel clamps and was made from reinforced wire inserted marine grade rubber tubing. Below the waterline hoses were always extra heavy duty and reinforced. You didn't want one of them giving way or springing a leak. Well, not until today anyway. The hacksaw from the workbench storage cabinet made short work of the half inch hose. It separated cleanly, allowing ambient sea pressure an easy path into the engine room and bilge. The rate of inflow appeared to be about right. Leslie needed the engine to run for another five hours or so before the seawater eventually covered the air intake, stopping the engine. The half inch opening should allow the boat to continue on course for at least the next several hours. There was a lot of boat down here to fill up. Taking a little longer would not be a problem. The end result would be the same.

By Leslie's calculations, assuming it took about five hours to kill the engine, the Southern Cross should be about thirty miles off shore in deep water when it went down. Once the engine was choked by rising salt water, the boat would finish sinking fairly quickly by itself, and that would be the end of that. Leslie could go about the business of daily life, this chapter closed and out of the way forever.

Leslie grabbed the Betamax tape from the cushion and went back up to the cockpit. He thought about putting a bullet in each one of them but decided not to. He was afraid the noise might carry a little too much, and he was still too close to shore to risk drawing any attention with gunfire. "Let 'em drown," he thought to himself.
250

Satisfied that the Southern Cross was maintaining a steady westbound course and that the boat was indeed sinking, he decided it was time to get off. He was still close enough to make it back to shore easily in the dinghy. The sailboat would simply continue heading out to sea and into the darkness. Even if the autopilot failed somewhere along the line, the rudder would remain in the center position, keeping the soon-to-be-drowned passengers heading westerly out into the Gulf of Mexico. Leslie scanned the horizon and was satisfied that they had no company in the immediate vicinity. There was only one smaller fishing boat that had already passed eastbound heading into the channel.

The dinghy was tied to the aft port cleat and dutifully following behind. Leslie pulled the little boat closer until the bow was touching the sailboat and retied it with a slipknot. He climbed the short distance down the swim ladder and into the rubber boat. After he pulled on the slipknot, the dinghy drifted to a halt as the Southern Cross continued along its doomed course.

The little motor fired up on the first pull, and it only took ten minutes to get back to shore. Alexander kept glancing back at the Southern Cross, confirming her westerly course. "Damn it," he thought, I should have checked the compartment the tape was in. I'll bet the money was there too. Oh well, too late now." The sailboat would soon disappear out of sight completely.

Seeing no activity at the county boat ramp near the mouth of the river, Leslie decided to pull in there. He got out of the small boat at the end of the dock, and still alone, he opened the three air pump fill valves on the little craft just enough to hear the hissing air escaping from the inflatable tubes. With one good push of his foot the inflatable boat was caught up in the outgoing current of the river while it was deflating. The channel was over 20 feet deep here, plenty of water for the dinghy to disappear.

The dinghy went down by the stern first due to the weight of the outboard motor, and Leslie Alexander was just about to lose sight of the boat as it drifted away in the current toward the open Gulf. He was able to see the last little portion of the bow just before the final bit of air exhausted itself, allowing the dinghy to complete its voyage to the bottom.

Walking up to the main road, Leslie held the Betamax tape tightly, feeling his frustrations beginning to ebb. He would get a cab to take him back to his car near the marina. "Things were beginning to look up" he thought.

***

The damn buzzing sound just wouldn't stop. Somewhere between his conscious and subconscious mind, Pete was becoming very annoyed at the sound. He was in that not-really-asleep-or-quite-yet-awake state of confusion. Was it that stupid watch under his boat in the marina again? Was he back home? Was Frank's fine timepiece beeping again? No, this was different, a bad sound. He just knew that damn noise needed to stop — it was quite disturbing. The wetness was strange too, and he was also in a lot of pain. Everything seemed to hurt at once. Nothing was making much sense. Confusion quickly enveloped Pete Mitchell.

It was painful, but Pete was able to force his eyes open, which didn't seem to help much. Everything was dark. The screeching buzzer was even more annoying when his thoughts began to collect into something akin to order. He was trying to focus his eyes, blinking harder to get them to clear. He tried to rub his eyes and couldn't understand why his arms wouldn't move. He was able to move his legs a little bit, but the sensation of water was really baffling.

As he took a couple of deep breaths, his head began to clear and his eyes to focus. There was not much light, but enough to start to make out shapes. He was able to tell he was on his boat as things became recognizable. There were LED lights on his right giving a little more illumination, and the moon was providing some more light down into the main salon. "Yeah, that's where I am," he thought, "in the main salon. But what is all this water doing here?" It was about at his chest. Pete was able to lift himself up a little more and lean against the engine room bulkhead. His hands were still caught somehow in the ladder and he couldn't move them.

A few moments passed, and his mind began to get clearer. He could now tell that his hands were tied together by large plastic wire ties, one of which was cutting off most of the circulation. His hands were numb. The second tie wrap was looped through the first, keeping his hands locked together. The engine was running, he could tell that, and the annoying noise was now beginning to make sense — the bilge high water alarm. The water was about twelve inches deep and shifting from side to side. He was underway and the boat was gently rocking sideways on light seas. He didn't like what he was seeing, but it was starting to make some sort of sense.

Pete heard a slight cough, muffled by water. When he heard it again, he was able to lean over and see another person lying on the floor, a woman, and she was holding on to the mast underneath the folded table. When the boat heeled slightly to the starboard side, the water would slosh over and partially cover her mouth. It wasn't until the boat rocked toward the port side that her face was free and she was able to breathe again. "Janet!" Memory flooded back. It was Janet on the floor and she was handcuffed to the mast. He tried to slide his foot toward her head but she was too far away.

The thought that they were sinking suddenly gelled into reality. The water was steadily rising, and he had to get free. The adrenalin coursing through his veins thrust Pete into the present. Pulling on the tie wraps only caused his wrists to bleed. His hands were numb, however, and he didn't care about the blood. He just needed to get free. The companionway ladder was held in by two

254

slide locks on the top with wing nuts securing the bottom. It was intentionally designed to be easily removable, thereby allowing easy access to the engine room past the forward bulkhead. His hands were between the second and third steps from the deck, and so he was unable to reach the wing nuts with his hands and he tried with his toes. That wouldn't work. Pete began to look for something, anything he could use as a tool. Janet was beginning to have more trouble breathing. He heard her gurgle and cough as the boat gently rolled with the waves. The water was slowly rising, covering her mouth and nose a little deeper with each passing minute.

The next time the boat rolled a little to the starboard, a tennis shoe floated by and he was able to catch it momentarily with his right foot. The next wave brought it closer, and he was able to bounce it off his knee to bring it a bit closer still. The third wave brought it past his chest, and using his knee, he was able to pin the shoe against his chest and under his chin. Moving his upper body toward his hands, he grabbed the shoe. Pete started to pull the shoelace out of the eye holes one by one. His hands hurt like hell and his wrists were beginning to bleed a little more freely now, but every water-choked cough from Janet made him pull the lace out a little faster.

Once the lace was free, he let the shoe float off in the next wave. Pete was able to tie one end of the lace to the handhold cut out on the side of the ladder below his hands. That part was almost completely underwater now. It had been dry a few minutes ago. The water was rising a little quicker than he thought, and Janet's head was almost completely under water now, but she was semi-conscious and fighting to keep her head up and to breathe. He could see she was losing the fight, however. The battle was about over.

Pete slipped one end of the shoelace through the flex cuff that was securing his left wrist while bending his right hand until it brought tears to his eyes. The pain was shooting through his entire body, causing him to grunt while suppressing the need to scream. Once the lace was through the cuff and dangling, he used his right hand to lift the lace to his mouth. He clinched the lace as tightly in his teeth as he could and pulled it as tight as he could without breaking a tooth.

Pete then began a short fast sawing action, pushing the plastic of the tie wrap tight against the shoelace. He was only able to make his hands move back and forth six to eight inches as he feverishly sawed away. The effect he was looking for could be felt on his wrist. The burning sensation created by the friction against the lace confirmed that the sawing was working. The heat was literally melting through the plastic, which was the reason the police flex cuffs had several strands of steel wire imbedded in them. This was an escape tactic Pete had learned during his POW escape and evasion training during the Ranger course. They called that portion *hell week* for a reason.

Janet was now constantly gasping and coughing up water when the waves shifted the boat to the port side. One or two more minutes and she would certainly drown. Pete sawed a little faster and was, after what seemed an eternity, rewarded with his hands snapping free. Pete immediately lunged forward toward the V-berth. This only worsened Janet's situation for a brief moment as the wake he created cut off her breathing even more, but it was very necessary. "Hold your breath, just a little longer," he silently pleaded.

Pete fumbled a little with the zipper of his dive bag that was on the bed in the V-berth. Some feeling was beginning to return to his left hand, just enough to get it to cooperate and work the zipper. After opening the bag, he grabbed the spare air miniature scuba bottle. As he sloshed back through the water, he saw that Janet's head was completely covered and he pushed the small regulator into her mouth. Jabbing the purge button on the top forced the water in her mouth to be expelled through the exhaust valve of the regulator. Janet instinctively inhaled deeply and then coughed water through the regulator. She took several more deep life-giving breaths as her eyes opened slightly underwater and she looked toward Pete.

Her eye caught his when he looked back in the dim light through the saltwater. Pete was sure he could see into Janet's inner core. She had just communicated something to him that could never be put into words. The spare air tank would not last long, three minutes maximum, and Pete needed to get busy if he was to keep her alive.

Pete went forward into the V-berth stateroom again. This time he pulled the normal size scuba tank out of the rack, pulled the regulator rig from the dive bag, and attached it to the first stage on top of the tank. He made his way back to Janet and laid the tank next to her in the water. She was still trapped but able to breathe. He lifted her left leg slightly and slid the tank under, then pressed on her leg to get her to hold the tank in place. He didn't want it sloshing around with all the other stuff and beating her to death.

Pete held the spare air with his left hand and the main scuba tank regulator with his right. Janet's face was completely submerged now. Some feeling had returned to his left hand with the tie wrap cut off, but circulation to the right was still cut off and it was numb. He accidentally dropped the regulator twice because he could not feel what his hand was doing.

Pete grabbed the small air tank and started to pull it out of Janet's mouth. She suddenly got very wide eyed with panic and stared directly at Pete through the dim sloshing water. Pete leaned in and told her what he needed to her to understand with his eyes. There was now some kind of a connection, and his silent instructions were relayed. Janet's look of terror turned to one of trust and her expression softened.

She inhaled and then held her breath as Pete slipped the small spare air regulator from her mouth. Pete slipped in the normal regulator and tapped the purge button on the front, forcing the water inside the regulator out the exhaust ports. Janet gratefully inhaled. She knew she would be safe now. Janet was confused and didn't feel very well, but she discovered that she could only move her legs, and she was confident that Pete would get her out of this. Janet felt a calm that reassured her with every fresh breath.

Pete got up knowing Janet would be fine for a while. She had at least 60 minutes of air in the tank, and he needed to take care of the rising water situation immediately. He made a quick mental priority list. The first thing was to cut the engine. The water was nearly high enough now to enter the intake and kill the engine permanently. Making his way over to the engine room, he opened the door, and with the flashlight, he easily found the bright orange spring-loaded engine kill switch, now submerged, on the side of the engine. Holding it in rewarded him with the Yanmar shuddering to a stop as the fuel was choked, and the engine silenced.

The rising water was the next problem. Pete illuminated the circuit panel and turned on both bilge pumps. He quickly discovered that neither one of his electric bilge pumps was working. The manually operated electric pump was on a shelf above the engine. It didn't energize and begin pumping when he turned it on, and he had no idea why. He immediately thought of using the manual hand-operated pump, which worked very well. This type of pump required that you to put a metal pipe in the top slot for a handle and pump back and forth. He would not be able to suck out the water faster than what was coming in, assuming he could even hang onto the handle, so that was not an option just yet. Then he thought of it.

There was a shower drain on the floor of both the forward and aft heads. The little room was designed to be a shower, so everything was waterproof in there for a reason. Both of the deck drains met in the bilge under the main salon just aft of the fresh water tanks. The open compartment held the grey water from the shower in the 15 gallon open tank. There was a sump pump lying in the bottom of the tank to pump the shower water overboard. The top of tank was open to the bilges, which meant that, with the water this high, the pump would work. Pete was praying when he flipped the shower circuit breaker.

The little pump ran quickly at first and then slowed as it picked up a prime and started to move water. Pete took a deep grateful breath as the little diaphragm sump pump worked as hard as it could. He still had to stop more water from coming in. Without the vibration of the engine and the Southern Cross slowing to a halt, the waves inside the boat had became almost still. Once Pete pushed the disable button on the high water alarm, the boat also became very quiet. The only sound was Janet breathing with the scuba tank, and right now, that was a wonderful sound indeed.

Scanning the surface waters inside the boat with the flashlight, Pete found what he was looking for — a bubbling on the surface in the engine room near the forward bulkhead. The small artesian well gave away the location of the breech easily. The seawater had kept the engine cool as Pete wedged himself over the top of it where he could feel around the bilge for the opening. He found the cut hose and stuck his fingertip in the hole to be sure.

Pete then reached the emergency plug bag, which was hanging on the engine room wall. There was another bag under the sink in the forward head and another in the aft head. Each bag contained 4 wooden dowel plugs of various sizes. One end came to a point and the other end was large enough to be hammered on. The plug was designed to be used for hose breeches through the hull or when a through-hull fitting gave way. They were standard on any properly equipped seagoing vessel. Pete got the plug pushed into place enough to stop the incoming flow of water. He would do a proper job of plugging the hole once the water was gone and he could swing a hammer. For now, this would solve the problem. He would know in a minute or two by watching the water level if this was the only hole.

Next he had to get that damn plastic cuff off of his right wrist and get the feeling back. A pair of end cutters from the workbench made short work of the plastic tie wrap. His right hand actually began to hurt worse now that blood was rushing back into it. "No time for pain," Pete thought.

He quickly poked his head up the companionway and scanned the darkness. One quick scan and he was assured there was no immediate threat up there. They were not going to hit anything and the intruder was not on board, but he was already pretty sure of that since he had not been stopped while he was busy saving Janet and his boat.

Checking Janet's hands, he confirmed that she did in fact have metal handcuffs on. He scanned the water's surface but could not see anything that would help him here. He went over to Janet and felt her pockets but found no keys. She was breathing steadily and appeared to be trying to watch him. He could tell she smiled at him by the way her eyebrows crinkled together.

Pete got the hacksaw from the workbench and started on one of the handcuff links. Hack sawing underwater with bloody wrists and numb hands wasn't easy, but he was determined. He only had about 25 minutes left before Janet was out of air for good.

***

Leslie Alexander arrived home shortly after 3 a.m. utterly exhausted yet unable to sleep. His mind was extremely busy recounting the day's events. Finally satisfied that this danger was behind him, he popped two 10mg sleeping pills. He deserved a good night's sleep, he told himself.

Pete had eventually cut the cuffs loose, allowing him to pick Janet up out of the water. They sat on the settee holding each other for a long time. Janet was shivering, and Pete tried to warm her with his still adrenaline-filled body while reassuring her that they had made it through the worst part. Janet had quietly cried for a short time, releasing trapped emotions. The stark realization of what had just happened was beginning to manifest itself in her consciousness. She had just intimately faced death, and it was ugly.

Janet's mind was riddled with questions, but she was unable to make any words form upon her lips. She decided she was content for now with just being alive, and that she was truly grateful to be looking into a friendly face.

There wasn't much on board that was dry anymore, but Pete wrapped Janet in a fairly dry blanket and laid her down on the settee. Pete then began to check the regular bilge pumps and found where they had been cut at the breaker. He stripped the wires and added a short jumper, putting power back to the pumps. With the pumps running, the lower deck would be dry when daylight finally reached them. Now that he had time to look, Pete had found Janet's purse among the other floating debris. He dug through it and came up with the handcuff key that was on a ring with four other keys. He got the cuffs off and covered her with the blanket again. Janet rubbed her wrists and was grateful to be free of the painful pieces of metal. She knew that the next time she handcuffed a prisoner, she would be reminded of this night.

There was something reassuring about the sunrise. It erased some of the previous night's evil while giving them both hope that this would all end well for them. Pete now had to figure out where they were. The water was almost down to the bottom of the cabin floor, and with the daylight arriving, some clean up could begin.

Pete found his portable GPS, which was waterproof, and he carried it up to the center cockpit and placed it on the instrument panel while it acquired a location. Pete took the opportunity to scan the horizon to see if any help was close by. Seeing none, he thought about calling the Coast Guard on the radio, but then he recalled that he had no radios. They had all been removed and the wires had been cut. He found his cell phone, which had floated into a corner. When you live on a boat, you bought everything you could find that was waterproof. The cell phone came alive, but he had no signal. "We must be too far from shore," Pete thought.

The GPS beeped, indicating it had acquired its position on the planet Earth. He took the wide area chart up to the cockpit with him because there was now enough daylight to read by.

They were 43 miles west of Charlotte Harbor, Florida. "Alright," Pete thought. "Now I need options." Pete started to formulate his plan for the day. He heard the shower sump pump start to suck dry air, which was a good thing, and he went below and turned that pump off. The automatic bilge pump would finish drying out the bilges. He needed to get to work on the plugged hose and make sure it would not come loose again. Forty-five minutes later the Southern Cross was underway, the Yanmar humming peacefully along. This time they were eastbound, heading toward shore.

Sixteen

Janet awoke and felt the need to be outside in a large open space, so she joined Pete in the cockpit. "You look like hell, Mr. Mitchell," Janet said.

"You don't look so snappy either, Miss Cantu." Pete instantly wondered why he said that. He was actually thinking how pretty she was. "What would you say to a good cup of coffee?"

"You have no idea how good that would be right now.... "

The coffee was percolating on the stove in a matter of minutes. Pete had put the silverware drawer back, but only after pulling his .45 out and placing it on the countertop within easy reach. "I'll not repeat last night," he thought. The back-up electric bilge pump started to suck air, so he turned that one off, and the automatic pump shut itself down about ten seconds later. Pete picked up a few other things and straightened up a bit while the pot finished perking, then hollered up to Janet, asking if she took anything in her coffee.

"Maybe a little Bailey's," Janet said, only half joking.

Pete put in a few drops of honey and a little fresh milk. He didn't have any Bailey's on board. He would have to fix that in the near future.

Sitting in the cockpit sipping coffee, they needed to get some things figured out. The autopilot was doing fine, and it would be six or seven hours before they would see the shore or get into cell phone range.

Pete looked at Janet. "I think I can trust you now," he said with a smile.

"I should hope so, Pete. I should really hope so."

Pete began to relate the story from the start. He told her how he accidentally found the airplane when the anchor got stuck. He let her know about the bag and all the contents, including the cocaine. He was holding nothing back. Janet had asked clarification questions along the way, and the story lasted through two cups of coffee as they discussed details leading up to last night.

Janet told him that she had come to the boat to have a look about, thinking that she would just meet him there. When she got to the boat around 6:30 p.m., she walked around the top deck a few times, looking at the blood and bullet holes. She went below to look around, and when she got to the bottom of the ladder, she saw a shadow move out of the corner of her eye. She explained, "I really didn't know what to expect. I've never been on a sailboat before. This has been one hell of a first experience."

Janet said that was all she remembered, then added, "Oh yeah, something hit me, and hit me hard." She unconsciously rubbed the very tender spot on the side of her head where there was a small butterfly bandage at the hairline to keep the split skin closed.

"I patched you up this morning," Pete said. "But you're going to need a couple of stitches."

"You still have a gash on the back of your head," Janet reminded him. "Bring the first aid kit up with a refill and I'll repay the favor."

While Janet cleaned and bandaged the back of his head, Pete started to fill in small pieces of the story he had unintentionally left out the first time. So much had happened over the last couple of days that it was only natural to miss a part here and there. He told her about how he had the Betamax tape converted to a DVD, which he had forgotten about the first time through his tale. When the thought struck him, he jumped up before Janet was finished dressing his wound.

Pete found his laptop wrapped in the garbage bag on the settee with some of his other stuff. He went back up to the cockpit while the computer was booting up. "I think I have something you need to see."

Janet leaned in as Pete brought up the Windows Media Player. The DVD was still in the drive bay. When the DVD started, Janet sat very still as the scenes started to materialize on the screen. When the guy spitting the chewing tobacco was leaning forward, Pete hit the pause button, freezing the face on the screen. He now knew why the intruder from last night looked so familiar. He tapped the face on the screen with his right index finger and said, "That's the guy who tried to kill us last night. He's about 20 years younger in these images, but that's him."

"Oh my God... Do you know who that is?" Janet said.

"Yeah, he's the SOB that tried to kill us." Janet noticed that a hard tone had developed in Pete's voice.

Janet took a deep breath and explained. "He is Major Leslie Alexander, Pinellas County Sheriff's Office. He's destined to be the next sheriff when Colbert retires in a year." Janet unwittingly made the mental connection. The earlier notation on S/A Wojcik's desktop notepad, POS LA, had suddenly formulated into a clear meaning — Piece of Shit Leslie Alexander. Apparently Wojcik was not a fan of their key suspect.

"I guess that would explain why he wants the tape so badly," Pete said. "It would probably cripple his campaign."

"He wants it bad enough to kill for," Janet added.

Janet watched the rest of the tape in awe as the scenes popped in and out on the screen. When the screen went black, she said, "That's it?"

"Yep, that's it," Pete said. He told her what the guy at the video shop had said about the rust inside. He also told her about how it might be possible to reload the tape onto another reel, but they no longer had the tape. Janet agreed that they would probably never get an opportunity to touch it again.

"I've got to find out who the other people are on that tape." Janet was talking like an FDLE Agent now. She told Pete about the steps that led to her involvement in this case, and she told him about the corruption investigation, leaving out the classified details of EPIC. She shortened that part, telling him only that she had received information from a source that tended to confirm the law enforcement corruption investigation. She admitted that she had no clue as to who the other cop in the tape was.

"Where are we going now, specifically?" Janet asked.

"There is a nice quiet little anchorage I know of behind a golf course." Pete had the navigation chart open now and pointed to Gasparilla Island at the mouth of Charlotte Harbor. "This cove is behind a very exclusive, and gated, community. I don't want to go to any of my usual places right now," Pete said. "Until we get Alexander locked up, we need to stay out of public view for a bit."

Janet agreed. She needed some more time to think this through. "If you have no objection Pete, I would like to cook my first breakfast on a sailboat."

"That would be fantastic — let me show you where everything is."

Pete kept himself busy while breakfast was cooking getting his boat back in order. "It smells pretty damn good," he thought. He hadn't realized that the last decent meal he had was with Sam on Pine Island, which seemed like an eternity ago. One of the first things he needed to do when he got to shore was call Amy and see how his buddy was doing.

Breakfast was delicious. They decided to eat up in the cockpit to enjoy the fresh air and spacious view. The foldout table provided plenty of room. After breakfast, Pete showed Janet how to operate the forward head and shower. He found a pair of cotton deck pants with a draw string for a belt and a tank top for her to wear. Janet said she wanted to rinse out her clothes in fresh water, and Pete did the same thing in the aft head. Pete marveled at how a little soap could make you feel like a human being again.

Janet's clothes were laid across the top of the boom in the sun. They would dry nicely there while they motored toward shore.

It was early afternoon when the western shore of Florida came into view over the horizon. Janet told Pete that she could actually start to smell the land. "That's civilization you smell," he told her. It was amazing how clean real fresh air smelled out at sea.

Pete checked their location on the chart and saw that they were on course for the entrance to Charlotte Harbor. They were starting to see more boat traffic in the distance as well. They had discussed all the options that would be available when the anchor was dropped.

The plan, as it stood now, was for Janet to call her friend Tim at FDLE once they got anchored in the bay. She had complete trust in him. Pete was going to be placed into protective custody until Alexander was arrested and the other suspect in the tape was identified and taken into custody.

"You can't see his face on the tape. You don't know who he is. How will you find him?" Pete asked.

Janet said that she was sure once Alexander saw he was facing the rest of his life in jail he wouldn't want to go alone. Alexander's type of personality dictated that he would try to take as many people as possible with him on the ride down. The same was probably not true on the ride up.

The afternoon thunderstorms were forming along the coast, the tops reaching over thirty thousand feet and the upper edges being whisked away and forming that familiar anvil shape. The water was beginning to fuss a little with the building winds that went with the storms. "Nothing to worry about," Pete said. "I have done this a million times before." He needed to get the aft hatch covered to keep the rain out. He had a piece of Plexiglas on the navigation station table that would fit for now. He could secure it in place with a couple of wood screws driven into the teak frame until a replacement piece was ordered.

It was slightly past 2:00 p.m. when the Southern Cross passed into Charlotte Harbor and calmer waters. The thunderstorms were winding up and going to present one hell of a show in a few minutes. The onshore breeze was fueling the towering cumulus clouds until they were ready to bust with rain and lightning. The bottoms were dark and had that ominous heavy appearance that always preceded a cloudburst.

Turning left after passing Gasparilla Island, Pete could see the intended anchorage just short of two miles to the north. The ultra exclusive mansions filled the end of the island, the homes of the elite who resided along the west coast of Florida. The water in the bay was a little choppy but nothing the Southern Cross couldn't handle. Janet enjoyed watching Pete work with his boat. "They're a good team," she thought.

They arrived in the small bay, stopping next to the exclusive but now empty golf course. The golfers had recently fled with the arrival of the first few cracks of lightning. Pete had already explained to Janet how to work the engine controls when it came time to anchor. He had the boat slowed to a crawl in eight feet of water and eased the anchor over the bow with his left hand. His right shoulder and hand were still too sore to lift the heavy anchor.

When the anchor splashed, he gave her the signal to back straight up, which she accomplished like an old pro. After 40 feet of anchor line was let out, Pete wrapped the line around the front bow cleat. The rearward motion of the boat caused the Danforth anchor to take a hard bite in the sand and to set deep. They were securely hooked. "Okay, neutral," Pete shouted.

Their timing couldn't have been any more important. The moment Pete stepped back into the cockpit, a bolt of lightning hit somewhere on the golf course nearby. "That was a little too close. Let's get below," Pete said, but Janet didn't need any prompting. She was already scurrying down the ladder. "How about lunch?" asked Pete. "It looks like we are going to be here a while."

***

Debora Hayes pushed the intercom button for Major Alexander's office. His door had been closed most of the afternoon. He got back a little before lunch and was his usual arrogant self. "What?" he barked over the office intercom.

"Detective Rawlerson with Homicide is on the phone. He said he needs to talk to you."

Alexander tapped the intercom button, killing the connection with the secretary, then picked up the phone and tapped the button next to the only blinking light that indicated a holding call.

"Alexander."

"Major, sorry to bother you," Rawlerson said. "I just located that boater you wanted me to interview, the guy that found the airplane off of Egmont Key."

"What?" Alexander was momentarily confused. "You found who where?"

Rawlerson went on to explain that he had received a State Attorney's investigative subpoena for the phone number belonging to Mr. Mitchell, the guy that found the airplane. He had immediately faxed the subpoena over to the Sprint security division office. He informed Alexander that the case was being transferred to the Lee County Sheriff's Office and wanted to know how the Major would like him to proceed. He had just received the GPS location of Mr. Mitchell's cell phone.

"That's old information, Detective." Alexander started to breathe normally again. "Lee County is going to close the case in conjunction with FDLE."

"Ah, no sir, it's not... It's not old I mean. I just got the call from Sprint," Rawlerson added. "They have been watching for the cell phone since I sent them the subpoena the other day. I was originally told it was off and they had no signal."

"So what's the problem?" Alexander asked.

"I was told that we were turning the case over to FDLE and the Lee County Sheriff, and so I let the matter drop and forgot about the subpoena, but a few minutes ago the loss prevention specialist with Sprint called and said he found the phone I was looking for. It was strange at first, but after looking at a map, it made sense. According to Sprint, the phone first appeared about six miles west of Charlotte Harbor and was moving toward shore. That's when they figured out it was on a boat and had been out of range the past couple of days. Well, he's stopped in Charlotte Harbor next to Gasparilla Island. He just arrived. What would you like me to do with the location information?"

Alexander's heart was pounding to the point of skipping beats and his face had become flushed. He was having trouble controlling his voice and sounding normal. "Exactly where is it?" he said. "I'll pass the information along to Lee County."

"Yes sir. The signal is stationary at 26 degrees 45 minutes 31 seconds north, 82 degrees 15 minutes 17 seconds west." Alexander noticed his hand starting to shake as he wrote the numbers down.

Alexander terminated the call, trying to be polite to Rawlerson, but every blood vessel in his head was about to explode. His blood pressure had risen to a dangerously high level and his vision was closing in. The entire phone shattered when it hit the wall. His rage was building to a dangerous level.

Debora watched Alexander storm out of his office, slamming the door extra hard behind him. "Less than half a day, a new temper tantrum record," she thought.

Alexander made it to his house in record time. The dash-mount blue light and corner strobes helped clear the few clogged intersections that slowed his progress. There was absolutely no time for delays.

Once at home, he found the phone number he needed in a safe concealed under the carpet of his walk-in closet. He grabbed a navigation chart off of the table in his study prior to dialing. The phone was answered on the second ring.

Alexander told the man on the other end that his services were needed immediately. The man lived in Sarasota, close enough to get the job done in a hurry. The friends Alexander had made along the way had served him well over the years, more than a few of them unsavory people without any conscience at all, like the man on the other end of the line. He had not talked to this particular special friend in almost two years.

"I need this done immediately, now, this evening, no delays," Alexander said. "Fifty thousand, cash." Leslie explained who the targets were and where they were located as he looked up the little bay on his own navigation chart. It coincided with the coordinates Rawlerson had given him. "I don't care what it looks like; they just need to be very dead, very quickly. There are two of them, a middle-aged white guy and a Hispanic woman."

"Seventy-five thousand, if it's a rush job."

"Do it. I'll expect to hear the good news tonight."

"And I'll expect payment the first thing in the morning," the man replied.

"Agreed," Leslie replied. "They are on a sailboat, the Southern Cross. They're anchored behind the Gasparilla Country Club golf course, the one on the south side of Gasparilla Island."

"I know the area," the man said, and he hung up.

***

The afternoon thunderstorms began with a fury and held until late evening. The lightning was frequent and the drops heavy. Pete and Janet spent the afternoon below deck. There was no sense dying of a lightning strike, especially after all they had been through.

Janet had found her cell phone, but it was worthless. The salt water had shorted out the internal workings of the small circuit boards. She would have to replace it. Pete's phone had died when they tried to make a call, the attempt draining the last of the battery's charge and the charger cord was nowhere to be found. "We can call

Tim when we go to shore," Janet said. "Just as soon as the lightning stops."

The storms followed the usual Florida pattern and began to abate around 7:30 in the evening. They were moving inland, driven by the sea breeze, and taking the lightning with them. The last couple of strikes had been more than 10 minutes ago. It was time to head to shore.

Without the dinghy, and being in eight feet of water, meant a short swim to shore. They were pretty close to the golf course, so distance was not a problem. Janet didn't want to walk through town dripping wet, and for that matter neither did Pete. The problem was solved with the small cooler. Janet's clothes had been brought in just before the rain, and the afternoon sun had dried them completely. They were folded and put into the cooler along with a clean pair of shorts and t-shirt for Pete, one beach towel, the DVD, shoes, flip-flops, and Pete's .45. Janet's gun was nowhere to be found. "Alexander probably took it," she thought.

"You wouldn't happen to have a nice two-piece bathing suit lying around by chance, would you?" Janet asked.

"Nope, sorry, I generally don't have such attractive guests onboard." Pete smiled at her.

Janet told Pete to pretend she was wearing a proper swimsuit and stripped down to a blue lace bra and matching panties.

"Victoria's no longer got a secret…" Pete chuckled as he stripped down to his skivvies.

"And I guess that answers the boxers or briefs question," Janet shot back with a grin.

The duo swam to shore in their underwear as they floated the cooler alongside them. Pete handed Janet the beach towel first after they climbed up onto the small dock. There was only room for one towel in the cooler. "I wouldn't mind going for another swim." Janet winked at Pete. "Once this case is closed. I have a policy about dating…" A screaming bullet slapped the towel from her grasp and Pete pushed Janet backward into the water as the next bullet split the night air between them, passing where Janet had been standing a millisecond ago.

Pete grabbed his .45 and rapidly put one round in the general direction of the shooter. He wanted the shooter to know he would fire back and he would be wise to keep his head down. Pete then grabbed Janet's hand and pulled her out of the water, dragging her down the beach line away from the gunshot. She managed to hold Pete firm for a brief nanosecond while she grabbed the DVD from the cooler.

One more shot came from behind them as they rounded the southern corner of the golf course along the beach. There was a small bay to cross that would get them off the golf course and into the exclusive neighborhood. The little bay was only about fifty feet across and turned out to be only a foot or two deep. When they arrived at the opposite shore, a second man appeared. He was out of breath and dressed in dark clothing. "He is trying to flank us," Pete thought.

The second man raised his semi-automatic handgun at the pair. He was only thirty feet away and the distance was closing rapidly. The second guy's gun spit one projectile toward the duo as Pete's .45 erupted into a flurry of four rapid-fire shots. Pete's shots were the result of extensive training, precision, and control in a high stress hostile situation. *Whap, whap, whap, whap.* They heard all four hit the man in the upper body, all grouped near center mass. Pete automatically kept count, two shots left. Pete's barrel stayed pointed at the crumpled mass on the grass as he got close enough to make sure the target posed no further threat.

Janet picked up the dead guy's gun, a .9mm Beretta. She had no idea if it was the high capacity magazine or not. In the middle of a gun battle was the absolute wrong time to figure out how much ammo you have. She would really like to know, but there was not enough time to look now.

The pair ran along the southeastern shore of Gasparilla Island, trying to put distance between them and the first shooter, who had gotten closer and fired another couple of rounds at them. Pete and Janet passed a four foot brick wall separating the manicured backyards of two rather lavish island homes. Neither appeared to be occupied and only had the minimal yard security lights on, enough light to give the shooter something to aim at, which was a bad thing.

Two more rounds pinged off the brick wall Pete and Janet were using for cover. They could not determine if only one shooter remained now or not. That's when Pete saw the way out in the yard behind him, a small Robinson R-22 helicopter near the rear of the mansion. Pete had flown this model a couple of times a few years ago and was familiar with the craft's basic operation. "Hold him off for a minute or two," Pete whispered to Janet.

Janet had used the opportunity to push the magazine release, dropping the nine-round magazine into her hand. "Only the one missing," she said and snapped the magazine back up into the handle. "We may not have a minute, Pete. Whoever is out there is pretty damned determined to see us dead."

Janet saw the unknown shooter move out from behind his own wall to maneuver into a better firing position. She fired two rounds at him, driving him back behind his protective wall. Pete sprinted toward the little helicopter while trying to remain in a low crouch. "I hope he knows how to fly that thing," Janet thought as another bullet chipped a piece of brick off the wall. The shooter was moving for position again and Janet returned fire.

As expensive as aircraft are, they are the least secured of any motorized vehicle. The little helicopter did not have the standard aluminum doors on it, but two snap-on clear vinyl rain covers, which

282

easily pulled off. Pete saw that the rotor blades were not tied down when he jumped into the right seat, the pilot seat in a helicopter. He reached over the top of the left seat and moved the fuel valve into the on position. With his left hand, he grabbed the collective stick next to his thigh and worked the throttle open a crack. No key was necessary. He flipped the magneto switches into the on position and pressed the ignition switch. Pete was rewarded with the engine springing to life.

The main rotor began to immediately spin up as he prematurely engaged the rotor clutch. "No time for standard procedure," he thought. The usual start-up time from engine cranking to take-off was usually about six minutes. Pete was going to do it in less than 90 seconds. The clutch squealed in protest but was rapidly bringing the rotor speed up to 100 percent. It still seemed to take forever as Pete watched Janet return fire again, once more keeping the shooter behind his wall. "Just hold him there a few more seconds," he thought — time seemed to stand still.

Pete released the control lock friction knob while the rotors continued their agonizingly slow climb to full speed. When Pete saw the Rotor RPM and Engine RPM needles climbing over 85 percent, he tried to wave Janet over to him but she was busy holding the shooter in position and wasn't watching him. Pete had to flick the landing light on and off twice to get her attention.

The shooter saw Janet run toward the helicopter and came out from behind the protective cover of his wall and ran toward them.

Just before Janet jumped into the left seat, she fired the last couple of rounds from the borrowed gun. The slide locked back on the weapon, confirming the magazine was now empty. The shooter ducked behind Janet's wall as her rounds whistled within inches of his head.

Janet was barely all the way in her seat when Pete lifted up on the collective stick by his left side. The rotors changed pitch, complying with the command, and began to develop lift. As they did, the torque increased, requiring Pete to push down on the foot pedal to increase tail rotor side-vectored thrust to counter the torque. While doing that, he manipulated the cyclic stick, bringing the little chopper into a low hover. This was where they were most vulnerable.

Pete had to push the pedal hard enough to turn the nose of the helicopter away from the house, and he was applying forward pressure on the cyclic stick at the same time to begin forward movement of the aircraft. The spinning rotor began to bite into undisturbed air that was clear of its own downwash and began passing through translational lift, which caused the helicopter to accelerate more rapidly and gain altitude.

The downside to all this was that it presented a pretty good target for the shooter. They had to fly directly past him and toward the water to avoid hitting the tall palms lining the yard. The only hindrance the shooter found was from the swirling fallen Banyan tree leaves and fresh-cut grass clippings.

Three rounds hit the helicopter. Janet had grabbed Pete's .45 off of her seat as she jumped in, and she fired his last two shots as they turned and headed toward the shooter, which prevented him from hitting the helicopter a few more times on their way past.

Pete was gradually picking up airspeed and altitude as they rapidly put distance between them and Gasparilla Island. Janet leaned over toward Pete and spoke loud enough to overcome the noisy open cockpit. "I'm sitting in a stolen helicopter in my underwear. I need stitches in my head, and people have been trying to kill me for the past couple of days. I'm not sure if you're good luck or bad luck, Pete."

"Let's hope it's good luck," Pete yelled back as he tapped the gauges with his left finger tip. "Were losing oil pressure, fuel is pouring out, and were over the middle of the bay without life jackets. But for what it's worth," Pete added with a devilish grin, "you look absolutely stunning in the moonlight…"

Seventeen

Crossing over dry land at six hundred feet brought a sense of relief to the occupants of the struggling helicopter, but the engine was starting to develop a vibration that could be felt through the seat and pedals. A red warning light had illuminated on the instrument panel. Yellow lights generally meant caution and that you were supposed to proceed to the nearest safe landing area for repairs. A red light simply meant land immediately because bad things were about to happen.

Pete was looking for a clear place to put the helicopter down, which was tougher than most people would imagine. There were power lines everywhere, and striking lines in this small helicopter would mean certain disaster. The Robbie only weighed 985 pounds when empty. Pete thought he saw a possible location as they were approaching the town of North Port, which is west of Port Charlotte. Pete was trying to avoid large populated areas intentionally, which is getting pretty tough to do along the Florida coastline.

Pete thought the shape of his proposed emergency landing area looked like an old drive-in movie theater. He hadn't been to one in years. Most had turned into flea markets and such with patrons electing for the comfortable air-conditioned, mosquito-free viewing offered by the megaplex theaters. But drive-ins didn't usually have power lines crossing overhead, not near the screen anyhow, a couple of street lights illuminated the lot too, which appeared to be empty. Pete had no way of knowing, but the drive-in was generally only open on weekends.

Pete lowered the collective, beginning their descent. He wasn't looking for a textbook landing, just a safe one. They had been through too much to get killed in a helicopter crash, he reminded himself. The engine was struggling, by the sound of it, but it was still providing sufficient power to perform a safe emergency landing. Pete brought the helicopter over the middle of the big screen and pulled sharply to the right while descending the last fifty feet. He saw some power lines running from the concession stand toward a power pole near the back row, which he was able to avoid, and he stopped in a low hover ten feet over the ground between the screen and concession stand.

"Yep, I must be lucky," he thought at the same time the engine gave its last burst of power. One minute sooner and an autorotation into here could have been quite disastrous. The small helicopter settled onto the ground with a slight bounce as the rotors bled off the last kinetic energy while expending any remaining lift. It was a hard landing nevertheless, which caused Janet to let out a grunt, but they were upright, and more importantly, alive.

Pete flipped several switches off, shutting down all electrical power. It became unusually quiet as the blades slowly spun to a stop. The pair simply sat there and stared at the blank screen for a few moments. Janet looked over at Pete and broke the silence. "This movie sucks. I want my money back..."

They found a pay phone next to the concession stand. The 800 number to the main FDLE office in Tallahassee was for agents to use when they needed to make long distance business calls from outside the office. It was very handy today, as neither of them had a quarter. For that matter, neither one had any pockets.

Janet dialed in a six-digit password, which rewarded her with a dial tone, allowing her to make the call. Tim answered his cell phone on the second ring.

"My God, Janet, where are you? Everyone at the office is worried about you."

"It's a very long story. I need you to pick us up. Can you run this phone number in the reverse directory and find us?"

"Sure, what's the number?"

She read it from the phone. "I think the name of this drive-in is the Silver Moon."

"I'm on my way — I'll find it."

"Oh, and Tim, don't tell anyone I called until I've had a chance to fill you in, and bring two blankets with you." Janet concluded the call after describing the drive-in theater's general location the best she could, and she added that they were at the concession stand, which was closed.

Fortunately, traffic was light, and Tim made the trip in record time. He could see the pair had been battling mosquitoes and losing for some time now. Tim handed out the blankets and glanced at the bullet holes in the helicopter, then back to the exhausted duo standing before him in nothing but their underwear. "This is going to be one hell of a story, isn't it?"

Tim was introduced to Pete as they climbed into the air-conditioned car and drove off. The ride back to Janet's apartment was filled with explanation, and by the time they arrived, Tim had a pretty complete picture of the past few days. He said he would head to the office to start things in motion. Janet and Pete needed to clean up and have something to eat. They were absolutely worn out and frazzled.

Tim watched the DVD of the Betamax tape on Janet's computer while she made him a copy. She wasn't letting go of the one she had. It had become very expensive, if a price could be put on a human life.

Tim would get the local police coordinated with the shootings at Gasparilla Island and have the helicopter dealt with. The owner probably wasn't going to be too happy about getting his machine shot up. Tim said that he would be back to pick Janet up at 7 a.m. Her car was somewhere in south Florida and would be recovered later. He would bring some clothes for Pete as well. They were about the same size.

Pete had already had his shower and climbed into bed, following Janet's instructions. She needed a few minutes alone to talk business with Tim. There were not many choices of where to sleep because Janet had a one-bedroom apartment with a queen size bed. He would have to find out what kind of sheets these were. "They feel so damn good," he thought as he easily drifted off into a deep sleep.

Just under an hour later, Tim was ready to get to work. He had a long list of things that needed to be handled, and it was Janet's turn to slow down a little. She took her shower and saw Pete's boxers hanging on the shower rod drying. "He must have rinsed them off in the shower," she thought. She was drained as well. The past couple of days were catching up to her physically. "When in Rome," she thought, draping her towel over the hook on the door. Pete unconsciously rolled over and snuggled up to Janet. They fit together well, and she felt safe in his arms. Within minutes, she was peacefully asleep, breathing in rhythm with Pete.

***

By 9:00 a.m., everyone had arrived at the FDLE Office for the emergency meeting that had been set up. Everyone was assured that this was of the highest priority and their attendance was most important, and they were further advised that this could not be discussed over the phone.

On one side of the conference table was Sheriff Colbert and his Chief Deputy. Directly opposite was the elected Pinellas County State Attorney along with his chief prosecutor. The St. Petersburg Chief of Police was in attendance, as were two Regional FDLE Supervisors. Tim and Janet were present, of course, along with her immediate supervisor, SAC Hollis, who had called this meeting.

Someone had provided the requisite dozen mixed doughnuts and coffee in the break room. When the owners of all the puzzled faces were seated, Hollis introduced Janet. Most of the folks here either knew her personally or by reputation.

Janet stood at the front of the room and began to lay out the case to the group. She related the events as if on trial, neither adding emotion nor leaving out critical components. When she specifically detailed Major Leslie Alexander as the prime suspect for their attempted murders, everyone knew why the pre-meeting secrecy was necessary. There were lots of little unnecessary details, like flying in her underwear that she didn't need to bring up at this time. She advised that the witness, Mr. Mitchell, was presently at a secure undisclosed location. Janet could see some shadows of skepticism on several faces during her oration.

Janet played the DVD from a laptop connected to a large wall-mounted plasma display. Expressions visibly changed.

The presentation had left no doubt in anyone's mind as to what had happened over 20 years ago. The tape seemed to affirm her narration of the past few days and solidified what had to happen in the very near future. It was time for a group discussion, and until now, this group had been eerily silent.

The State Attorney talked about an indictment for suspicion of homicide with regards to the skeleton, two counts of attempted murder, destruction of evidence, violation of the law enforcement corruption act, and the list went on. The attorney then answered a question with, "Yes, there is the possibility of the death penalty here."

He went on to explain that the rest of the charges would guarantee life in prison at the very least. The deaths of the man on Gasparilla Island along with the death of the boat burglar would most likely be connected to Alexander as well. The present count had him responsible for three bodies and two attempted murders. The evidence was overwhelming.

Sheriff Colbert was stunned at the news. He never had a clue. He was wondering how he could fend off the massive amount of national media attention that was sure to strike. Visions of aggressive media snoops crowding his private entrance sent a shiver down his spine. He had longed to get his turn on FOX LIVE, but Colbert had hoped it would be over something like an apprehended child rapist or found missing kid or something, not his corrupt organization and murderous senior staff members. Colbert sat a little lower in his seat, wishing this would all go away. He wanted this to be nothing more than a bad dream. He needed a drink, several.

His chief deputy, however, was actually quite elated at the news. His slot as the next sheriff had instantly become a reality — it was guaranteed and his day was off to an absolutely wonderful start. During the rest of the meeting, he was busy visualizing his name on stationary, parking lot signs, and over the door of the main office.

Alexander lived within the city limits, and the St. Petersburg police chief was only too happy to help. Due to the sheriff's office being involved in a corruption investigation with unknown additional co-conspirators, the SPPD would provide the SWAT team to effect the actual take-down and arrest of Alexander. FDLE would execute the search warrant at Alexander's house subsequent to the arrest.

The State Attorney explained that he needed a few hours to draw up the necessary warrants and get them signed. Everyone agreed to meet again at 1500 hours at the St. Pete PD briefing room. The warrants would be given to the SWAT team and the operation would begin.

Everyone was admonished by the FDLE regional director to maintain a strict level of confidentiality until the arrest had been conducted. No one was to discuss the merits of this case outside this meeting room, no exceptions, no excuses.

***

When Pete got out of bed, he found a sticky note on the bathroom mirror: "Don't leave. Make yourself at home."

There was a pair of shorts and a light button-down linen shirt folded on top of the sink. The brewed coffee smelled pretty good and led him to the kitchen.

***

It was just after 1:30 in the afternoon when the phone in Alexander's study rang. Leslie held out little hope that it would be good news from Gasparilla. Too much time had transpired without hearing his much desired news. Something had probably gone wrong in Gasparilla and he would have to start figuring out how to clean up yet another mess.

"Leslie," the male caller said. Alexander immediately recognized the voice, which belonged to the last person he had expected to hear from today. "Something is about to go down. You need to meet with me ASAP, Weedon Hammock, the usual place, *now*." The line went dead.

Leslie instinctively knew he had no choice. He set his private line to forward all calls to his cell phone. He was still hoping to hear some good news from Gasparilla Island, but that hope was dwindling steadily.

Weedon Island, sometimes called Ross Island by the locals, is a nature preserve on the east side of St. Petersburg. A lone road leads around the island to the bay side where there is a small parking lot that is usually empty on weekdays. Bird watchers like this place, but they only seem to appear during early mornings and weekends.

Alexander recognized the car as it approached. Nobody else was around as the newcomer pulled up, driver's window to driver's window, as cops across the nation have done since they began patrolling in cars. Alexander rolled his window three quarters of the way down. "What's so damn important? I'm busy."

"I thought you told me that you took care of Vince and that damn tape 20 years ago. What the hell went wrong? How did you screw this up?"

"Hey, goddamn it, I did take care of it. How the hell was I supposed to know he would get so close to Florida?" Alexander had immediately become agitated.

"Well he did, and you have really caused some problems this time. Do you have any idea what's coming your way this afternoon?"

"What? What the hell are you talking about?" Leslie was starting to sound scared.

"FDLE has a copy of the tape you took from the sailboat. You couldn't even kill two tied-up unconscious witnesses. You have always been a lower-class screw up, you know that?"

Leslie completely understood the implications of what had just been said and why he was at this meeting. His contact had failed last night in Gasparilla. The FDLE agent and Mitchell arrived safely and they were talking. "I have the tape," Leslie forced out. "They don't have any proof without that."

"You goddamn idiot!" The man had gotten louder. "They made a copy of your Betamax tape."

"Screw you, asshole. You're on that tape too." Leslie was pointing a finger at the other driver. "You're going down with me, and so are the other sorry asses that were part of this. I'll be dammed if I'm the only one taking all the heat for this!"

"You're wrong, Leslie, the tape was corrupted by saltwater and time. You're the only one on the tape."

Leslie was pissed, and every pore of his skin suddenly felt hot. He stiffened in his seat as his racing brain was rapidly piecing things together. "You lousy piece of dog shi…"

The 9mm slug pierced his skull a quarter of an inch above Leslie's right eye. The semi-jacket hollow point began to mushroom immediately after entering the brain, and the projectile's speed and energy was spent in the span of 4.3 inches, terminating near the back of the skull. The internal shock wave through the brain caused by the rapid deceleration scrambled Leslie's brains and he simply slumped down in his seat, his head lying back on the headrest. Leslie's stoic expression revealed nothing more. The terminally injured brain immediately stopped sending signals to the heart telling it to keep beating.

There was very little blood.

Epilogue

Pete had cleared the harbor and raised the mainsail. This was a nice morning for sailing. The breeze was light, seas were calm, and the temperature was perfect. Pete had plotted a course that would take him back to the one preprogrammed spot on earth that required his immediate attention.

When he arrived, Pete donned his dive gear and slipped over the side. After following the anchor rode to the bottom, he began a circular search pattern until he found the sunken airplane once again.

The dashboard clock inside the cockpit put up very little resistance. The retaining screws had long ago succumbed to the ravages of rust. The clock would be on its way to Sam's house as soon as he got to Key West and put it in the mail, and Pete would take the time to give it a good cleaning while on his way south. Janet had promised to send the official report on the sinking of the airplane to Sam once it became public record.

***

Janet had returned to her apartment late in the evening a few days before. She had told Pete about her day, which turned out a little different than he had expected. The arrest team arrived at Alexander's house and executed the warrants, and there was no resistance when they entered the home as Alexander wasn't there. The FDLE team was still processing evidence at his home when Janet received the word that Leslie Alexander's cell phone GPS signal had been traced to a stationary position on Weedon Island in the nature preserve. The SWAT team mobilized and performed a perfectly executed felony take-down on a corpse in a car.

Alexander had been murdered, she explained. There was burnt gunpowder residue on the outside of the driver's window, and the blast pattern revealed that he had been shot from a distance of three or four feet. The position of Leslie's body indicated he was killed by someone he had trusted to get that close.

Pete had a choice, according to Janet. He could either be placed into protective custody, or get lost for a while. Alexander's killer, it was believed, was one of the other people on the Betamax tape. Janet had said that she very much wanted to see Pete on a more personal level, maybe even go sailing for a week or two when this was all over, but that couldn't happen until this case was closed and he was no longer a witness. She did, after all, have rules about dating.

FDLE needed to find out who had killed Alexander and determine for certain if Pete was still a target or not. Until that happened, St. Petersburg, Florida and the surrounding area was unsafe for Mr. Pete Mitchell.

Pete's choice was obvious. He was going to get lost for a while.

***

When Pete got to Key West, he walked to the post office and mailed the package to Sam. Key West was a pretty good place to get lost, and he was enjoying an afternoon stroll on his way back to the Southern Cross when a navigation chart displayed in the Mel Fisher Treasure Museum window caught his eye. The chart had his undivided attention as his synapses made the connection. The answer had quite unexpectedly presented itself.

"Well I'll be dammed, that's it!"

Pete made his way to the museum window with the small piece of paper that had a long string of numbers on it. The paper from the PVC tube had largely been ignored by everyone. Too many more important things were happening that had seized everyone's attention.

Reading the numbers from the paper, Pete matched them to a location on the old Loran C navigation chart that was in the window. Following the coordinates revealed a small atoll in the Bahamas. Nobody used the land-based radio navigation system anymore, which was outdated when the much more accurate satellite-based GPS system came into civilian use.

The reference lines intersected on the east side of one tiny island lost among its larger neighbors. The entire string of islands was part of the eastern Bahamas, uninhabited, and in the middle of nowhere.

Six days later, Pete arrived at the small spit of land in the teal blue waters of the island chain. His had been the only boat navigating the waters for the past 24 hours. He was quite alone. There was not much land for him to search. It was no more than one city block long and only half as wide. If anything had been sticking up marking the spot, it had been erased by the passage of time long ago. The metal detector was about to become a valuable asset once again.

He was a little east of dead center on the island when the detector barked at him. The small hand shovel easily removed the top layer of sand and pieces of broken coral. When he hit metal, the remaining layer of sand was brushed away, uncovering three waterproof military-style ammo boxes buried one and a half feet deep.

All three were stuffed with cash, once again all older bills. There must have been a couple hundred thousand here. An oilcloth rag had been tied with cotton kite string around a book shape object. With very little force, the string popped and the oil cloth fell away. Inside was one perfectly preserved Betamax tape with the word "ORIGINAL" written across the face.

Pete was kneeling next to the open containers of cash when he held the tape up toward the heavens inspecting its pristine condition. "Case closed," he said to a passing seagull. "Case closed."